Si...

Sib...
Copyright © 2017, re ... **, by Jack L Knapp**
Cover by Mia Darien
Stock photos from Fotolia.com

Book Five, the Wizards Series

Siberian Wizard

A Paranormal Thriller

By Jack L Knapp

Siberian Wizard

Jack L Knapp

Table of Contents

Jack L Knapp

Prologue

Ray was worried.

Had T been killed? It seemed impossible, and yet...

What made the newspaper article worrisome was that Tagliaferro, the man reported killed, had been one of T's aliases. And he alone had not returned from the past. He was phenomenally strong, but could even he survive a lightning bolt? *Someone* had been there, that much was clear from reading the article, but after the lightning strike there was no sign of the man. People who had been there during the storm thought his body might have washed into the Sound.

But reading the article a third time wouldn't make things any clearer. Ray cleared his screen and joined Ana Maria and Shezzie on the patio. His gloomy mood today called for scotch.

Shezzie noticed.

Despite Ray's silence, there was no hiding his concern. Shezzie was a not only a strong telepath, she possessed a high sense of empathy and Ana Maria, Ray's domestic partner, was almost as strong. Neither missed what Ray had just done; the tumbler, which had moments ago held a good four fingers of scotch, was now half empty.

"You brought Libby back, Ray. Don't blame yourself; T made his own decision," said Shezzie gently.

"Yeah, but he only went back in the first place because Libby needed help! In his place, I wouldn't have let someone else take the risks either."

"His choice, Ray," Shezzie insisted. "Was your trip dangerous?"

"Maybe. I don't know, it could have been, but it wasn't particularly dangerous except for not being sure any of us would ever get back. But I agreed with T, we couldn't abandon Libby. For all her abilities, she's still a kid. As to how I found her, I finally thought of taking short teleports and trying to comm her as soon as I got where I was going. She answered and we joined up. That's when I got to wondering if changing direction would make a difference. It worked. I'm pretty sure now that teleporting interacts with the Earth's magnetic field. Going west took me farther into the past and going east brought us home. Although it's possible we were being pulled back, which is what Shorty thinks."

"I don't understand how direction could be important, but then again I don't really understand how we do the things we do! Physics doesn't have the answer," confessed Shezzie.

"No," agreed Ray. "Sometimes I wonder whether the magnetic field is as important as T believed, but it's all we've got and it's not as if anyone is experimenting. Q.E.D; Reversing direction reversed our movement in time. It worked. But next time, who knows?"

"We can't tell anyone," Shezzie agreed. "I don't suppose it matters, though. The abilities are spreading whether we like it or not, and sooner or later, we'll have to go public. I'm surprised we've been able to hide this long! But I'm afraid of what might happen if others started traveling into the past."

"It might be worse than you think," Ray said thoughtfully. "Suppose somebody from the 19th Century had learned to read minds just from being around me? Or learned how to teleport when I did? I understood the possibility of causing a time paradox, but I wasn't willing to leave Libby back there. And to be honest, I wanted to come back too, so I took a chance and it doesn't seem to have made a difference. If anyone developed Talent from being around Libby or me, it never made the papers."

***

A faint breeze stirred the tall conifers. A heavyset man dressed in rough clothing glanced up at the tall tree. Drawing back his axe, he swung again, a powerful blow driven by the man's thick muscles. Again and again he struck, alternating his blows so that wedge-shaped chips popped free from the cut.

A reddish light, followed by a light pop, interrupted the steady chopping. The woodcutter swore in Russian and froze, axe upright. Had lightning struck the tree? The low-hanging clouds didn't look stormy, but still, who could say what the weather might do? That flash of red had come from the north...

Across the clearing stood a man dressed only in tattered remnants of clothing. Most of his coat was gone, the collar no more than a fragment and the sleeves missing entirely. The body of the coat gaped, revealing a vest that was in slightly better shape. The shirt had also suffered damage and most of the man's hair appeared to have been singed off.

Had he been in a fire? But no, that didn't seem right. Except for a torn knee, his trousers appeared to have suffered little damage. A shoe was missing and the other was totally unsuited for walking in the forest. Where had he come from?

"Kto ty? Otkuda ty priyekhal?"

The strange man looked back, no sign of comprehension on his face.

"Ty *idiot*? The woodsman's tone revealed his exasperation.

The man's expression changed. It appeared he had understood at least some of the words.

"I...do you speak English?"

The astonished Russian lowered his axe.

"Angliyskiy?"

The stranger blinked, trying to understand the unfamiliar word. "Not English. That doesn't sound right. I'm...American, I think."

"Amerikanskaya?"

The man nodded and spoke one of his few words of Russian. "Da."

***

The Russian stood his axe by the door and called out to someone inside the log house. A heavyset woman dressed in a long, loose skirt and wearing an apron hurried out in response and gaped at the stranger. "Is he a soldier, Mischa?" Her voice showed concern.

"I don't think so, Mother. He has no uniform, but that doesn't mean much. A lot of Semenov's soldiers don't wear uniforms. They all have guns, though, and this one doesn't."

"I will send for your father," the woman decided. "He will know what to do. Ekaterina, go to the fields and bring your papa!"

An older man, heavily bearded, arrived ten minutes later, accompanied by the young girl who'd gone to fetch him. He was dressed much as the woodsman and there was a distinct family resemblance. The older man's beard was as dark as his son's, except for streaks of gray. He man took in the scene at a glance. "Mischa, you should not have brought him here! If he's one of Kolchak's men and Semenov finds him here, they will kill us. If he comes from Semenov, *Kolchak's* soldiers will kill us, and even if he's a Bolshevik, he could bring the Cossack soldiers on us and then they would take you away. We would starve if they didn't kill us first. This man is dangerous; I say we kill him and bury the body in the swamp!"

"Father, he has done us no harm! Look, he seems dazed and he does not understand Russian! He cannot be a Bolshevik and he does not look like a Cossack."

"That does not matter! Do we not owe it to ourselves to survive? We owe this stranger *nothing*!"

Mischa shook his head. "Father, we will offer him soup. It is time for dinner, I am hungry, you are too. Mother has made soup, there will be enough for all. I will decide what to do after we eat. Come, we will take the man inside and give him food. It is what we have always done, be hospitable to strangers."

The older man frowned. "Mark my words, nothing good can

come of this! Look how ragged he is! He's no more than a beggar who will eat us out of house and home!"

"Father, *I* will decide." Mischa's voice was respectful but stubborn. "I respect your words, but we have our traditions! Sometimes I think it is all the revolution has left to us. Only the food we grow ourselves or gather from the forest is left, and the Bolsheviks will take that if they learn we have it. The stranger will share and after we've had our soup, we will speak again."

The old man, unconvinced, muttered as he led the way inside. Mischa beckoned and the stranger followed. A rude table, small but sturdy, stood beside a wood-burning stove. A large pot simmered on the stove, and a hand-carved wooden ladle hung nearby from a peg on the wall. The woman dished up the soup, ensuring that the stranger got a full bowl. The family muttered and crossed themselves before eating.

"Pork? This contains pork, doesn't it?"

But the stranger's words were no more than nonsense. The family ignored him and ate, wiping the bowls clean with slabs of heavy dark bread thickly spread with butter. Cups of tea, sweetened with honey, followed the meal. The stranger noticed that the soup pot was empty and that there was no more tea in the teapot. Even the samovar had been set aside. The family was obviously very poor, and yet they had shared what they had.

"Thank you, ma'am. I was hungry. I don't know who you are, but I get the idea you folks aren't well off. Would it offend you if I offered to pay? I think you need the money more than I do."

The man reached for the last button on his shirt and opened it, losing the button as the thread snapped. Sighing, he fumbled open a pocket on the belt he wore beneath the shirt. Taking out a coin, he laid it on the table, then pushed it toward the woman, looking at her expectantly.

"Mother, that is...is that *gold*?"

"I think it must be," the old woman whispered. "But it is not Russian. Will we get in trouble for having it?"

"We can get in trouble for drinking tea, Mother!" Mischa said.

"Take that and hide it, quick!"

"Mischa, he may have more of those things! I still say we should kill him and hide the body, but first we look beneath his clothing!"

"Father, I have decided! I will leave as soon as we are finished. Mother, make up a packet of food. I will be back tomorrow."

"Mischa, take your axe," urged the older man. "After you kill the stranger, search his body for the rest of his gold. Then bury the body deep so the wolves don't dig it up."

"Father, I won't kill him!one I'm going to turn him over to the soldiers."

"Mischa, they will kill him and probably kill you too! Semenov's guerrillas are beasts!" The old man appeared panic-stricken.

"I will not give him to Semenoff's men, Father."

"The Bolsheviks are almost as bad, Mischa. They're *all* murderers, too lazy to work!"

"I will take him to the foreigners, Father."

"There are others like this one? In Siberia?"

"Yes, Father, Americans like this man, and also many more strangers. The Americans build a railroad, but the Chinese, Japanese, Czechs, and English have come too. This is what the revolution has done. Russia is overrun with foreigners!"

"Won't they kill you, Mischa? How can we trust foreigners?"

"I will not trust them, Father. I will take this man to them and let them decide what to do with him. Perhaps they will give me food or maybe a new shovel. They might even give me a gun, so that if the Cossacks come I can shoot them."

***

The American struggled, unable to match Mischa's pace. Mischa patiently waited until he caught up. Perhaps the boots, a pair Mischa had outgrown several years before, were not a good fit.

They crossed railroad tracks late that afternoon. Two hours later, they came to a cleared space that was almost half a mile across. In the center stood a wall made of upright tree trunks, slightly taller than six feet.

Ahead was a pair of sturdy gates that met in the middle. The wall curved away on each side. In appearance, except for the trench surrounding the wall, the fort would have looked at home in the old American west.

"First Sergeant, you better come see this! There's a Russian at the gate and he's got somebody with him. The other fellow looks like he's been run over by a truck or something!"

"Dammit, Heintzelman, can't you make a decision for yourself? You're a *corporal* now!"

"Want me to just shoot these two?"

"Hell no! Well, not unless they've got guns. Hang on, I'll be right there." The First Sergeant, judging by the stripes on his sleeve, set down the cup of coffee and picked up his trench shotgun. "Heintzelman says there are a couple of Russians at the gate. I'll be right back, but you three pick up your rifles and watch what happens. Smithers, if this is some kind of trick, you'll be sorry you were ever born!"

"It's not, Top," said the mortified Smithers. "It's just like I told you."

"Back me up, Heintzelman. Be ready, but don't shoot unless I do."

"*Me*, First Sergeant? Can't I do better if I stay behind cover?"

"*With me*, Heintzelman. That's why they pay you the big money now. Or will, one of these days."

"Shit, I should'a stayed a *private*!"

The ragged man with the Russian heard this exchange. "Are you Americans?"

"Son of a gun, this character speaks *English*!" exclaimed Smithers.

"Well, sort of. It don't sound like Boston English, so maybe he's with that English regiment that's up north of us," suggested

Heintzelman.

"We're Americans. Are you English?" The First Sergeant looked doubtful, then continued. "You're not a Czech, are you?"

"No, I'm pretty sure I'm American. What are you doing here? Isn't this Russia?"

"I guess you could call it that. We're part of the AEF-S, Army troops assigned to Siberia."

"I don't think I knew that there were Americans here! But I don't remember much of anything. I don't even know how I got here! But I found this man, and he fed me and brought me here. The fur coat and cap are his, the boots too."

"I guess we'll take charge of you then. Heintzelman, you speak Russian, more than I do, anyway. Tell that fellow thanks and send him on his way."

"Okay, Sarge." Heintzelman rattled off a string of words and the Russian answered back. "Top, he says he's hungry. He also wants to know if we can give him a shovel for finding the American? If we don't have a shovel, can we give him a rifle?"

"Aye, we'll be giving him both! Take one of the extra rifles in the lieutenant's hut. We'll replace it from that shipment the general is refusing to turn over to Semenoff. Ammo too, give him a case if he's willing to carry it. He *does* look hungry, so have the cooks feed him too before you send him on his way."

"Wait a minute. I've got something for him too." The stranger pulled out two coins from a money belt and handed them to the delighted Mischa.

"Are you part of the 31st Infantry, Buddy? Or maybe the Russian Railroad Service Corps?" Smithers asked. "They're Americans."

"I don't know. I don't think so. Wouldn't I remember if I was?"

"Maybe not," Heintzelman said. "More than one good man has gone crazy over here! It's the ass end of the world, Chum. Why the hell President Wilson ever decided we should be sent here is beyond me! Maybe he's crazy too. It was bad enough, heading for

France to be part of the Ass End Foremost, but Siberia? We just this past Christmas got our wool uniforms!"

"You can give that Russian back his coat and hat," decided Mac. "They're mostly so poor that they need everything they've got, not to mention that one probably has cooties. You come with me, we'll get you a uniform. I reckon we can get you a rifle too. In this part of the world you need a gun of some kind! You ever shoot a rifle? The Springfield is guaranteed to put a Cossack down if you hit him in the right place, and when it does he won't be getting up again."

"I don't know. I don't remember."

"You got a name, Buddy?"

"I think so. I would have to, wouldn't I? But I don't remember what it is."

***

"Major, I've got a fellow here who says he doesn't remember his name. He wasn't wearing a uniform, just some scorched rags. Lucky he wasn't caught out overnight! He'd have got pretty damned cold if a bear didn't get him first! Anyway, he says he's American and I believe him. He sounds like us, some of us anyway. Maybe he's from Texas or someplace like that. He doesn't sound eastern."

"One of ours, Lieutenant?"

"Not as far as I can tell, Sir. Like I said, he wasn't wearing a uniform when he showed up. He was wearing borrowed Russian clothes over a ragged coat with a label inside that said New York. You want I should send him on to Vladivostok?"

The major drummed his fingers on the desk and thought. "Could he be one of those railroad people?"

"I don't think so. He was surprised to find us here, so that makes me think he's not one of our missing or killed in action, body not recovered, guys. He couldn't remember his name, but when I tried to use letters to see if anything jogged his memory he said 't' sounded familiar. So maybe his name starts with a T.

Except for not remembering his name, he seems pretty sharp."

"Didn't the 2nd Battalion lose a Corporal Tyler last month? They never found the body, so they reported him KIA-BNR. He could be Tyler, or one of the other people we never got back. Let me think for a minute."

The major took a full minute and more. Finally, he decided. "He could be Tyler. Any sign of recent wounds?

"None I saw. Most soldiers pick up scrapes here and there, but if he's got any wounds or scars I didn't see them."

"The important thing is he's American, or at least he thinks he is, so we can't just tell him to hit the road. At the same time, we can't keep feeding him if he's not on the morning report. Tell you what, send him into Vladivostok and let the doctor examine him. If he pronounces him fit for duty, ask him if he's willing to enlist and point out that if he doesn't, he's on his own. Either way, that should work, and we can always discharge him later if we find out he's English or a civilian. But don't make him a corporal, at least not yet. Let's see how he does first. He might be Tyler, or for all we know he might be Tippecanoe!"

The First Sergeant, who had accompanied the lieutenant, smiled at the joke, saluted, and went off to follow his orders. He was a happy man; casualties hadn't been replaced, meaning the work had been shared among fewer men. The ones in hospital might come back at some point, assuming they got over the cholera, but in the meantime, one more warm body would help. And if the new soldier didn't know how to soldier, well, teaching him would be just the thing for Corporal Heintzelman! About time that slacker earned his new stripes!

But after that, assign him to a veteran NCO who knew the ropes. Two inexperienced people in the same squad? No, that was a recipe for disaster, even though it might be necessary when a unit was in the lines.

Aye, Corporal O'Brien could certainly use him!

Chapter One

The squad went to ground as soon as they heard the shot. The first bang was followed by several more as the riflemen sought better cover, clicked off safeties, and waited. The Chauchat automatic rifle chattered briefly, then fell silent. Private Tyler glanced at Private Smithers, who lay sprawled half-atop the weapon.

"Tyler! Get that gun into action, *now!*"

"I'm on it, Corporal!" Tyler rolled over three times, that being the fastest way to reach Smithers. Dragging the weapon from beneath the man's unconscious form, he fitted the stock into his shoulder and looked for a target. But there was no sign of life in the fringe of bushes that lined the far rim of the arroyo.

"Shoot, Tyler!"

Corporal O'Brien fitted a clip of five cartridges to the open breech of his Springfield and pressed down firmly, stripping the rounds into the rifle's magazine. Chambering a round, he fired at the base of a bush that showed a faint trace of smoke. Moments later, Tyler's Chauchat joined in, the bullet strikes kicking up dust as they pocked the ground from left to right.

A cloth hat tumbled out from behind the bush, followed moments later by the body of a man. Tyler thumbed the release, dropping the depleted magazine. He fumbled a replacement from the pouch at Smithers' waist, slid it into the weapon's well, and cycled the bolt to feed a round into the chamber. Smithers groaned and tried to sit up, then fell back.

Tyler watched the far side of the arroyo. But there were no more targets and the shooting had stopped. He looked deeper into the trees beyond the screening brush. Nothing stirred.

Thirty yards to the squad's left stood the sturdy wooden railroad bridge they'd come to check out. If there was damage, nothing showed from where they had gone to ground. Across the ravine, Tyler noticed that the man he'd shot looked strange. Something was wrong with his head. He suddenly realized that one of his bullets had smashed the man's jaw, knocking it askew before penetrating the skull.

"We'll wait a while before we take a look." Corporal O'Brien's voice was calm. "Tyler, check on Smithers."

"He's alive, Corporal. Got a lump on his skull and he's bleeding. I think he's waking up."

"Then put a bandage over the wound! *His* bandage, not yours. That'll have to do until we get back to camp."

Tyler, usually called T by his squad-mates, eased the compress into position and tied it in place. Glancing again at the dead man, T remembered that today was an occasion of sorts. He'd joined the US Army's American Expeditionary Force in Siberia just three months ago.

***

"Where in the world did you dig that one up, First Sergeant?"

"The major handed him to me as a gift and I immediately thought of you, Corporal. Now I know you're convinced I hate your guts, but that's not true. No indeed, I thanked the major and immediately thought of you. Mac, says I, Corporal O'Brien is just the boy to make Private Tyler into a soldier I can be proud of! After all, didn't I take *Private* O'Brien and make *him* a soldier? One that major Herne could promote to corporal and trust to lead my First Squad?"

"Some squad, Sarge! 'Tis me and four privates fresh off the boat! And now, Tyler! He fits right in. He's clumsy as *Paddy's pig*, so he is, and in poor shape to boot! We but hiked down to the railroad, no more than five miles it was, and he was puffing like...well, I thought the train was coming, that I did! I doubt the man's ever done an honest day's work in his life! I handed him a maul and told him to reseat a loose rail spike, but somehow, he managed to break the handle! He's strong, I'll give him that, but no endurance to speak of. He's fair *useless* and next week I've got to take him to the rifle range! He knows how to march in step, I'll give him that much, but better 'twould have been if Heintzelman had taught him to shoot!"

"Train him, me boy, train him! Just think, now you've got *five* men in your squad, and any day the major's going to send a letter up to regiment mentioning your name for sergeant. 'Tis a compliment to me, it is." The burly first sergeant's eyes twinkled at the disgruntled corporal.

"Now if ye're done drinking that excellent Army coffee and crying on me shoulder, how about being off and earning that excellent salary that the Army will pay you one of these days?"

"*What* pay? We haven't been paid for three months! I think old Black Jack sent us to Russia and then forgot about us!"

"Don't ye fret, lad. Doesn't the Army feed you well and give you a warm blanket to sleep under? And aren't you able to cut the finest spruce tips for a soft bed at night? Why, you're living better than you *ever* did in the ooold country!" The sergeant's voice changed. "Now suppose you round up that miscreant and the other four and get out on the square. I want to see them properly executing the manual of arms for the Springfield rifle by sundown, or you can lead them in another round of drill after dark. Do ye take my meaning, *Corporal*?"

Corporal O'Brien sighed and stood up. "I'll be about it, but ye're a *hard man*, Mac MacAuliffe, that ye are." The corporal picked up his Springfield, checked that the safety was on by habit, then shouldered the piece as he left the hut. He squared his campaign hat and immediately bawled out a command. "Aw right, you people! Form up and try to look like *soljers*, even though you're a disgrace to the uniform! You'll never *be* soldiers, but as God's my witness, you'll look enough like one to fool someone from a distance by the time I'm through with yez!"

Tyler was the first to take position. He muttered to Private Dyson as the corporal approached the three. "Is he always like this?"

"Naw. Sometimes he's mad at us. You can tell by the way he talks. When he gets upset, that brogue is plumb hard to understand!"

"Shut your gob, Dyson! And Tyler, there'll be no more hiding from honest work! You're assigned to First Squad now and you'll work, or I'll know the reason why!"

***

But three months later, Corporal O'Brien's opinion of Tyler had changed.

"T'was a fair bit of shooting, Tyler. How's Smithers doing?" Corporal O'Brien's voice was soft, barely louder than a whisper.

Tyler matched the corporal's volume. "Says he's all right, Corporal. You still intend to cross that bridge?"

"And didn't First Sergeant MacAuliffe himself order me to? He'd be disappointed if I didn't, and Mac MacAuliffe is not the man you want to disappoint. I'll give it half an hour more, and then we're heading across, watching the rails in case the guerrillas decided to pull a few spikes before we got here. They were up to something, no reason for them to be here otherwise."

"Suggestion, Corporal. How about I move down the arroyo a ways and cross over before you move onto the bridge? I'll just have a look and if that far side's clear, I'll signal. But be careful; I'd hate to get shot by accident."

"'Tis too chancy! If anybody's over there, they might spot you as soon as you start moving."

"There's enough underbrush to hide me," Tyler argued, "and they won't be watching if you and the others keep them busy. Fire a shot every couple of minutes and stop in...twenty minutes, I should be in position by then. As soon as you stop, I'll sneak up to where that one was hiding. They're not really soldiers, they're bandits for the most part, and they'll run as soon as I start firing. "

"We'll keep them busy, then. Are ye sure you want to try this alone? I could send Dyson with you."

"I'll make less noise alone. He has big feet."

"That he does," chuckled O'Brien, "and he's not all that careful where he puts them. Go ahead, then. We'll shoot up the bushes for twenty minutes. Tell you what, just before we stop, I'll have

Smithers burn through a full magazine. I wish I had somebody else to send with you, but..."

"Yeah. Too bad McKinney caught the flu. He's pretty good in the woods."

"That he is. Well, lad, 'twas your idea, so off you go. We'll do our bit." Corporal O'Brien studied the far wall for a moment, then turned to voice one last caution to Private Tyler.

But he was gone, leaving no sign that he'd been there at all. O'Brien's worry lines eased; Tyler might just be as good in the woods as he thought he was. Low-crawling, O'Brien worked his way over to Private Smithers. "I want you to put a few rounds into the bushes, starting with that bush to the right of the dead man. 'Tis the one with the white flowers. And when I signal, change magazines. I'm going to want you to lay down a full magazine just above the edge of the ravine. No more shooting after that unless I tell you. Don't bother with that bush to the left of the body; if anyone else was there, you can bet he's gone by now."

"I see it, Corporal. Looks like a rhododendron, doesn't it?"

"I don't care if it looks like yer Aunt *Sally*, Smithers! Put a short burst at the base of it!"

"I don't have an Aunt Sally, Corporal."

Corporal O'Brien sighed. "Five shot burst, Smithers. If you can't control that gun, I'll give it to Private Tyler. You can be *his* ammo bearer!"

The Chauchat chattered briefly and the 'rhododendron' fell, cut through.

"Better, Smithers, better. Now let's be moving yer gun to the left. See that scrubby thing that looks like a young spruce?"

***

"Ye killed two of the bastards, Patrick? And what did you do with the bodies?"

"Dumped them in the arroyo, Mac, and destroyed their rifles. Old Moisins they were, not worth bringing in. I smashed the receivers and bent the barrels around a tree. The bolts I brought back; ye can have them for souvenirs."

"I'll send them up to battalion, that I will," First Sergeant Mac decided. "That intelligence lieutenant swears Semenoff's troops are a hundred miles west of here, so he does, and I'll let him argue with the evidence. No damage to the bridge?"

"None. We checked it over, nothing to worry about. Well, other than that it was built by Russians, not honest Irishmen."

"How did Private Tyler do?"

"Acted like a veteran, so he did, and 'twas himself that volunteered to clear the far side of the arroyo. That's where he shot the second one. Both shot in the head, Mac. He's as good a marksman as I've ever seen. Got a positive talent for it, he has. It's like he knows where the bullet's going to go."

"Good man to have around, then. Well, finish yer coffee and see to your men, Patrick. I'll be sure to mention your name when I telephone the Colonel."

"Telephone the Colonel, eh? Ye wouldn't be making fun of yer favorite corporal, now would ye?"

"'Twas bragging about our new telephone I was, Patrick! But I've been with the Colonel a fair few years now, since before the war. He'll want to know about the two guerrillas yer man Tyler shot."

"Then how about asking him if we're ever going to get paid when you pay your respects?"

"On your way, Patrick O'Brien."

***

"Sir, we're trying to play catch up without enough players on the field!"

Colonel Morrow commanded the 27th Infantry Regiment, newly-nicknamed the Wolfhounds. He had brought with him to the meeting an intelligence summary prepared by Major David Barrows, temporarily loaned to the AEF-S, which had been supplemented by a more-extensive intelligence appraisal from his own intelligence officer, Captain F.F. Meere. He had handed those to the general after reporting, who had laid them on his desk.

"Did you read my proclamation to the Russian People, Colonel?" asked General Graves.

"Yes, Sir."

"That's all, Colonel? Just 'Yes, Sir'? And stand at ease. Better yet, have yourself a cup of coffee. Brandy with it?"

The colonel shook his head. "Sir, I answered the general's question. It's not for me to comment on the general's proclamation."

General Graves chuckled. "I didn't like it all that much myself, but I don't have a lot of choice. Take a lesson, Colonel. One day, you'll be a general yourself and you'll be in a situation something like I'm in. I wrote the proclamation because that's what President Wilson wants me to do. The War Department has different ideas, and so does the State Department, and for my sins I'm responsible for those too. I'll get to that in a minute. I don't have nearly enough troops to start with, and they're spread out from Archangelsk to Vladivostok. Total, just slightly more than 7000 officers and men. The northern detachment is under British command, and when they're not guarding the supply dumps, they're fighting the Bolsheviks. Down here, we're trying to be *nice* to the Bolsheviks because they're fighting Semenoff's army!

"Semenoff was being paid by the British up until a couple of months ago. He used the money to recruit and pay his troops, but when he ran short of Cossacks he recruited others, and they're mostly bandits. Who have now stolen at *least* two, maybe three, locomotives and a number of train cars! Which Semenoff has *armored*! He uses the trains to raid towns *I'm* responsible for! But the British got tired of his raiding and stopped paying. The intelligence department says the Japanese are his new paymasters, but we haven't confirmed it yet.

"I mentioned the War Department. Their orders are for me to keep the Trans-Siberian Railroad and the Chinese Eastern Railway open to all traffic. You've got a little more than a thousand men, almost as many as Semenoff has, but they're spread out because that's the way it has to be. I don't have a single additional company I can give you! Not one! I thought of assigning my MP's to your battalion, but they've already had to break up a fight between American railroad workers and Semenoff's troops!

"I'm stretched to the breaking point, Colonel. You should have at least two regiments to cover the area you're responsible for, but all you have is two companies and because of the sickness they're barely larger than platoons. The only thing I can do is tell you I'll try to avoid turning over those arms to Semenoff as long as I can. But I may not be able to do that for much longer; if the State Department insists, I won't have a choice. Meantime, I *don't* want to know about it if bandits raid that arms shipment you're holding. Do you take my meaning, Colonel?"

"Yes, Sir!" Colonel Morrow stood and came to attention. "Permission to withdraw, General?"

"Granted. I would do more if I could, Colonel. One thing I *can* do if your people really get into a fight, I've got a few marines I can send you, temporarily. I keep them back until they're desperately needed, so you can't have them permanently. Meantime, I suggest you augment your forces with local hires. Laborers, kitchen workers, wagoneers and mule drivers, people like that; they can go out with your patrols and carry back supplies. My budget will support that."

"Thank you, Sir." Colonel Morrow saluted and held the salute until General Graves returned it.

By the time Morrow closed the door, the general had started studying the intelligence summaries the colonel had left on his desk.

Chapter Two

Second Lieutenant Thornton came to attention, saluted, and announced, "Lieutenant Thornton, Robert, reporting as ordered, Sir!"

"At ease, Lieutenant. Coffee?"

"Sir, yes Sir!"

"Relax, Lieutenant, this isn't West Point and you're not here for an ass chewing. Get your coffee and sit down. I wanted to ask about this report."

"Is there something wrong with it, Sir?"

"No, and I said relax! I just wanted to confirm a few things. How's morale holding up?"

"As well as can be expected, Sir. The men aren't happy. The rest of the AEF are either going into Germany as occupation forces, or they're heading home for demobbing. But we're stuck here, and the men wonder if they've been forgotten."

"They haven't," Colonel Morrow said. "Mail still arrives, it's slow but it's sure, and the paymaster will be around in a few days. Things will improve. This Tyler, your new man; how's he shaping up?"

"Better than expected, Sir. Corporal Heintzelman taught him a few things, how to wear the uniform and such, but as soon as he picked up a Springfield it was obvious that he'd done a lot of shooting. Outstanding marksman, as good as anyone in the company! He's equally skilled when firing the pistol and the Chauchat automatic rifle. Most have trouble with trigger creep, but not Tyler. He was squeezing off careful three-round bursts within five minutes. First Sergeant MacAuliffe is impressed!"

"Old Mac; I'm surprised he's still in," Colonel Morrow mused. "He must have 30 years in the Army now."

"Yes, Sir. But he doesn't want to retire, Colonel; I gather there's nothing for him at home."

"Yeah. The Spanish flu hit his family hard. I don't know if he mentioned it, but they had three boys. The kids got it first. His wife

25

Flo...the flu turned into pneumonia and after that, it took her too.

"But about Tyler; you wrote that according to Corporal O'Brien, he's steady under fire and shows commendable initiative?"

"Yes, Sir. Send me as many more like him as you can find. My A Company is the best in the First Battalion, I'll make it the best in the regiment!"

The colonel leaned back, making the swivel chair creak. He looked across the desk at Lieutenant Thornton, making up his mind about something. Thornton waited; whatever it was, it probably wouldn't be good. "I've got a problem, Lieutenant, and you're just the fellow to help me solve it. The battalion only has two short-handed companies and the general has no troops to spare. I asked and he explained, which was more than I expected. Our orders are to control the port of Vladivostok and keep the Trans-Siberian and Chinese Eastern railroads open to all customers. I don't have enough troops and my men can't maneuver. We're stuck guarding the railroads, but the Cossacks are cavalrymen who can hit us wherever they've a mind to. The only good thing is that at least half of Semenoff's so-called army are simple bandits. As for the railroad, as soon as we get more rolling stock Semenoff steals it. He's got at least as many men as I have and intelligence says the Japanese are paying him now, which may allow him to recruit more. His former British paymasters were fairly tight-fisted. So tell me, Lieutenant; in my shoes, how would you multiply your forces?"

"Guns, Sir." Thornton's answer was prompt. "Employ artillery and massed machine gun fire at critical points." The earlier uncertainty had gone.

"That's the West Point solution, Son, but it won't work here. I don't have artillery to give you, for one, and there are no massed troops to use it on for another. Semenoff's people don't stand and fight, they raid, sabotage, and if they run into opposition, they fade back into whatever crack they crawled out of. But I'll mention in passing that we're holding on to an arms shipment. It was supposed to go to Semenoff, but the general doesn't want to give it to him. Arm an enemy that's opposing us in the field? Madness! But the State Department might not leave him the choice. The shipment contains rifles, mortars, automatic rifles and machine guns, and ammo. The rifles are in a locked building and the explosives are in a bunker a short distance away. You might mention that to First Sergeant Mac.

"But there's another solution. The Boche had more and better machine guns when the war started, but when we showed up the AEF had something they didn't have. Ever hear about that fellow from Tennessee, Alvin York? I hear he's a sergeant now."

"Sharpshooters, Sir? But we still have that maneuver problem you mentioned, and the guerrillas can show up anywhere. They were bent on mischief when Corporal O'Brien's patrol ran into them, I'm sure of it, but they took off after losing two men. I'm not sure that having a designated sharpshooter along would have helped."

"Keep thinking, Lieutenant. You're getting there."

"The enemy doesn't bother pulling a few spikes now," the lieutenant mused. "The American Railway Service--make that the Russian Railway Service, mostly Americans--just resets the rails and moves on. But they were definitely up to something when my patrol interrupted them! You think they intended to destroy the bridge?"

"That's the only explanation that makes sense," the colonel agreed. "Semenoff's got a serious tactical problem called the Czech Legion. They were fighting on the Eastern Front with the Tsar's Army, but the Bolsheviks turned on them as soon as they made peace with the Kaiser. The Germans pulled out most of their divisions and sent them to the Western Front, but there are still too many for the Czechs to fight their way through so they can't go home. Germans to the west, Bolsheviks to the east; they're essentially trapped. But they have been loyal allies, and President Wilson is determined to get them out. That's where we come in, and it's one of the reasons we're guarding the railroad.

"The Czechs are heading for Vladivostok. They've fought several small battles since the Bolsheviks made peace and won them all. They lost people, but the rest are here in Siberia. Which brings me to Semenoff. He has to stop them, or he loses control of the railroad, but they're soldiers, real fighters, and his people are mostly simple bandits. If the Czechs reach his headquarters in Chita, he loses control of several thousand square miles of territory. Without that base, Semenoff's no longer a general, he's just a bandit on the run, and there are several factions that intend to hang him if they catch him."

"Yes, Sir. It's not surprising that his men ran! Not only are they undisciplined, they're not good shots. Their rifles are old, and the only ones I've seen are Moisins with permanently fixed bayonets. Not very maneuverable in a fight, and not very accurate even when they were new."

"Keep going, Lieutenant."

"Yes, Sir. So if we can't watch the tracks, you think putting a sharpshooter to watch the bridges would pay off? Or maybe send out long range patrols?"

"Not a sharpshooter, Lieutenant; the Brits call them snipers. Something to do with gamekeepers and snipe, I'm thinking, but it's been working well for them. One man or a two-man team can tie up a lot of enemy forces! It's one thing to advance knowing that you might be shot at, it's quite another to realize that as soon as you break cover you're dead. A team, maybe the size of that small patrol you sent out, would work best. The British have been doing it for a few years now and they're training our troops, the ones around Archangel, as snipe-hunters. That's what made me think of this."

"Sir, you're asking me to divide my forces!" the lieutenant protested.

"*Custer* didn't have Lewis guns or Brownings, Lieutenant! You might point that out to First Sergeant Mac, because he's bound to complain. And don't forget about that arms shipment, he really needs to know about that. Make sure you tell him what's in it."

"Yes, Sir. I'll be sure to do that."

***

The message was duly delivered. Mac frowned, then grinned. "I take the general's meaning, Lieutenant. Now, if there's nothing more, I need to get to work."

"Dismissed, First Sergeant."

An observer might have noticed that Top MacAuliffe was busy for some time after he left the lieutenant.

And that later that afternoon, he led a small group away from the camp.

***

"Keep it quiet! Do you want to get us shot?" Mac was mad, and made even madder because he had to keep his voice down.

"Sorry, Top," whispered Corporal O'Brien. "But the guard's asleep, and the duty officer won't bother to check. He sacks out after midnight because he has to work tomorrow. Besides, Private Jensen doesn't have any bullets. Regiment's afraid he will shoot a local."

"But he *has* got a bayonet! And I said *keep quiet!*"

Sensibly, O'Brien decided that if his first sergeant wanted to know more, he would ask.

The lock was Russian and far from new. Private Smithers had volunteered to pick it, a fairly simple process or should have been. But the lock stubbornly remained locked. He, along with Private Tyler who had been assigned to assist, huddled around the door. The others moved away to allow them to work. They would also keep watch for Private Jensen, who might decide this was the night to wake up and check the building he was supposed to be guarding.

Smithers fumbled at the lock again, frustrated. "The damned thing is *rusty!*" he whispered. "The shackle should have released, but nothing's happening!"

"I'll hold the body of the lock, you make sure you didn't miss one of the tumblers," Tyler offered.

"I'm sure I got them all, but maybe the tensioner didn't hold tight enough to keep one from slipping back. Okay, you hold it and I'll use both hands."

Tyler, called T by the squad, gripped the body of the lock, waiting for Smithers to do his work. Idly he wondered how Smithers knew what to do, then pushed the thought aside. If Smithers wanted to open up about his past, he'd do so without being asked. At least he *had* a past, unlike T, who sometimes had strange dreams. But didn't everyone? Especially dreams of flying, of soaring effortlessly across the landscape while feeling the stiff breeze in his face?

Of reality, there was no trace. Who and what he was...he might have been born anew that day he stumbled into the clearing. What was Mischa doing now? Did he really intend to use his new rifle to hunt bandits? If so, more power to him! While thinking, T had unconsciously kept tension on the lock body. Suddenly it popped open, the click as it opened sounding gunshot-loud to the men.

"Leave it unlocked and hang it on your belt," whispered Mac. "As soon as the door opens, get inside. And no talking!"

The hinges squeaked, but the sound was slight. Moments later, they were inside the rude building. Dim light penetrated through a small, barred window set just below the roof peak, revealing orderly stacks of boxes. "We should be safe enough now, but keep your voices low. Check the boxes; there should be labels somewhere. I'll be wanting twenty pistols and five BARs, so I will. Leave everything else and try not to create a mess. I may want to come back here again."

The crates were strapped with metal bands, but wire cutters worked almost as well on the bands as they had on the barbed wire of the Western Front. Using a pair of trench knives to pry open the lid, they carefully opened one of the wooden crates. Long paper-wrapped packages were stacked side by side, held apart by wooden spacers. "Replace the Brownings with those damned Chauchats!" Mac murmured. "I'm glad to see the last of them! How are you doing with the pistol crates?"

"I got them open, Top," said Tyler. "I think I can carry the twenty you want and one of the BARs. I'll just run a wire--there was a spool on that shelf against the wall, along with a hammer and some other tools--through the trigger guards. That'll do until we get back to the camp."

"Good thinking, Tyler! Smithers, you carry one BAR, I'll carry one, and Dolan, you carry the other two. What about that steel strapping? We can't just leave it."

"Put it in the case with the other BARs," suggested Tyler. "We'll put the cover back in place, tap the nails in, and no one will notice."

"Tyler, I swear you had to have been a thief somewhere before you joined up! Do it and let's get out of here."

"Just one thing, Sarge. I'm not carrying two fucking automatic rifles. Those damned things are heavy!" Dolan stopped speaking suddenly.

Corporal O'Brien had produced a toad sticker, a weapon that combined a cut-down bayonet and a heavy brass knuckle-guard. The needle tip now rested against Dolan's chest.

"Recognize it, Dolan? It used to be a Lebel bayonet, one of the triangular ones. But I might not stick you; I might just see whether the knuckleduster can break a jaw. Feel like eating mush for a month or so, Dolan?"

"I..."

"Don't kill him here, Patrick! Make him walk; if he gives you any lip after that, just make sure it's deniable. I doubt anyone will ask questions." Mac's voice left no doubt that he meant precisely what he'd said, that he'd just given Corporal O'Brien permission to murder Dolan if he caused further problems.

"I'll carry thim, but begorra, I should be the gunner! 'Tis *wrong* I should carry a gun for somebody else! You need a big man to carry that heavy damned BAR!"

"We'll talk about it back at camp," Corporal O'Brien whispered. "But make no mistake, Dolan, you try shirking in my squad and yer mother will get a nicer letter from the lieutenant than she deserves."

Dolan fumed, but picked up the two wrapped weapons, which together with the accessories brought the combined weight to almost a hundred pounds. He suddenly realized that Tyler, who probably weighed no more than a hundred and fifty pounds, had to be carrying almost as much weight. And those pistols, even hung across his shoulders, had to be an awkward load.

"Patrick, lead the way," MacAuliffe ordered. "Dolan, you stay with the corporal. If ye cause trouble, *I'll* find you. My trench knife works as well as that fancy French toad-sticker, and you don't like the steel, now do you? You keep that in mind!

"We'll be along as soon as Smithers replaces the lock, Patrick; don't stop until you're back at the camp. Put the BARs in my quarters. I'll see that the guns are put where they'll do the most harm. O'Brien, you and Tyler hang onto the pistols. Clean the new weapons tomorrow after morning drill, and we'll see about test firing them in a day or so."

He was answered by silent nods, barely visible in the dimness, and the two men slipped away in the darkness. As soon as the two were far enough away, Tyler, whispering, voiced a concern. "We could have left one of the BARs. We only had four Chauchats."

"We could, but I doubt anyone will check the numbers and I wanted to make a point. Dolan's a bad actor, been in the stockade more times than I can count! Give him his due, he fights when fighting is called for, but he's also got the disease; he's got a thirst as big as he is and he's a brawler even when he's sober. Corporal O'Brien will do what's necessary, so he will, but *you* two need to be careful! He'll take out his temper on the two of yez if he gets half a chance. Ye might see about picking up a toad-sticker of yer own, but they're not easy to find in Russia. If ye can't, trench knives are common enough and Dolan doesn't like the steel, he fair doesn't. He'll kill a man with his fists, but the cold steel is not to his liking!"

"I'll watch him," said T. "He won't cause trouble."

Sergeant Mac nodded; there had been no doubt in Tyler's words. What did he know? Was his memory returning? Well. The team would be going out in a few days, as soon as the lieutenant gave his approval. After that, it would be up to Corporal Patrick O'Brien.

And just maybe, Private T if he was as good a fighter as he thought he was.

Chapter Three

"You up for another midnight requisition, Tyler?" asked Sergeant Mac.

"Sure, Top. More BARs?"

"Not this time. The lieutenant wants a sharpshooter, and the colonel has a Springfield that was set up especially for him by the regimental armorer. It's capable of minute of angle or less."

"Really? An inch at a hundred yards? If I ever shot anything that accurate, I don't remember. But then, there's still a lot I don't remember. Some things have come back, but not everything."

"It happens," Mac agreed. "Some of the boys have it worse. I remember one, got caught in a mortar barrage while we were stationed in the Philippines; I don't think he ever spoke another word, just sat staring at the wall. The Army shipped him home."

"Poor guy," mused Private Tyler. "I keep hoping the rest of my memory comes back. I have dreams, but they don't make sense."

"Dreams of fighting?" asked Sergeant Mac. He had dreams of his own. And some were nightmares.

"Not exactly. There's an eagle, not a bald eagle but one of the brownish ones like you see over here, and I'm flying alongside it."

"'Tis a strange dream indeed, Lad! Anyway, back to the colonel's Springfield. There's only one like it in the regiment. 'Tis the colonel's personal weapon, but he never checks it out, not even to go hunting. Lots of officers do that, you know, some of the troops too. Plenty of deer and bear around here, and the cooks are glad to get the meat. But the colonel wears a Colt auto on duty, one of the new M1911A1 models. I figure you need the rifle more than he does, and if we replace it with a Springfield from that shipment he'll never know the difference."

"You think I need it? I'm pretty good with the one I was issued."

"Are ye? You fired the standard known-distance course, but only out to 600 yards. I'll hand you this much, you did pretty good considering the rifle. Now I know a thing or two about precision marksmanship, so I do. I tried out for the Army Marksmanship Team in 1907. I thought I had a chance, but I lost out during the final practice match. The point is that we fired at targets that were 1000 yards away. That's over half a mile, me bucko, and at that range the 30-inch bullseye is but a dot that's less than half the width of the front sight. The slightest breeze can throw you off, so it can. That's what happened to me, I doped the wind wrong. I was cut from the team, so I was, but I never forgot. A Springfield will kill a man as far as you can see him...if yer a good enough shot."

"Top, you're probably a better shot than I am! Why don't you take the colonel's rifle?"

"Two reasons, me boyo. I like being the company first sergeant, so I do, and one of these days I'll be a master sergeant. But if the colonel got word I was shooting his pet rifle, I'd be busted back to private before I could sneeze. The other reason is that I've got a reinforced half-company to take care of right now, and maybe later on I shall have a full company, and that reinforced too! If I volunteered for this special mission, somebody else would get that promotion, so he would."

"But what happens to me if the colonel finds out I have his rifle?"

"How? Yer not going to tell, I'm not going to tell, and Smithers is yet a private. Nobody listens to privates, Lad. Even if the colonel heard about it, yer *already* a private so he can't bust you. And I hear tell the chow in the stockade is better than what we get, plus you don't have to fill sandbags in the rain."

"Put that way, why not? I'd rather shoot a Cossack when he's a thousand yards away. Much better than trying to bayonet him when he's about to whack my head off with a sword! But how are we going to do this? The regimental arms room is bound to be better guarded than that storage shack."

"Oh, it is, me bucko, but we're not breaking in. We'll take a Springfield from the shipment, aye, and clean it properly. But then we'll waltz into the arms room big as you please. *If...*"

"If, Sergeant Mac?" T was suddenly suspicious.

"*If* ye have two more gold coins like ye gave to that Russian! The armorer will do the exchange, but he's taking a chance, so he is, and he expects a little extra for his time and trouble. He'll change the serial numbers in the records, but if he changed the colonel's serial number and substituted *yours*, the which is on the detachment's property book, 'tis possible some nosey might find out. Now it could just be that there's a record somewhere that says it was issued to you, or to A Company, at least. 'Tis why we'll have to steal one from the shipment. There is no list of serial numbers, just the model number and quantity."

"But won't someone wonder if the count comes up short?"

"And why would they? *Our* officers won't care, so they won't! The arms are probably going to the Russians anyway. They might say something about a missing rifle, but they also might not. If they hope to get more later on, ye ken, they'll keep mum. 'Tis a piece of cake, Lad!"

"So why would we be going to the arms room? We need a reason, don't we?"

"*Maintenance*, me boy! I've noticed that the front sight on your rifle is a wee bit worn, and the armorer, who's school-trained, is the only one who can decide if something needs replacing. Now 'tis true that most of the time a bottle of rum or a few beers will do when a fellow needs a favor that's off the books, but this time he's being a bit skittish. 'Tis the colonels personal rifle, d'ye see. He's a buck sergeant and likes being one, but for a pair of double eagles he's willing to do what's needed."

T nodded understanding. "So when are we going to do this, Top?"

"I'll let ye know. You do have the gold, right? Two double eagles?"

"I don't know. The few I've got left might be eagles or even half-eagles. But forty bucks worth, I think I still have that much. Maybe. I'll have to sneak out of camp to get it."

"Don't get caught, lad, especially not by an officer! In the meantime, I'll just have a chat with my friend and have him take a good look at the colonel's rifle. If it needs a new sling or something, he'll see to it before we stop by for a visit."

"Now that you mention it, Top, have him put a new sling on the one we're taking. Take the colonel's *old* sling and transfer it to the rifle we're substituting! The colonel might not notice the serial number of his piece, but he'll notice if the sling is different. Or at least *I* would."

"And so would I, my lad, so would I! Ye're another born thief, me boy. You'll go far in this man's army, mark my words! If ye can stay out of Dolan's way, that is. He been bothering you?"

"Not so far. I hear he gets mean when he's had a snootful."

"Aye, and the lieutenant wants you four to have a couple of days off before you leave. He'll have his chance at the whiskey, so he will. Be careful; you don't look like a pug, me boy. Yer nose is too straight and yer ears still look like ears."

"I don't think I ever boxed, if that's what you mean, but Dolan's clumsy. I saw him in the ring two weeks ago when he fought that machine gunner from B Company. His footwork stinks."

"That it does, but don't get overconfident! He's bull-strong and quick. He knows about his footwork, it's why he only fights in local matches. The regimental champ would tear his head off and feed it to him backwards, so he would."

"He's strong," T agreed. "But he telegraphs his punches. It was like I knew what he was going to do before he did it! But I don't have any reason to start trouble. If he leaves me alone, I'll do the same to him."

***

T and Smithers sat cross-legged by a scrap of canvas, once part of a shelter half. They had disassembled two of the 'requisitioned' pistols and were meticulously removing the grease that had been put on while preparing the weapons for overseas shipment. Neither noticed Dolan's approach. Smithers spotted him first and his eyes widened, but he had no time to call out. T never saw the kick coming.

Dolan was drunk, which may have been why his kick missed T's head and struck his left shoulder.

Numb, left arm useless, T rolled clumsily to his feet. He backpedaled, trying to work feeling into the arm while avoiding Dolan's left-handed punch at his face.

But the tingling arm refused to cooperate.

"I don't like your goddamned face, Bucko!" Dolan panted. "I think I'll just improve it!" He followed the first punch with a powerful hook from his right hand. It might have ended the fight, but T stepped inside and lifted a vicious knee into Dolan's crotch. Dolan hunched over and grunted, shocked by the sudden agony. T stepped back and measured the man. Balanced, feet slightly spread, he took a half-step forward with his left foot and brought up his right foot, kicking Dolan on the point of his jaw. Teeth rattled against the ground and Dolan slumped bonelessly, already unconscious and bleeding from the nose and mouth.

From the first kick to the last, the fight had lasted less than half a minute.

"Shit, you killed him!" exclaimed Smithers.

"I don't think so, but you'd better run and get someone just in case. See if you can find Corporal O'Brien and if you can't, tell Sergeant Mac. After you explain what happened, bring the medic."

"No medic, T; he's in Vladivostok seeing about the sick men and won't be back until tomorrow. I'll fetch the corporal. He'll know what to do."

Smithers trotted away. T gathered the pistol parts and stored them in the hut. Mac and the corporal would understand, but suppose an officer heard about the fight? Some things were better not mentioned. He laid his Springfield and Smithers' BAR out on the canvas.

Dolan was breathing loudly, bloody bubbles on his lips, as T field-stripped the weapons for cleaning.

***

Corporal O'Brien was having coffee with Sergeant Mac when Smithers found them. Gasping, he attempted to explain what had happened.

"Well, well; ye don't say? Dolan's been asking for it and 'twas only a matter of time until he found someone who would give it to him. Ye say T kicked him?"

"Yeah! He did something else before that, but I didn't see what it was. By the time I noticed Dolan, he had already kicked T. The kick knocked him over, but T rolled right back up. He never even put up his hands! Now that I think about it, I'm pretty sure Dolan was drunk. He didn't say a word, just tried to kick T in the head and the next thing I knew, Dolan was holding his crotch. T never threw a punch, although Dolan sure tried to! T just took a moment like he was deciding what he wanted to do, then kicked Dolan upside the head. I heard a crack when T's boot hit and I thought the kick broke Dolan's neck for sure, but T says not. Even if Dolan is still alive he probably has a busted jaw, and for sure he lost some teeth!"

"Ye don't say! Well, we should probably go see in a bit. Ye're sure Dolan's down?"

"Oh, yeah! If he's not dead, he's at least out cold. If I was him, I'd stay that way! After that kick..."

"Well, then! There's no reason to hurry, is there? Want a cup of coffee, lad?"

"I don't know, Top; shouldn't we see about Dolan?"

"Ye can if you want to, but I'm going to finish my coffee first. Patrick?"

"Pretty good coffee, Sergeant Mac. Be a shame to waste it," O'Brien agreed.

"I think I better go back, Top," fretted Smithers. "Thanks for the offer, but T told me to find you and tell you what happened. I should be there if Dolan wakes up."

"Go ye ahead, then. Tell T we'll be along directly, and don't you be mentioning this to the lieutenant. 'Tis NCO business, d'ye understand?"

"Got it, Top. What if Dolan wakes up?"

"Tell T to kick him again, but harder. Dolan's got a thick skull, so he has."

***

Dolan was duly hauled off to the train stop, and none too gently put on the train for Vladivostok. He was awake by then and in considerable pain from his swollen jaw. If anyone was sorry to see him go, no one mentioned it.

"It leaves me with a problem, so it does. I kind of wish yer boy T had just whipped Dolan bad, not put him in the hospital. The colonel wants a squad out on patrol, and I don't have anyone else to give you. At the same time, I don't like the idea of putting three men out without backup. I wouldn't even know about it if ye needed help."

"There's a lot more to Tyler than shows on the surface, Mac," Patrick said. "Tell you what, let me talk to him and Smithers; I'm ready to go out with just the three of us. Dolan would have been more trouble than he was worth anyway."

"I don't like it, young Corporal! Too damned many bandits out there, aye, and Cossacks too. I don't think it matters anyway; the lieutenant won't send just the three of you out."

"What if we leave before he gets back?" Patrick asked.

"No," Mac decided. "For one thing, ye haven't finished cleaning those weapons, and for another, we'll need to check them over good before I'll be willing to issue them. I need the extra firepower, so I do, but a weapon that might malfunction is worse than no weapon at all. Losing people if ye run into an ambush...well, there are none too many of us as 'tis. One of these days, Gospodin Cossack is going to come calling. They hit a detachment up north of here at Romanovka, ye know. They killed and wounded a bunch of the boys, the dirty spalpeens, and they could do the same to us. But if I can get those BARs into the hands of my boys, we'll give them a whipping they won't soon forget!

"And they've already had desertions, so they have. Did ye know that hundreds of Cossacks showed up asking for our protection? With Hetman Kalmikoff and a couple of thousand others hot on their heels? Which may be why Semenoff started recruiting bandits; they don't care who's in charge or what they're ordered to do, so long as they're paid and they get to rob and rape. But by the same token, they'll take off just as soon as they run into regular soldiers. They'll be like Villa and his bunch, so they will. 'Twas down in New Mexico, barely spitting distance from the border.

"They snuck into Camp Columbus in the wee hours, started shooting with niver a word of warning. They killed a couple of the lads, then took off as soon as one of the boys got his machine gun going. Bandits, they were, and niver soldiers. I was a new corporal back then. I had an old Hotchkiss gun at the time, and as soon as I saw a target, I gave him a burst. I kept on shooting and the lieutenant kept the boys busy bringing me ammunition. The barrel was fair useless after that. I fired close to 3000 rounds that night, so I did. The lieutenant said that any man who would spend that much of the taxpayer's money on ammunition ought to be a sergeant, at least. So he gave me Sergeant Dobbs' stripes. Blood stripes, they were."

"Heard about that fight. I was a kid when it happened, still going to school," said Patrick.

"Ye're *still* a kid, corporal. But if ye pay attention, I'll make you into a real soldier one of these days."

"So you want us to clean and test-fire the weapons? After that we can go?"

"You'll go when the lieutenant says, young Corporal, when the lieutenant says. Just you be ready, and if I can find you another man or two between now and then, I'll see you get them. Now why don't you go give the pair you've already got a hand cleaning those guns? One thing, Lad; I wouldn't be letting myself be fooled by Private Tyler! He's not like Dolan, all bullying and bluster.

41

"That young man is dangerous, so he is."

Chapter Four

"What the devil are you doing?" Corporal O'Brien's voice showed his irritation.

"Something you should do, Corporal. If you ever want to hear your grandchildren's voices, that is." T had been systematically stripping threads from the tattered edge of the worn canvas scrap while they talked. Finished, he wadded up balls of thread and carefully inserted them into his ears. Unslinging the rope around his shoulder...the carry wire had bruised his shoulder...he laid the pistols on the canvas. Smithers had been opening boxes of the fat cartridges while T made his earplugs. Briefly inspecting each cartridge before loading it into a magazine, he systematically prepared the pistols for firing. The members of the proposed sniper team would get pistols as part of today's exercise, five others would be given to the company officers and NCOs to replace worn pistols, and the rest would be issued as the lieutenant and Sergeant Mac thought best.

"If the army had wanted us to use earplugs, they'd have issued them! Besides, an empty .45 case works pretty good." Patrick took two brass cases from his pocket and carefully inserted them into his ear openings.

Corporal Heintzelman had come up with his Second Squad while the discussion was ongoing. They had brought the rest of the automatic rifles and two cases of ammunition. Hearing the comments, Heintzelman used his trench knife to cut a swatch of cloth from the shrinking piece of scrap. Keeping two small pieces for himself, he passed the rest of the cloth out to his men while issuing orders. "I'll have twenty-eight long paces, Johnson. Albertson will help you put up the posts and nail the two long boards between them. The short nails are to tack the canvas to the boards.

"Morris, you'll mix flour and water to make the glue that will hold the targets to the canvas. I want one target chest high, and a smaller target just above it. The third target will go below the big

43

one, just above the ground. When you've done that, step off to the side and pace off twenty-two more yards. Put up the second set of posts, but this time I only want two targets. The big target will be chest high and the smaller one head high."

"No lower target, Corporal?"

"Nope. The two upper targets are for the pistols, but we'll zero the BARs at 28 yards. That's what the low target is for. The BAR shoots the same round as the Springfield, so sighting in at 28 yards will mean the weapon is dead-on vertically at just under 250 yards. It's the best we can do with the hasty range we're building. 'Tis a good combat zero for the automatic rifle. Ye must hold a little low out to 200 yards, on target from 200 to 275, and a little high out to 300. I wouldn't expect great accuracy; the BAR might be better than other machine guns, but I'll wait until I've had a lot of practice before I try precision shooting. A good marksman can hit a man out to 1000 yards with his Springfield. Think you can do that, Tyler?"

"I guess we'll see, Corporal. As for the pistols, I'll be happy to be on the target out to 50 yards."

"I thought you were supposed to be a good shot?"

"I guess we'll see, Corporal," Tyler repeated. "How about you?"

"I'm fair with a pistol, so I am. I can keep on target out to 25 yards. Farther than that, I'd use a rifle anyway."

"Count your people and make sure everyone is back," Corporal O'Brien said. "When you're ready, choose a pistol for yerself and let yer men choose too, but don't load until everyone is accounted for. And keep them back from the firing line!"

"I'll take care of my people," Heintzelman responded testily. "You just worry about hitting the target."

***

Corporal Heintzelman fired his last shot, emptying the magazine, then lowered his arm. Like most pistol shooters, he'd learned to put his left hand on his hip and extend the right hand, pointing the pistol at the target by turning sideways. He laid the pistol on the canvas. The slide had locked back after the last shot and thin tendrils of smoke rose lazily from the muzzle and the open action.

"Ready to take a look?" T asked.

"Yeah, I think I did pretty good." The two walked downrange to the 28-yard target.

"Looks okay. Any problems with the pistol?"

"It felt good. No rattles and the sights looked steady."

T frowned at the target. "You've got one in the bull, two in the three ring, and five just outside the ring. You're on paper and no flyers, so yes, I'd say that was okay."

T took a pencil from his pocket and carefully marked each hole with vertical and horizontal lines.

"You gonna do better?" asked Heintzelman.

"Why don't we find out?" T led the way back to the line, then picked up the pistol Heintzelman had used.

Glancing around to ensure that everyone was behind the line, he adjusted the pistol's grip so that it fitted snugly into the web between the thumb and forefinger of his right hand. Corporal O'Brien watched carefully, making mental notes; he'd never seen this done, but quickly understood why T was doing it. "I do things a bit different," offered T. "Why don't you just tell me when you're ready for me to start?"

"Sure thing, Tyler. Ready?" Heintzelman avoided smirking, but only just.

"Anytime you are, Corporal."

"Then...go!"

T swept the cocked pistol up, watching the front sight as he brought up his left hand and cupped it around his right hand, the little finger underneath to support the pistol butt. Crouching slightly, he squeezed off round after round until the slide locked to the rear. The recoil from each shot caused the muzzle to rise, but it sank back into shooting position before T squeezed the trigger again.

"What the hell was *that*, Tyler? You cheated!"

"That's how I learned, Corporal. Why is it cheating?"

"They'd never even allow you on the line during a match, and that's *not* how you qualify with the pistol! And eight shots that fast...hell, I doubt you were even on paper! It can't have taken more than seven or eight seconds!"

"Let's take a look." T laid the pistol aside, then joined the corporal as they went forward to examine the targets.

Despite his doubts, Heintzelman was impressed. "Little high and off to the left, but I can't argue with the group. Six inches?"

"About that, I'd say. I'll make a note to adjust the sight on this one. Couple of taps will move the sight in the dovetail. For now, I'll just hold a couple of inches to the right. As for being two inches high, that's what you want at this range. We'll see how it does at fifty yards." T took out a sheet of paper and recorded his observation and the pistol's serial number. He then made the same set of vertical and horizontal identifying marks through the new target holes.

"Can you show me how you did that, Tyler?" asked Corporal O'Brien.

"Sure. Corporal Heintzelman was using the old duelist's stance. Mine was developed by a man named Weaver."

"Never heard of him. T, are ye getting your memory back?" O'Brien asked.

"I think so. I'm having a lot of dreams for one, nightmares too, and I don't think my name's Tyler. But I remember people calling me T, so maybe it is."

"I don't suppose it matters, but you might want to keep it quiet if you do remember. For all we know, you could be some kind of murderer. Maybe you're on the run."

Funny you should say that, T thought. *That's exactly what I am. That much I remember. Although I don't think I'm running from the law, at least not here in Siberia!*

But he simply nodded to the corporal and went on with his work. "Let me check the sights and functioning on the rest of these, Corporal O'Brien. As soon as I'm satisfied, I'll hand you a pistol. You check it over, make sure I didn't miss anything, and as soon as you've got enough you can start qualifying the rest of the squad."

"I'll do that, but after I'm done, I want to learn that funny style of shooting!"

***

T was tired at the end of the day, but this time he didn't have to carry the pistols back to camp. The corporals had apportioned them out to the rest of their men, and they were happy to carry the extras.

He and Smithers lugged two BARs each, but the automatic rifles now had slings so it was a simple matter to carry one over each shoulder.

Sergeant Mac was waiting when they got back to camp.

"Got you a present, Tyler. With luck, the colonel will never realize what happened."

"This is the colonel's rifle?"

"That it was, lad, and if I hadn't promised it to you I'd have it for meself! 'Tis a sweet weapon, so 'tis, and I don't think the colonel would bust me. He needs a good first sergeant, so he does."

"Thank you, Sergeant Mac. I'll put it to good use."

"I'm depending on it! Sight it in carefully, lad, it will take care of ye when ye need it most."

T nodded and accepted the rifle. Outwardly, it showed no sign that anyone had worked it over. Thoughtfully, he opened the bolt and looked inside, making sure the chamber was empty. Closing the bolt, he carefully squeezed the trigger. The action and trigger were much smoother than would be expected from an issue weapon. T nodded to himself; if the rifle shot as well as it functioned otherwise, it might well be all that Sergeant Mac had promised. "I'll see if Smithers is available to go back to the range, maybe Corporal O'Brien too. The corporal will let you know how well it shoots for me."

***

"Thought you would want to see this, Sarge." Corporal O'Brien was carrying a crude target made by painting a large black circle on the front of an old uniform shirt.

Mac looked at the target, then leaned forward and placed his hands side by side, covering the holes in the shirt. Leaning back, he asked quietly, "How many shots? At what range?"

"Ten, Sarge. That's them, all of them, the ten rounds he fired for record. Range, an estimated eight hundred yards. He had already checked the zero on the piece. Pretty close in windage, elevation...well, he had to do some sighting shots. It had apparently been zeroed at two hundred, so that took about a half dozen rounds to get it to where it was right.

"No wind, not even a breeze; just a cool day without a lot of mirage visible. I set that shirt up at an estimated 750 yards and when we paced it off, it ended closer to 800. I'd say that's good enough for a combat zero."

"Just under half a mile, then. If he can shoot that well at an estimated distance, and at a target that might shoot back..."

"Yeah. He's done all right so far, and we're going out tomorrow. I'll set up an ambush where we can see that railroad bridge, probably stay out for the day, and come back in around midnight. If that's okay with you, I mean."

"That should work out. The lieutenant will be back by tomorrow afternoon, so if he gives you permission you can go out for a longer patrol next time and stay overnight. What about rations? Water? Ammo?"

"We'll have enough for the day. Shouldn't be a problem, except that we'll be loaded down with bandoleers. The BAR goes through ammo pretty fast. We'll reload the magazines in the field. If we need to, I mean. With luck, Tyler can bag a guerrilla or two and put the fear of God into the rest."

"Where are Smithers and Tyler now?"

"Cleaning their weapons. I told them to get some sleep after that."

"Okay. One day-long patrol approved, be back by dark or shortly after. If ye're late, I'll tell the cook to save dinner."

***

Tyler's sleep was normal, uninterrupted, in the beginning. That soon changed, but this time it wasn't the nightmares he'd recently experienced.

His shout woke Smithers, who found Tyler sitting straight up in his bed. He was wide-eyed and shaking.

"Tyler, what the hell are you doing?"

"I...I'm sorry, I didn't intend to wake you up."

"You damned well did! What was that about?"

"What did I say?" Tyler asked, suspicious.

"Nothing that made sense. What was going on?"

"I don't know how to explain it, but I could swear I heard Dolan!"

"Dolan? He's still in Vladivostok! You had to be dreaming. Was it about the fight?"

"Not exactly. Maybe; Dolan accused me of being some kind of spy! He said I was a fraud, and he was going to kill me when he got back. So I knew he was still in the hospital, but at the same time I could hear him. His voice was as clear as yours is right now. What did I say?"

"I didn't hear everything, because I only woke up after you started shouting, but I heard that last. You yelled, "Get the hell out of my head!"

"That doesn't make *sense*!" said Tyler.

"I know. But that's what I heard."

Chapter Five

Corporal O'Brien's voice was soft.

"Time to get a move on. Semenoff's people, assuming they're out there, won't be stirring this early but 'tis time we did. A weather front has moved in, and we've got light rain. Which is usually followed by fog. I let you two sleep as long as I could, but if we're going to reach the bridge by daylight we've got to get started."

"What time is it?" asked T, still groggy.

"'Tis gone half past three. There's coffee and breakfast in the kitchen. Don't dawdle."

"Meet you there, Corporal. Is Smithers awake?"

"Yeah, you two woke me up," Smithers grumbled. "Is that rain?"

"Aye, it is, but it's letting up a bit. The which is to the good, because we can move faster without being so concerned about noise."

T pulled on his uniform, appreciating the warmth of the heavy wool this morning. The sweater went on over the blouse, followed by his campaign hat. "Poncho?"

"Leave it in your pack, Lad. The rain is just a drizzle now, and 'twould be a fine evening in the old country! The fog is moving in, that it is, but we'll follow the tracks. We'll get to the bridge in plenty of time." Corporal O'Brien's brogue was more pronounced this morning.

"If you say so, Corporal." Smithers fell in behind as T followed the corporal to the mess tent, which was lit dimly by a single kerosene lamp. A cook was waiting to dish up their breakfast of hard bread, fresh eggs, bacon, and potatoes. "Beans ain't ready yet. How many eggs you want?"

The men asked for four each. The cook nodded and cracked them into a bowl.

Heavy mugs, locally manufactured, waited by the coffee pot. T poured coffee into three, then added sugar. Locals occasionally supplied milk as well as eggs and potatoes, but it wasn't available this morning. He carried the mugs to the table and handed the extras to Corporal O'Brien and Smithers. They ate quietly and soon finished the meal. Metal trays and utensils went into a heavy steel basin that was already heating atop a wood-fired stove. They would be washed later by a soldier detailed to help in the kitchen.

Packs on, weapons slung muzzle-down, they walked silently toward the gate. The guard nodded but said nothing as they headed down the muddy path leading to the railway.

"We'll stay off to the left of the tracks," Corporal O'Brien whispered. "No need to go into the woods, we'll just stay close to the edge. I'll lead, Smithers in the middle, T follows. Watch out for bushes, they're hard to see in the fog, and keep the noise down."

Soft moonlight, diffused through the fog, showed spectral pines at the edge of the cleared zone. The rain had turned into mist, but the mud made walking a chore. The three shrugged their packs into more-comfortable positions, then headed for the railroad bridge. If Semenoff's men were out and about, they'd have the same problems with the limited visibility and sticky mud. The patrol didn't know if anyone was waiting by the bridge, but on the other hand the enemy wouldn't expect an attack. Perhaps it all equaled out.

***

T was weary by the time Corporal O'Brien called a halt, the only one he'd allowed during the hike. A pale glimmer showed that dawn would arrive soon.

"We'll move into the edge of the woods now, and be sure ye keep quiet," whispered O'Brien. "I figure the bridge is about half a mile ahead, no more than that, but it could be closer. And the enemy could be anywhere. There'll be no speaking aloud until we're back at camp, understood?" The other two whispered assent. "Shuck your packs here. Check the safety on your weapons and make sure your muzzles are clear of mud and rain. We'll take a fifteen-minute break before we move closer to the bridge. Take a crap, water a bush, do what ye need to. We'll fill our canteens at the spring on the way back, but there will be no more food until we get back so be sparing. Questions?"

"Not a question, Corporal, but they're ahead of us and moving. I can hear them," T whispered.

"*Damn*! I don't hear anything; are ye sure?"

"Hang on for a moment..." T concentrated. "There are four of them. They're talking, but I don't think it's Russian. Mongolian, maybe. They're in front of that low knoll on the far side of the ravine. Smithers, can't you hear them?"

"I don't hear anything. Just the dripping of the trees." Smithers slipped the BAR off his shoulder, feeling for the safety.

"Tyler, I hope you're right, but it just means we have to be extra quiet from now on. We'll keep the same order when we move ahead. I'll scout, Smithers follows twenty yards behind me with the BAR, and Tyler, you'll be ten yards behind him. Keep that safety on and yer finger off the trigger until I tell you otherwise, Smithers. Tyler does the killing, ye're security in case they figure out where the shooting is coming from. I'll drop back and be yer assistant as soon as Tyler shoots. Tyler, if you can hear them then they can hear us. They can't be more than three hundred yards away and maybe less than a hundred, it's hard to tell in this fog. If you spot them before I do, tap me shoulder. I'll figure out what to do then. If ye're wrong about the numbers, we'll just find a nice safe place to hole up and wait for a better chance."

"Got it, Corporal," Smithers whispered. His finger touched the safety, making sure it was on. The automatic rifle was fully loaded, needing only to have the safety released to be ready to fire. T simply nodded, the motion barely visible in the dim moonlight. He understood the corporal's caution. "One thing, Corporal," whispered T. "This fog is a good thing. They won't know where I'm shooting from."

"Aye. Well, four of them and but the three of us! If ye can take out the trailing man and at least one more, I might be able to do for the rest. I'll pot the one behind the leader as soon as you shoot. The shooting should freeze the others in place just long enough, so take whichever one you can see after they go to ground. With a wee bit of luck, we'll bag the lot of them. And Smithers, save yer ammo unless they rush us, understood?"

"Yes, Corporal."

"Tyler, any idea how close they are?"

"It's a ways yet. The other side of the ravine, bottom of that knoll, but coming this way."

"I didn't think we were that close! We move out in--twelve minutes. Take care of your personal business, but be careful. Keep yer weapons with ye at all times."

***

Break over, O'Brien led them to the edge of the woods. Hearing nothing, other than the occasional drip from the trees, he eased ahead. Where was the damned bridge? They should have reached it by now...unless Tyler was imagining things. But he'd sounded certain of his information; how could he have heard the guerrillas talking?

Slow anger began growing. If Tyler had spooked enough to believe he'd heard the enemy...

A tap on his sleeve halted him. "They're crossing the bridge now," T whispered. "I can hear them clearly, but I don't know what they're saying. It's not Russian, I can make that much out. Could be some kind of Mongolian dialect or Chinese. We're not far from the border."

"Find ye a place to shoot from then, and make every shot count. I still don't hear anything, and I can't see a sainted thing in this fog!"

"It's hanging close to the brush, Corporal. Looks like it's thinner up above. I'm going to climb a tree now, and see if I can see better. I suggest you let me pick off as many as I can, then if they come toward us you and Smithers open up."

"Are ye sure, Tyler? 'Tis just barely gone daylight! The fog will lift as soon as the sun comes up."

"I'm sure. As soon as the fog clears, they'll move closer to cover. I'll take what I can get while they're being careless."

"Go ahead then." Patrick's voice revealed his tension.

He signaled to Smithers, pointing to a tree where he could set up with the BAR. Whispering directly into his ear, he said, "Under those low branches. Keep your body behind the trunk, it may help protect you, but make sure you can cover your front. I'll pass fresh magazines if ye need them. If they *do* come this way, they'll avoid that depression off to the left and I'll be covering yer right flank. Got it?"

Smithers nodded, then eased to his knees and from there to fully prone. Creeping slowly ahead, he avoided the limbs as much as possible while crawling to the position O'Brien had indicated. Making himself as comfortable as possible, he settled down to wait. A faint rustle to his right indicated that Corporal O'Brien was also in position. Of Tyler, he heard no sound; which tree had he decided to climb?

They waited, tense and silent. The fog continued to lift as the ground warmed.

Fifty yards to their front, Smithers saw movement for the first time. The enemy soldier, likely a guerrilla or a bandit, walked confidently along, unworried. After all, this was territory claimed by Ataman Semenoff and the Americans were miles away. He was followed by two others.

Was there a fourth, as T had claimed? If so, where was he? O'Brien tried to aim, but his vision was obscured by a low eddy in the drifting fog. He attempted to track the leader, then gave up and switched to the second man. He was squirming into a slightly better position when T fired.

The oncoming figures froze, then dropped to the ground. Had T missed? Moments later, a puff of smoke announced that one had fired his rifle but there was no crack of a passing bullet. Had they spotted T and shot at him?

Realizing that the corporal's simple tactical plan was blown, Smithers eased the BAR's safety to "A" and waited. He couldn't tell where the enemy soldiers were, but they couldn't have gone far. Well, they hadn't tried to charge and if Corporal O'Brien wanted him to lay down suppressive fire, he would say so. Smithers waited, relaxed, finger on the trigger.

T fired again, startling him anew. Of the figures who had gone to ground, he saw nothing; they were hidden by low-growing bushes and vines. Had T seen them from his perch in the tree?

T fired a third time. Moments later, an enemy soldier stood up, no longer carrying his rifle. The man turned and sprinted back in the direction he'd come from.

T's fourth shot struck him in mid-stride. A pinkish mist hung in the air, reflecting the early sunlight, as the man fell. "That was the last one. There were only four." T's voice came from somewhere high and off to the side.

"Corporal? You think he's right?" whispered Smithers.

"He's been right so far." Corporal O'Brien stood up and reached down to give Smithers a hand, helping him back out from under the branches. The BAR made it more awkward backing than entering had been. "If he got all of them, that's some shooting! That last shot was at a running target, and from the blood spray I'm guessing it was a head shot at more than a hundred yards. But we'd better take a look; they might be carrying something intelligence would want to look at. Check your safety, Smithers."

Remembering guiltily that he'd switched to automatic, Smithers clicked the lever to "S".

The two waited, looking toward where the enemy soldiers had fallen, until T walked up. "Be ye sure they're all dead, T?"

"I'm sure. They stopped whispering after I shot the first one. Just like you said, Corporal, I took the last man first, then the leader."

Corporal O'Brien stared at T, then glanced at Smithers who was looking back at him, wide eyed. "I never heard a word! What about you, Smithers?"

"Nothing, Corporal! T, you've got to have the damndest ears I've ever heard of!"

"They're pretty good, I guess," said T absently. "But if we're going to check the bodies, I suggest we be about it. There were only four in this group, but others may have heard the shooting."

Patrick nodded. "Aye, let's see what we can find. If nothing else, we need to destroy their weapons."

***

Ray Wilson was currying his new stud, an American Quarter Horse. Unlike many owners, Ray enjoyed working with his animals. It gave him time to think.

The stallion was shedding. Great swatches of black guard hairs had loosened, thanks to Ray's efforts, and rolls of hair now littered the ground. The summer bay color beneath the guard hairs was striking, the russet blending into black below the hock and knee joints and with only the barest trace of white above the two front hooves.

He'd become increasingly concerned about T. Was the newspaper report accurate? Was T the 'Tagliaferro' reported killed? But thinking produced no answers and there was no one he could ask. Deciding he couldn't simply refuse to act, he commed Shezzie. <Meet at our place tonight? I'm thinking you, Ana Maria and me, and Bobby.>

<About T? I'm worried sick, Ray!>

<Me too. Six o'clock?>

Shezzie agreed and they dropped the connection. Ray commed the other two and arranged the meeting. He briefly considered inviting Libby, but her trip back to the 19th Century had been accidental. His intervention had rescued her; otherwise, she would probably still be there. So no; she would likely have nothing to contribute. His thoughts were suddenly interrupted.

<Don't worry, Uncle Ray. I'll listen in anyway, and if I think of anything, I'll tell you.>

<Libby, you shouldn't be listening to our thoughts! We've *told* you about that.> Ray commed resignedly.

<I don't listen unless you're thinking of me! Your secrets are safe.> Libby's mischievous tone came through. <But you're

forgetting something. I don't know anything about time travel except what you showed me, but I'm better at telepathy than anyone. *Lots* better, and that includes Uncle T. If you're going back to rescue him, you're going to need me.>

<Out of the question!> Ray's irritation showed.

<Uncle Ray, it's not your choice. You can't stop me.>

<Libby, you're just a *kid*! It's dangerous!>

<Just a *girl*, you mean. Get used to it, Uncle Ray; age doesn't matter, only ability. Which I have, and it's my choice. One thing, please don't tell Grandpa. He's not well yet and there's no reason to worry him.>

<I won't,> Ray agreed. <But changing the subject won't work. You opened the discussion, but I haven't agreed to your going with me. Assuming I decide to go myself.>

<I know what you're going to decide, Uncle Ray. You do too, but I'll let you figure it out on your own.>

<Libby, you can do that? Deep-read my mind?>

<That, and a lot more. It's been...very educational. Some of the minds I've contacted...>

<Libby, you can't go raking through people's minds!>

<I can't *stop* it, Uncle Ray. It's like turning off my eyes, I can't do it. I understand what's bothering you, you're thinking that I'm just a girl, but I'm not. I grew up the hard way after the kidnapping. That man was prepared to kill me, for no other reason than that I might identify him to the police! And I've found others like him since.>

<Libby...>

<You have your secrets, Uncle Ray, I have mine.> The coldness came through clearly, leaving Ray appalled.

What had they done? He realized that 'they', including T himself, had made no conscious choice. The Talents were loose now, for better or worse. They had always been there, latent, but now they were breaking free. That was another reason to go back after T. He might well be the only person in the world who could face down the next Solaris when one popped up.

That was the corollary for knowing the Talents had escaped; some of the new ESPers were evil and others insane. There would be another Solaris, and another after that.

Possibly stronger than the first had been.

Chapter Six

Ray swirled the scotch around in his glass, concentrating. "I've been thinking."

"I know," Shezzie sighed. Bobby just nodded. Ana Maria had elected to stay home; she already knew what Ray had in mind.

"It's been almost six months. I can't wait any longer."

"Ray..."

"The longer I wait, the more likely it is that whatever happened will cause a paradox. We have no idea what that means; for all we know, we're *already* in a different timeline."

"Does it matter?" asked Bobby. He sipped at his scotch and waited.

"I would say no," replied Shezzie. "If the theorists are right, somewhere there's another timeline that's just a little bit different. It will continue to diverge from ours, but we won't know and we have no reason to care. We're us, the only version there is as far as we can know, and we can live on only one timeline at a time."

"Except that in *this* timeline, T went back looking for Libby and has never returned," said Ray

<That bothers me too, Uncle Ray,> Libby chimed in, her voice clear to all three.

<Libby, it's not polite to listen in!> sent Ray.

<Mostly I don't, but I was studying math and you distracted me. You mentioned my name and my mind locked in.>

<You're in now, you might as well stay,> Ray said resignedly. <I've waited long enough. It will take me a few days to get everything together and do some planning. Soon as that's done, I'm going.>

<I'm glad,> sent Libby. <I intended to go anyway. He only went back in time because of me. I'm with you, I think he needs help!>

<You can't go, Libby, and anyway there's no reason to. What can you do that I can't? I'm an adult, I've done a time trip by design. You went back by accident, and to be honest you were

lucky. You're only here now because I found you.>

<That's true, but it doesn't matter now. I know everything you know about time travel, which isn't very much. I learned it on the way back. I'll admit there are things neither of us know, but I've got one advantage. Uncle Ray, I'm *way* stronger than you are. Not just telepathy, I've been practicing levitating and I've also done a dozen short teleports. I just wanted to get a feel for what it's like, but I did it and I always returned immediately. You need me!>

<Libby, you're still in *school*! You can't just go off whenever you feel like it!> Ray protested feebly.

<Sure I can! Who's going to stop me? Anyway, I'm studying for my math final, and I've got most of it down. All those trig transformations! But the teacher said I'll need them next year for calculus, and if I run into problems I'll just read his mind. School's out in another eight days anyway, Uncle Ray. I already intended to go, but I'd rather go with you.>

<And what about your parents? Are you just going off without telling them? What does Shorty say?> Ray was running out of excuses, and felt a sinking feeling as soon as he realized that she knew.

Shezzie and Bobby had caught wisps of the conversation. Recognizing that it was ongoing, they waited. Ray would explain when he finished comming with Libby.

<Grandpa suspects. I didn't want to worry him, but he's pretty smart and he knows me better than you do. He just said to be careful. As for Mom and Dad, I'll leave them a note just in case, but I intend to be back before they know I've gone. Time travel is that way; if I work it right, I can return to the exact second I left.>

<Libby, you're asking me to be responsible for you! You just turned 15, and I'm not really your uncle!>

<Uncle Ray, you were responsible last time. *This* time, it may turn out that *I'm* responsible for *you*.>

Ray sighed in defeat and dropped the connection. He drained his glass, then explained to Shezzie. "It's a done deal, apparently. Libby's coming with me as soon as school's out. She thinks she can return right after she leaves so her parents won't ever know, but there's no use in taking chances. She can take her finals while I get things together and work out a plan.

"I'm not exactly sure which track T followed; I might have to hunt around a bit, but if that article was right I know the date he disappeared. That means I know when and where I can find him."

"Ray, you mentioned time paradoxes. That may have already happened; the report said T died," Bobby said.

"That's not what it said. It said that a *man named Tagliaferro* was lost, after the lightning strike and during the flooding. We assumed it was T because he had used that name before, but no body was found. I checked every edition of that newspaper, starting the day that Tesla's transmitter was destroyed and continuing for six months afterward. If there had ever been a body it would have shown up by then.

"If it was washed out to sea, there wouldn't have been anything left by that time but bones, so I stopped researching. Here's the thing, who's to say that I didn't get there before the lightning hit? What if I snatched T away? That would fit the news report, and it means I *have* to go back to the past."

"Ray, Libby's a young woman now! You can't take her!"

"You tell *her* that, Shezzie. Let me explain..."

***

Ray begged off next morning when Ana Maria suggested they go for a ride. She shrugged and headed for her office, where her latest book was taking shape. There was still quite a lot to be done before it was ready for a publisher.

Ray used his computer to download several books, most of them histories dealing with events during the turn of the Twentieth Century. Scanning through them, he made notes and listed references in the bibliographies to see if he could acquire those. Before departing, he would use the books to do an in-depth study of the period. It might be unnecessary, but hope was not a plan; Ray intended to be prepared for whatever happened. Despite

Libby's brash comment, he understood what she did not, that the only substitute for experience was knowledge.

Finished with his preliminary work by lunchtime, he ate a sandwich and headed for the mine. He wanted to talk to Bobby, then visit one of the cache sites. Bobby probably had contacts among mining professionals, so maybe he would know someone who could convert one of the gold bars to gold coins.

***

"It's medicinal rum, Corporal. You look like you could use a drink," said Lieutenant Thornton.

"Thank you, Sir! Aye, I could!"

"After the ambush, you checked the bodies? And there were four of them?"

"Yes, Sir. It was just like Tyler said, but..."

"But what, Corporal? I agree, after the ambush it was advisable for you to bring your patrol in. Someone would have heard the shots and at the least, informed Scmcnoff. You had only three people, and with your presence known the danger was too great for any results you might have achieved."

"Sir..." Corporal O'Brien's words came with a rush. "Ye should know that I was there, and I can't explain it. Tyler did things that just aren't possible! How could he have heard people talking from almost half a mile away? And separate the voices enough to know that there were four of them?"

"Sound can play funny tricks, Corporal. I visited a Roman amphitheater once; you could stand at one end of this big open area and speak normally. Someone at the other end could hear you perfectly, and when he responded I understood him. The two ends must have been at least 100 yards apart. You reported that it was foggy, and that can change sounds too. But here's the thing, you and Smithers confirm that Tyler said there were four and that's how many there were, and they also showed up just about where he said they would. We know he was right, because he killed them."

"Yes, Sir, and with head shots. *Four* men, in fog, and at ranges I paced off! The first man he shot, the one that was following behind the others, was 120 long paces away, the which is why I niver saw him. The closest one was only 50 paces, the one that was running was farther! 'Tis not *possible*!"

"I agree, it's unusual. But do you have another explanation?"

"No, Sir."

"Thank you, Corporal. Why don't you take your men over to the kitchen and tell the cook I said to feed you? Steaks, if he has them."

"Aye, I'll do that, and thank you, Sir." Corporal O'Brien came to attention.

"Dismissed, Corporal." O'Brien turned and left, closing the door quietly behind him. Lieutenant Thornton poured shots of the rum into glasses and handed one to Sgt. Mac. "What do you think, Top?"

"There's a word for it, Lieutenant, but I don't know it. It means that the facts speak for themselves. Ye should know that O'Brien is reliable; if he said he paced off those distances, he did."

"And we don't know much about Private Tyler, do we?" mused Lieutenant Thornton. "Other than a Russian brought him in and said he thought he was American."

"Aye, Sir. Yet Tyler's steady under fire and a reliable man, I've seen that for meself."

Lieutenant Thornton nodded. "But I've got a report to write, Top, and I can't tell the colonel that Tyler does impossible things. The colonel will have my *ass*, if the report even gets that high! There's a captain and a major that will see it before it goes to the colonel, but it will probably end up on his desk anyway, because sending out sniper teams is his baby."

Lieutenant Thornton was gloomy.

"You've got a problem, Lieutenant," Sergeant Mac said with a noticeable lack of sympathy. "Meantime, 'tis thanking you I am for the hooch!"

"You're welcome," said Lieutenant Thornton absently. "Do

you believe Corporal O'Brien? Because I don't! I *can't*, because I have to write a report that the colonel will accept, or he'll just make me write it over. That's the way the army is."

"I'm glad to learn that, Lieutenant," said First Sergeant Mac, an old soldier who'd been in the army since the lieutenant got his first pair of long trousers. He suppressed a smile with difficulty, but Lieutenant Thornton picked up the sarcasm and flushed.

"Between you and me, Top, the stress of the engagement caused Corporal O'Brien to misjudge the distances. That's what the report will say, and as we both know army paperwork is never wrong. Dismissed, Sergeant."

"Yes, Sir." Sergeant Mac came to attention briefly, saluted, and left the office.

Lieutenant Thornton was already thinking about how best to word the report so that no one would question Corporal O'Brien's judgment. Mac was right; he was a good man and he showed promise. With a bit more seasoning...

Lieutenant Thornton, barely 'seasoned' himself, saw no reason to question his opinion of Corporal O'Brien.

***

Matters settled back to normal and the camp was quiet. Around the post, vegetation had been cut back out to a distance of 100 yards. Conceivably, Semenoff's irregulars might try to use the trees beyond that point for cover, but marksmanship was not their forte and the dead zone behind the trees was too small for adequate cover anyway. Corporal Heintzelman took out a patrol, as did others; there was no sign of Semenoff's men, and the daily train's crew had reported no problems.

Mac had things to do, so the question of what Tyler had done or not done on the patrol was pushed to the back of his mind. He spoke to Corporal O'Brien from time to time and watched Smithers and Tyler as they worked about the camp, but paid them no special attention.

He had seen to it that the new BARs were now an integral part of the camp's defenses. Timbers had been used to construct fighting positions just inside the palisade, then covered over with dirt. Slits had been cut for the weapons to fire through, only a few inches high and barely wide enough for the gunner to traverse the barrel to cover his area of responsibility.

The BAR teams had also drilled with the other troops, manning the strongpoints as soon as the alert sounded and preparing to defend their assigned quadrant. Although Lieutenant Thornton and First Sergeant MacAuliffe had no way of knowing it, the camp was perfectly safe. Semenoff had his hands full elsewhere.

***

The Czech Legion continued their remorseless advance east. They had fought White Russians, Bolsheviks, and now, Semenoff's army on the way. They had captured towns, rested and regrouped, then moved on. Always, they had remained close to the railway and used the trains whenever possible.

The Bolsheviks had now pulled back, cowed by Semenoff's armored trains, but they would return. Little by little, they were consolidating their hold on Siberia. Treat with Semenoff they would, but if he weakened they would move in. And if they got their hands on him, they had every intention of treating him to a quick trial and a quicker hanging.

Beset on the north by the Bolsheviks, on the northeast by Kolchak's forces, and on the west by the oncoming Czechs, Semenoff had no resources to spare to attack the troublesome Americans.

Disgusted by the actions of his bandits, British paymasters had given up on Semenoff in disgust. But the Japanese soon took their place. The promise of regular funding allowed him to hire replacements and even augment his numbers. The Japanese considered the money well spent; the unrest caused by Semenoff allowed them to strengthen their influence in the region. Korea, Siberia, and conceivably a large part of Russia itself might become part of the empire. Mongolia had no appreciable army, but it did have abundant coal resources.

Japan schemed, Semenoff dreamed, and the US Army's farthest-west outpost prepared for the day when Semenoff attacked.

***

Mac was certain the current lull wouldn't last. Simply put, there were too few Americans and they were surrounded by too many enemies. Sooner or later, one of the competing Russian factions or Japanese-influenced groups would achieve military superiority. The dominant faction would then take over the Trans-Siberian railroad, the key to extracting wealth from the vast territory. Which was being kept open at the moment by a few Americans, operating from small and widely-separated camps. No, it couldn't last.

Their only hope was that someone in Washington would remember that the war hadn't ended for the American Expeditionary Force in Siberia. And that the War Department would then order them home, hopefully before they got rolled over by one group of Russians or another.

Chapter Seven

"Go slow! I don't like this!"

The small farm appeared deserted, but the smell indicated it hadn't been that way for long. Corporal Brennan waved and two of his soldiers circled to the right, rifles ready as they approached the log building. They moved from one bit of available cover to the next, checking their surroundings carefully before moving again. The approach took almost ten minutes before they reached the door.

One of the scouts pointed to a broken hinge. At Brennan's nod, he pushed the door with the muzzle of his rifle. It swung open, creaking, long enough for him to peer inside, then swung closed again when he withdrew the pressure.

Brennan waited with the remaining two men. If he was right about the smell, no one was going anywhere.

The scouts stood upright and waved the others in. "Two or three days, I'm thinking. Somebody put up a fight, probably that young guy over by the barn. Not much left of him now. Wolves have been at the bodies. They just shot the old man, but the old woman they raped, probably more than once. She was inside, so the wolves never got to her. I didn't see any sign that she was shot or cut up. There may be wounds on the back side, but I didn't turn the body over. Could be she died from a heart attack."

"Semenoff's God-damned *bandits*!" said Brennan, his tone bitter. "I wonder what they were after?"

"They don't have to be after much, Corporal. Out here, just having food can get you killed. The farmers don't have money, they just swap produce with their neighbors. Of course, if they were supplying our kitchen they might have had a few coins put by," observed Private Simpson, who had discovered the old woman's body near the fireplace. "If they did, the raiders found them. There's a stone in the fireplace that was pulled out. Not much room underneath, just a small hollow, but they probably never had much. For that matter, they might have had nothing. The raiders could have dislodged the stone while they were at her."

"But look what else I found!" Private Perkins held out a handful of empty cartridge cases.

"The headstamps are the same as ours, and that's an empty US ammo carton leaning against the shed," Corporal Brennan pointed. He put the cases in his pocket; the first sergeant would want to know.

"I've been here before," Perkins mentioned. "I was on a provisions detail; we bought early vegetables from this family a little over a month ago. The father was a crotchety old rascal, but the young guy was okay. Hard worker, I thought, and the old woman was a lot like my grandmother. There was a daughter, too; she might have gotten away."

"Maybe. Sergeant Mac gave a rifle and ammo to the guy who brought Tyler in. Could be this was him," observed Simpson."

"Whoever he was, he put up a fight! That's probably why they hacked him up," said Private Perkins. "Maybe he got one or two before they killed him."

Corporal Brennan nodded. "We'll bury them. Look around; they probably had a shovel. Axe too; we may need it. There should be at least one, if the bandits didn't steal it. I'm guessing they searched the house, but they might not have bothered with the outbuildings. Miller, take Perkins and see what you can find. Simpson, you're with me." Corporal Brennan headed past the curtain into the bedroom, looking for something to wrap the bodies in.

***

Ray left early the next morning to visit a money cache, one of several he and T had planted around the ranch. Paranoid as ever, they had sold most of the remaining Doc Noss gold bars long ago and converted the proceeds to gold coins, mostly double eagles and eagles. Circulated coins were cheaper; collectors preferred the uncirculated or lightly-circulated. For their purposes, bug-out money, circulated coins were actually better, so they'd bought a selection from what the dealer had on hand.

T had taken about half of the US coins while preparing for his trip. Ray shrugged mentally and took the remaining ones. The Liberty head and Indian head types, all that were left, were stamped with the same value, ten dollars. They should be relatively easy to spend. Coins, unlike paper money, had changed very little over the years. He decided against taking the Krugerrands. They were readily exchangeable nowadays, but they would raise eyebrows in 1905. The last thing he wanted to do was attract attention!

After considerable thought, Ray had decided that April of 1905 should be his target date. There was no way to be sure; Distance, direction, and the relationship between their departure point, the Earth's magnetic field, and their arrival point made precision impossible. Having Libby along was likely to help; if T was there when they arrived, she would be able to comm him. The three could then return to the present before the storm hit Tesla's tower later that year.

As to when T had reached New York, there was probably no way to tell. If he hadn't arrived by the time they got there, they would have to wait. They might be able to take shorter teleports just before reaching New York to narrow down their arrival time. Conceivably, Libby might contact T in 1900 or 1901, but even if they were forced to wait, visiting 1905 New York would be a real education for Libby. She'd landed in 1870s Nevada during her first accidental trip and had spent almost all her time there, living among the Paiutes with Sarah Winnemucca. New York of 1905 was certain to be very different!

Ray shook his head at what he intended to do. Selling millions of dollars worth of impure bars had made sense at the time; they couldn't spend the bars, and if they'd had to abandon their current identities, having transportable wealth that could be easily exchanged was a better option. Now he intended to spend the Liberty head and Indian head coins at their face value of $10 each! Such a waste! Ray grinned; it was only money so long as you had it, and they did. But the coins might not be enough, and he was loath to raid a second coin cache.

<Bobby? We need to visit the mine.>

<What, now?>

<You got something better to do?>

***

Libby had also been making plans. What to wear on the trip? Start with sturdy trousers, a long-sleeved shirt, and boots; depending on where they stopped first, she would need at least one dress, and not her usual mini! No indeed!. She giggled; that might get her tossed into an old-time jail on suspicion of being a hooker!

So something long, probably a dress, but maybe a skirt and blouse? A hat of some sort, not too outrageous? She opened a page on her browser and started researching fashion from the 1930s. Hats... Ridiculous! Women really wore those silly things? Maybe she should settle for a practical Stetson or a simple scarf? And what about underthings? She could do without a bra. Puberty had arrived a few months ago, but it hadn't brought the kind of breasts she was hoping for. Not yet, anyway. But long bloomers? Yuk! And definitely no corset!

What did teenagers wear back then? Surely not those foolish things! She needed advice, but who could she ask? Not a historian, of course. He or she would wonder why Libby wanted the information. And there was only one other time traveler she could call.

<Uncle Ray, got a moment?>

***

Sergeant Mac read the telegram and sighed. Things had been so quiet lately! Grabbing his campaign hat as he left his office, he headed off to find Corporal O'Brien.

He found the members of First Squad working at repairing the low firing step behind the parapet. "And where would I be finding yer corporal, Smithers?"

"He's sick, Sergeant Mac. I saw him throwing up. He's got a headache."

"I didn't ask you about his medical condition, now did I? I asked where he was!"

"He's in bed, Sergeant Mac."

"In bed, and it practically the middle of the *morning*? Saints presairve us!" Fuming, Mac headed for the bunkhouse, already thinking of just what he intended to say. A *corporal*, sleeping during working hours! What was the Army coming to nowadays?

But he bit off his words as he got closer. O'Brien was indeed still lying on his pallet. A damp rag lay across his eyes. Concerned, Mac checked his first impulse. "Lad, is it the cholera?"

O'Brien removed the cloth and blinked. "Sorry, Mac. No, I don't think so, nor the typhoid or typhus. There are no spots, d'ye see, it's just that my head is throbbing something wicked and the only thing that helps is a cool cloth. And the dark, of course."

"Hold still, Boyo." Mac felt of O'Brien's forehead with the back of his hand. "No fever, Lad. Ye say 'tis just the headache and that one time you vomited?"

"Aye, 'twas just the one."

"And were ye partaking of the creature last night, young Corporal?"

"Not a drop, Mac, I swear!"

So. That exhausted Sergeant Mac's limited medical knowledge. What to do? "'Tis not the cholera or typhoid, and 'tis not the Spanish flu. But here's the thing, lad. I need you to go into the village to meet the train. Do you think you can?"

"I'll try, Top. The headache might be letting up a bit, I'm thinking. I'm not shirking, but couldn't one of the other corporals go?"

"If you can't manage, I'll have to send Heintzelman or Brennan. But it's to do with your squad, d'ye see? Dolan's been released from the hospital, he has, and I'm a bit worried about what he's likely to do now. He'll be arriving on the train, and I thought of going meself to meet him, but 'tis properly your job. But since you're sick, ye will stay here. I'll just have a chat with him when he gets off the train, so I will, and if yer Mister Dolan doesn't toe the line he'll wish he had! But if you aren't better by suppertime, you'll be goin' into Vladivostok and seein' the surgeon. In the meantime, I'll have yer Private Tyler keep an eye on you."

"Thanks, Mac," O'Brien said gratefully. "When do ye expect the train?"

"'Twill be in this morning sometime, so I'd best be on my way. I'll take Smithers with me, and Tyler can keep working on that wall while we're gone. Aye, and I'll have him check on you from time to time."

"Thanks, Mac." O'Brien replaced the damp cloth as he lay back. Mac shook his head and left. *Not cholera or smallpox and probably not the flu...what else?* He was uneasily aware that any number of diseases might be endemic in this Russian pesthole.

Aye, and including even the black plague!

***

T nodded when Mac gave him the assignment. He had worries of his own, worries which included not only Dolan but O'Brien as well. Having time to himself would be useful. His memory had returned, as had his psi abilities except possibly teleporting. He'd had no opportunity to test that one. What he'd feared most, that the paranormal abilities called the Talents might spread due to contact with him, had happened. Dolan had at least rudimentary telepathy, as shown by the contact while T was sleeping, and O'Brien's headache might mean that he too was becoming a Talent. As time paradoxes went, this promised to be an absolute disaster!

Would he be able to return home at some time, or was he already on another timeline? Well. Smithers was gone, the firing step needed to be rebuilt, and no one was watching. Had they been, they would have been astonished. T was carefully avoiding notice if someone was looking his way by putting his hands on the half-rotted timbers he was replacing, but he was lifting them using psychokinetics.

Pull one from the ground, drop it on the growing pile. Lift a fresh-cut log that probably weighed two hundred pounds, position it carefully, then ease it into the hole. Wrap the reinforcing wires to hold it in place between the others, shovel dirt into the hole, and tamp it down firmly. Ensure that the dirt between the low wall of timbers and the parapet itself was smooth and solid enough to support the weight of men firing over the wall, then move on to the next.

Deciding he was far enough ahead, he headed for the barracks to check on Corporal O'Brien. And do a test on the way. <Corporal O'Brien?>

***

"How much do you want?" asked Bobby.

"How much is available?" asked Ray.

"Quite a bit, and I can easily refine more. It just takes time."

"You're refining it here?"

"In a side tunnel off the main adit. I couldn't use a big industrial crusher, because even this far back in the hills someone would hear and wonder what was going on. And maybe they *wouldn't* wonder, because a lot of people know what a rock crusher sounds like, but I came up with a work-around. I had months with nothing much to do while my leg grew in, so I dug. Okay, blasted and dug. I could do that."

"Still using ANFO?"

"No, I needed smaller, more controllable blasts. The easiest solution was to switch to half-sticks of dynamite. I found that punching a pattern of four holes in the tunnel face worked. I put in the fused dynamite, tie in a small ring main to detonate everything simultaneously, and set it off using sixteen-inch lengths of safety fuse. I've still got the roll I started with."

"Holy cow! Sixteen inches? You're crazy!"

"Ray! Think! How do you suppose I light the fuses?"

"Oh. Pyrokinetics?"

"Got it in one. Don't worry, I'm careful. I'm using small

charges, no more than four half-sticks at a time, and the technique is similar to what I did when I worked for the quarry except for the small size of the charges. The idea is to fracture the tunnel face, not blow off half the mountain, and it's easier to handle chunks of rock than gravel.

"But small charges or not, I'm at the tunnel mouth when I light the fuse, and I'm away from the tunnel opening when the charge blows. I prep late in the evening, set it off as soon as I'm out of the tunnel, and wait until the next day before I go in. The delay is to make sure the gases have cleared out. I also carry a small tank of compressed oxygen just in case, but so far I haven't needed it. Anyway, it's routine now; prep, blast, wait, muck out, and sort through the rubble.

"Next step, refine the ore. I'm only running the high-grade, the rest I'll leave for later. I bought a pair of laboratory-sized crushers and an industrial diesel generator to run them. The coarse crusher is just under four feet tall, and it breaks down the larger rocks. The fine crusher accepts the coarse output and reduces it to the consistency of beach sand. Since I'm working inside a tunnel, there's very little noise gets out. Sluicing the sand to concentrate the free gold is relatively easy, and I'm doing the final refining myself. I got the idea from T; he mentioned he could flake off paint, so I thought I'd try picking off bits of mineral.

"It worked, but after two hours I was exhausted and I only had about a tablespoon of gold-bearing mineral, mostly quartz. So I gave that up. I still do it during the final refining, but only after I've washed the sand through the sluice. It's efficient, even if it is boring. I also don't have a lot of water and that limits how much I can process. The spring only puts out a few gallons a day, and I use some of it for drinking, showering, and washing dishes.

"I recycle water as much as I can. The gray water I use for the sluice and if I need to, I go without showering for a day or two. I get free gold right out of the sluice, so the last step is to sort what's left manually. I'm not as good as T at sensing gold in the tailings. I can do it, but why bother? I've got a side tunnel filled with metal drums of stuff now! I couldn't melt it down for ingots, but it was too good to throw away. Processing it would take more time and resources than it's worth, considering how much I'm getting right out of the sluice."

"Where are you getting your supplies?" asked Ray curiously. "I would have noticed delivery traffic."

"No traffic. You should get up here more often, Ray! You really don't know what I've been doing."

"I knew you were taking it easy while your leg grew ou,t and I knew about mapping the deposit. I didn't worry, because you stopped in at my place or Shezzie's a couple of times and you would have commed me if you needed help."

"Yeah. Well, I got tired of living in a tent, so I built a cabin. Plenty of rocks for the floor and walls, and lifting them was easy. All I needed was cement, so I had a truckload of bags dropped off up near the property line. I told the driver I was constructing a ditch to bring water out of the mountains. As for other things I need, it's mostly food and household supplies and I go out shopping in Reno once a week. I get diesel and lube oil for the generator in Little Dry Creek, but parts for the crushers, mostly replacement jaws, are shipped to my post office box in Reno. They're pretty durable and I buy two sets at a time, so I have a spare when I need to change one out. I could have the cutting edges sharpened, I suppose, but why bother?

"I buy dynamite in Reno too, from a small construction company that deals with explosives on the side. I still have my ATF license, so buying dynamite and caps isn't a problem. I don't want anyone to wonder what I'm doing, so I always do my buying just before the office closes and break my trail by levitating. I could teleport, I suppose, but I've been afraid I might end up back in the wild west or something and anyway, I can make it to Reno in one hop now. I've had lots of practice!"

"You're hauling dynamite by levitating?" Ray said doubtfully.

"Why not? But I only do it when I'm heading back here. I rent a small truck when I pick up the explosives; it keeps the construction people from asking questions. I worked out a system; the required safety signs are magnetic and I keep them in a rented storage unit, so all I have to do is drive the truck to the storage unit, stick the signs on, and head over to the construction company. I handle the purchase in the office, but I have to go outside the city and pick the dynamite up at their trailer. It's surrounded by berms and only licensed people are admitted; they have to do it that way for safety reasons. They know me now, so it's just a straightforward purchase and pickup. What makes it even simpler is that I only buy small amounts at one time, no more than two boxes, and I put the dynamite into a trash bag when I get to the truck so people won't get upset if they look into the bed. I stash my signs at the storage unit, turn in the truck, grab my trash bag and walk away. No one pays attention. And as soon as I'm where no one can see, I levitate. Easy money."

"Wow! You've been a busy guy!" said Ray.

"You have no idea, Ray! That's just the high points, and I had a reason; I wanted to make sure there was enough gold, my share I mean, to do what I wanted. You might as well know; I'm tired of hiding out, and I'll be leaving as soon as I clean out the pocket I'm working on now. Don't get me wrong, I love what you guys did for me, but I've had enough skulking in the hills! I intend to come back and visit, and after I get settled in I'm going to want you guys to come visit me. In fact, the only reason I'm still here is because I don't want to start out broke. I figure I'll add a few hundred pounds to the gold stash, take my third, and go somewhere there are people. *Female* people."

"I can understand that," Ray said slowly, "and you'll always be welcome. You say you're planning to clean out that gold pocket?"

"It's only the most recent one, Ray, and for that matter it's not even the biggest one. T found that first one, but I've located two more since then and I think there are others. If we don't get stupid, there's enough gold in them thar hills...okay, this hill and the one behind it...to set us up for the rest of our lives! I made a map, it's in my cabin, so if you decide to do more mining you won't have a problem locating the other deposits."

"But you said...wait a minute, did you really say a few hundred *pounds*? Of *gold*?"

"Ray, I've *already got* almost three hundred pounds. It's raw gold, not as pure as if I'd electrically refined it, but pure enough. I'm casting it into six ounce ingots now, because it's a lot less work than casting one or two ounces at a time. Before I worked out my current system with the crushers and the sluice, production was slow enough to justify using the one- and two-ounce sizes, but not now. It's just too much work!"

"How are you casting them?"

"Sand molds. Put the washed gold into a crucible, heat it in a coal-fired furnace...you know there's coal on the property, don't you? Not enough to be a commercial deposit, but enough for what I'm doing. Melt it in the furnace and pour it into the molds. You've got to get it hot, and coal has enough energy. I thought of setting up an electrical refinery too, but that's overkill. I want the buyer to understand that this is *mined* gold and that's why there's no refinery stamp on the ingots."

"I'm having a hard time believing this!" exclaimed Ray. "That sounds like an awful lot of gold!"

"Believe it! Nevada's a world-class source of gold. Early miners shipped hundreds of tons of gold from Nevada and *thousands* of tons from California, which if you've forgotten is right next door. After I mapped the deposits and built my cabin, I didn't have anything else to do but mine and refine. In the beginning, the only time I left was to see Shezzie; she wanted to check my leg while it was growing back. And as I said, I go into Reno or Little Dry Creek about once a week now. But between trips, I've worked. Not gimping around on a stump helps, and you'd be surprised how much I can do by using Talent to speed things along. Mucking out and hauling the rocks to the crushers takes minutes, not hours, but even so I'm tired of it. Gold fever burns out after you've seen enough of it."

"I guess I am surprised, a little," said Ray. "So you've got gold ingots available?"

"Come on in and I'll show you."

Ray followed Bobby into the tunnel. He took a right jog, then a left, and from there another left into a side tunnel that appeared to have been abandoned. Some two hundred yards down the tunnel, they came to a roof collapse that appeared to have happened years before.

"Watch where you put your feet!" Bobby flicked on a flashlight, very bright in the gloom. "I don't want tracks in the dust. Levitation's better. Up ahead, behind the rockslide, is where we're going."

Ray followed close on Bobby's heels and suddenly stopped, stupefied. The flashlight, sold as a 'tactical model' that used a very-bright LED, lit up the room. The reflected light turned golden as soon as they passed the rockslide.

"Oh, my!" said Ray.

Chapter Eight

"Why not spend a month or two in Las Vegas? Maybe go out to California or Hawaii? I don't think you've thought this business of leaving through."

"I have. I told you, I'm tired of having to always hide out, always be looking over my shoulder!"

Ray sighed. "Believe it or not, I understand. I was just a retired soldier going to college and trying to figure out what I wanted to do next. I didn't have a worry in the world! Add in that I had just met an interesting girl and my life was looking up. And then I ran into T. Pure accident; I wasn't looking for him because I figured the Taliban had both of them. No idea of how they'd been captured, but that was the only thing that made sense. Anyway, after I left Afghanistan I had a lot to do. Retire, find a place to live, sign up for the GI Bill, and enroll at UTEP. Lots of paperwork and I had to get everything done before the semester started, so they slipped my mind.

"I didn't exactly forget, but they were part of the past and my time in the Army. But I had spent a week studying their files, so as soon as I saw him I knew that T reminded me of someone. It was just a thought, and I would probably have forgotten about it in a day or two, but T couldn't afford to. It wasn't just that he was hiding from the authorities, he was hiding from assassins! When you're that much on edge, it doesn't take much to make you suspicious and he had to worry about Shezzie too. He didn't know who I was at first, but he saw me studying him and followed me to the library where I was meeting Ana Maria. The melding was accidental and after that, one thing just led to another.

"Ana Maria was worried about her sister. Marisela was already dead, but none of us knew that at the time. That came out later on, after Surfer died. I helped T a little at first, just staying on the sidelines, until after he offed the guy responsible for Surfer's death. After that, T was the last one; Henderson, the guy he killed, had murdered or caused to be murdered a bunch of guys who were just trying to do what we did, serve the country. But then T located the gang that had murdered Marisela. I no longer wondered what I was going to do, I knew! People needed my help and I felt it would be a betrayal of my Talent not to do what I could.

"That was my thinking when I saved a mother and her baby. I got her husband up to where rescuers could reach him, but he didn't survive. Later on, we helped fight a wildfire and then we saved hundreds of lives after the quakes. *You're* complaining about having to hide out, but you're not like us! Nobody is looking for you, but the cops think I'm a drug dealer and the Army thinks T's either a POW or a deserter. Technically he *is* a deserter, and that's just what they know about, so we *have* to stay hidden. But you're different. You can always turn yourself in and become a lab rat, but I don't think you'll like it if you do. What you really want is to go back to the way things were before your Talents woke up. Is that it?"

"That's part of it, but so what?"

"So here you are. You're no longer a one-legged guy hopping around a blast site on a fake leg, doing the only thing you know how to do. You've got two good legs now, and you just mentioned accumulating gold in hundred-pound lots. Other people work their *asses* off to get a troy ounce or two, but you're sitting on a treasure King Midas would envy! And you're alive in a way you haven't been since you left Afghanistan! You want to give all that up?"

"I guess not, now that you put it that way. But I'm still going stir crazy up here in the boonies!"

"So take a vacation, all the time you need, but don't stay in one place very long."

"Why not? Suppose I meet a nice girl in Hawaii? Or even better, one who's not so nice?"

"Are you ready to create another Chupacabra?" Ray asked, "Or maybe something worse? The rest of us could leave too, you know, and we'd be safe unless someone checked our fingerprints and that's not likely. According to what the papers reported, the cops think we died when Battleship Rock fell. Jay's the only cop that even knows about us, and he can't afford to talk because he's a Talent himself. We've got new identities and unless someone gets curious, we can live relatively normal lives. But only in an out of the way place like this. Think about Ana Maria and Jay; they didn't ask for this. They got too close, or they stayed around us too long, and they changed."

"You're talking about the Talent. We can't stop the spread, Ray."

"Maybe not, but we can limit it, and we should. We stay in Little Dry Creek because the people we spend time with are already Talented. That's one of the reasons why I'm going after T; I don't know that he needs help, but if he stays in the past too long the Talent will spread back there too. T has created the most dangerous time paradox there is, just by existing in the past. So I'm going back to pull him out before the Talent spreads."

Bobby shook his head, then looked up. "I don't like it, but you're making sense. Don't be gone too long, or I'll head back to find *you*! Meanwhile, take as much gold as you want. T wore a money vest and a belt, so why don't you do the same? He thought having them in contact with his skin was important."

"Do I need both? I was thinking about just a belt. Libby will have her own."

"T thought he needed the vest. The ingots go in the vest's pockets, and he kept coins in the belt where they'd be easier to get at. Don't worry about pocket size in whatever you buy, I'll cast ingots to fit. I take it that you're still intending to take Libby?"

"I don't have a choice," said Ray wryly. "She's going by herself if I don't."

"So a vest for you, and two money belts. You can hide a vest, but Libby can't."

<My waist is 22 inches around, Uncle Bobby.>

Bobby looked at Ray in shock. Ray just shrugged. "Get used to it. She knows when one of us is thinking about her."

"Okay. She's slim and a belt with vertical pockets will make her look fat. I can cast thin ingots with a slight curve, so when you order her belt keep that in mind. Get one with horizontal pockets."

<So *not* fat!>

Ray shrugged, defeated.

***

T waited. He felt a faint, momentary, tingle in return, but nothing he would call a response.

The headache might have nothing to do with O'Brien's Talent, but people got sick from any number of causes and headaches were common. O'Brien's could be due to eyestrain or even constipation; it wasn't as if they ate a healthy diet, so constipation was one of the inevitable side effects of too few vegetables, too little fiber. He headed back to the wall to finish the repairs.

Twenty minutes later, movement at the forest's edge caught his eye. Corporal Brennan was coming in with his patrol. Routine, it happened all the time. T went back to work.

Brennan found him there half an hour later. He was munching on a strip of jerky and holding a piece of hardtack in his other hand. "Got some bad news, Tyler. The Russian fellow that helped you? He's dead. Bandits killed him and his parents. Perkins said there was a girl, but there was no body so she might have escaped."

T stopped and stood up, ostentatiously stretching his back. No reason to have anyone suspect the job had been easy.

"You're sure it was them? They live back in the woods quite a ways."

"Pretty sure. You gave him a rifle and ammo, right?"

"Sergeant Mac gave him the rifle; I gave him my last gold coin." There was no reason to let Brennan know there were others concealed a short way out of camp.

"The hut had been searched pretty good, so if they had money the bandits got it. But the reason I mention the rifle was that we found empty cases with US markings. Had to have been the same guy."

"You said bandits?"

"Part of Semenoff's gang, I'm thinking, It's not an army now, they're mostly just crooks who couldn't steal enough on their own. We buried the bodies, all we could do for them. I just hope the girl got away."

"Thanks. They were nice to me when they didn't have to be. Did the bandits head this way?"

"No, they went northwest. That was another reason I figured they were Semenoff's. If they were part of Kalmikoff's bunch, they would have headed northeast."

"You're probably right, Corporal. Thanks again for taking care of the bodies. I appreciate it."

"Well, we bought vegetables and stuff from them before," Brennan said awkwardly, "It seemed like the right thing to do,"

"Yeah. Doing the right thing is uncommon in this place!"

"Say, are you about finished? I can rustle up some help if you want."

"No, I'm done. I suppose I'd better check on Corporal O'Brien. He's sick."

"Oh, *hell*! How bad?"

"Sergeant Mac just wanted me to check on him every so often. I don't think he's worried."

"He should be! I've seen how fast disease can spread through a camp. Three-quarters of our guys got sick and a quarter died. That was in the Philippines and we had a hospital available."

"Tropical diseases," agreed T. "Not sure if it's that dangerous up here."

"It is. Some of my boyos volunteered out of the Eighth Division with General Graves. California's not exactly tropical, but they had outbreaks too."

"I'll go check on him," T decided. "Sounds like the guys that met the train are back, so I'll report to Sergeant Mac when I'm done. Thanks for letting me know, Corporal."

"Aw, no problem. You take care of yourself, Tyler."

"I'd better go." T walked away, leaving Corporal Brennan looking wide-eyed at the fresh section of wall. How had Tyler, working by himself, managed to get those logs into position?

T knocked lightly at the hut door, then opened it and looked inside. Corporal O'Brien was sitting up, the cloth gone from where it had protected his eyes.

<Tyler?>

***

Ray was on his way back to the ranch when the comm came in. <Uncle Ray?>

<Hi, Libby. Did you do what I suggested?>

<I sure did! I logged on to Etsy like you said, but none of what they were selling fit the description you gave me. But I found a woman on there that's a seamstress, and she can sew anything. I described what I remembered about women's dresses and bonnets from when we had that meal in Albuquerque, and when she asked, I told her I was going to be in a high-school play. I said that it was set in early Nevada and I wanted to look the part. I even mentioned Sarah Winnemucca. Best of all, the lady lives here in Las Vegas!"

"Good! No reason to let her suspect what you really need it for."

"I was careful. She suggested a dress, but when I mentioned that there might be dance scenes and maybe even some outdoor scenes, she said a denim jacket and jeans would work too. I'm going to her studio so she can get measurements later this afternoon. What do you think?>

<I think she knows more about that stuff than I do! I really never paid much attention to what women were wearing while I was in the past. I worked almost exclusively with men, and the women I saw were heading for church or they were like that woman in the cafe that you remembered. Most decent women spent most of their time at home.>

<So what did the not-so-decent ones wear, Uncle Ray?> Libby dropped the connection, only a slight echo of her teasing laugh revealing her amusement to the discomfited Ray.

***

T was gobsmacked. What to do? Should he respond to O'Brien's comm effort? The corporal was sitting up and looking directly at him. Uneasy, he decided to ignore it. It might have been an accident, after all. "Sergeant Mac told me to keep checking up on you. I'm glad you're feeling better."

"I am. The headache's gone and I feel fine. Where are my guys?"

"They went with Sergeant Mac. They just got back, but I figured I should check on you before I went over there. To report to Sergeant Mac, I mean."

<Dolan's dangerous! Be careful!>

T tried to hide his sudden start, unsuccessfully. He started to answer, then stopped. Was this deliberate, or an accidental thought? O'Brien's next comm removed all doubt. <Damn you, why won't you answer me? I can hear you!>

"Because I'm not the only one that might be listening! Use your voice!"

"You think someone else can do this? I don't believe it! It's got to be the magic working! Me gram had the power too, that she did!"

"It's not magic, and your grandmother had nothing to do with it. And yes, there may be others. In fact, I'm sure there's at least one. Look, I need to report to Sergeant Mac."

"I'll come with you. I need to thank him for picking up Dolan and for having you keep an eye on me."

"Voice only, okay? You've got to learn when to use the mental contact and only do it when necessary."

"Why? Are you sure we can be overheard?"

"Not absolutely, but I wasn't sure of you either until now."

"Wait a minute! I'm the corporal, you're a private. I tell *you* what to do, not the other way around!"

T looked at him. What to do? Deciding it was best to nip this in the bud right now, he reached out with his PK and lifted the corporal by the shoulders, allowing his feet to hang. Astonished, O'Brien attempted to reach the floor, but even by stretching his toes he was still left hanging in the air. "You couldn't be more wrong, Corporal. *I'm* the one in control, not you! Do you understand?"

O'Brien, speechless for a moment, finally whispered. "Tyler, what are you?"

"I'm not a witch and I don't have time to explain right now but I will, I promise. Say nothing of this, understand? I can take care of myself, but you can't! You can't allow *anyone* to know that you can talk using only your mind!"

"Dolan never had a chance, did he?"

"No, not after I realized what he was doing. Sergeant Mac's just coming in the gate. You take the lead." O'Brien nodded and pulled on his blouse. Picking up his campaign hat, he led the way to the gate.

"And there ye are, ye slacker! I was worried about you, Lad. Are ye all right now?" asked Mac.

"I'm fine, I am. Never better. I needed the sleep, I think. The headache's gone, that it has, and I'm back on duty."

"Good man! I brought yer man Dolan, who swears he's a reformed character now. Ain't that true, Dolan?"

Dolan simply nodded, but T noticed that his eyes had never wavered. He had listened, but during the conversation he'd been watching T. Despite the lump on his jaw where the swelling hadn't fully gone away, Dolan had not changed. He hated T. His words to Mac had been no more than a subterfuge; when opportunity presented, Dolan intended to have his revenge. The thought was fleeting, but T caught it.

Expecting something of the sort, he never changed expression. Dolan intended to wait until the next time they engaged with Semenoff's bandits. While T was concentrating on them, Dolan intended to shoot T in the back. The only surprise was the glance T got from Corporal O'Brien.

He looked at T and slowly winked.

s

Chapter Nine

His memories had returned, but T still had no idea of how he'd
come to be in Siberia. Teleportation? Time displacement? That
much was clear. The electrical storm and Tesla's machine had most
likely played a part, but he had no idea how. One moment he'd
been on Long Island in late summer 1905, the next he'd been in
Siberia. There was a hazy memory of something else, but it was
fragmentary; had he gone somewhere else in time before he ended
up in 1919? But except for that gap, his memories were complete.
Afghanistan, his friends in Little Dry Creek, it was all there.

But what had happened to Libby during his amnesia? Had she
somehow managed to find her way home, or was she still lost
somewhere in the past? She was a capable Talent, and possibly
much more than that; she'd discovered pyrokinetics and
teleportation on her own. She'd rapidly learned to levitate too, and
as for telepathy she was already stronger than Shezzie. Not to
mention possibly being able to influence the *weather*, which no
one else could do, so she was far from helpless. But what if she'd
teleported into a mountain or the midst of a natural disaster? Could
a child adapt as quickly as an adult to whatever circumstance she
found herself in?

The past had not been pleasant for children, especially poor
ones, and she wouldn't have had money. But workhouses or sexual
slavery were out! Pity the man or woman who attempted to abuse
Libby! One had threatened her and paid for it with his life.

Had he realized his mistake before he burned to death?

Even so, she had arrived in the past penniless, alone, and with no way to get back home. That was self-evident; she hadn't returned, which meant she couldn't.

T had already been worried about Libby, and now this. Dolan had at least a touch of ability, and Patrick O'Brien was a telepath, not to mention what had happened to the Russian family who had helped him. Despite their own poverty, they had shared the little they had, and Mischa had braved danger by bringing him to the isolated AEF-S camp.

Had Semenoff's bandits been watching the camp? Could they have followed Mischa home? Had helping T cost the lives of him and his family? Or had they found them by accident? And what of his sister? Had the bandits taken her with them? It could have happened to *any* peasant family; injustice was accepted in Russia, part of the everyday life of an exploited people in a land where the weather itself conspired against them. But regardless of how it happened, the end result was the same; three people were dead and a girl was missing.

Siberia had always been a harsh land; the weather itself is an almost-insurmountable challenge and Siberian peasants are born to hardship and suffering. So none of what had happened to Mischa and his family was new. T had been worried; now, overlaying that, was anger, the old familiar rage he felt when a child was threatened. Beneath his growing rage, T understood that he couldn't change the world. But he might be able to punish one particular group of murderers, and after all, wasn't that the real underlying reason why the AEF-S was here? Despite the high-sounding rhetoric and platitudes, the mission boiled down to fighting Semenoff and his band of Cossacks and criminals.

American soldiers fought *bandits*, not political slogans. The bandits that had raided the small farmstead were probably part of Semenoff's gang, not that it mattered. The dead were dead. But what about the girl? Had they already killed her?

Finding a particular group of bandits wouldn't be easy. Siberia is a vast land with few roads, but there are hard ways to get from one place to another and much easier ways. The bandits, traveling on foot, wouldn't have sought out the hard ways. And in any case, his mind was made up; children, particularly girls, endangered? For a moment his mind flashed back to Afghanistan, to a little girl caught in a firefight and blown away.

T would seek out the bandits. If the girl...Ekaterina?...was still alive, he would rescue her. As for what he intended, he'd done something similar in Afghanistan. The enemy was different this time, as was the terrain, but inside he was still the same man who'd gone on solo patrols seeking out Muj terrorists in places where they thought they were safe. The only real difference now was that he would search for one specific group of murderers.

But he was a private soldier now, not a warrant officer; questions would be asked if his absence was discovered. "Smithers, I need you to cover for me. I won't be gone long, a few hours at most. Corporal O'Brien is probably asleep, but in case he comes around, tell him I've got dysentery and I'm hanging around the latrine."

"T, what if he checks?" worried Smithers.

"He won't. Nobody goes there until they absolutely have to."

"Yeah, I'm surprised we haven't filled that one in and dug another! But if your rifle is gone, he'll notice."

"I'm leaving it in the rack. I won't be out long."

"Shit, you'll get *killed* if you show up in the village unarmed! I'd better go with you."

T didn't explain that he had no intention of visiting the small settlement. Let Smithers go on believing that. "I've got my pistol; you've seen me shoot, it's all I'll need. For backup, I've got my trench knife."

Smithers reluctantly agreed. T buckled the pistol belt on, adjusted the hang of the holster, and made sure the flap was closed over the bead fastener. He nodded reassuringly at Smithers and slipped out the door. Leaving the hut, he walked around back and paused, senses probing the darkness. Voices murmured in his head, but he couldn't separate one from another.

None of the thoughts concerned him. A few soldiers were smoking and telling yarns around a small fire, but they were a hundred yards away. Even so, sharp eyes might spot rapid movement. He drifted slowly up, not pausing his steady rise until he was well above the camp. Orienting himself by the half moon, he headed north. With luck, there would be other campfires.

Peasants didn't need them. They normally went to bed as soon as it was dark and if the evening was cool, a fire in the stove was enough. So there would be few campfires, and they would be easy to spot in the vast blackness of the Siberian night.

***

<I'm ready, Uncle Ray.>

Ray sighed. What to do? His attempt at convincing her to remain behind while he went back in time hadn't worked. Maybe a different approach would. <You really shouldn't be doing this. I *have* to go, but you don't.>

<I don't see it that way, Uncle Ray.> The stubbornness was clear, even through the telepathic connection.

<Have you thought about not being able to return? Of never again seeing your family or friends?>

<Why wouldn't I?> This time the emotion he sensed was wariness.

<Because you haven't thought this through! You're a middle school student who's barely scratched the surface of math!>

<High school next year, but so what? I got back the last time!>

<With my help!> Ray sent. <And after I had time to think about it, I realized I had been lucky.>

<Lucky how?> More interest this time, less wariness. And no trace of the stubbornness; he was discussing the issue with her and treating her like an adult, not a little girl.

<You know I killed a man back there, don't you? Maybe more than one?>

<I think I did too, Uncle Ray. So what? We were only

defending ourselves!>

<We were,> Ray agreed, <but if we hadn't gone back in time, it couldn't have happened. Oh, I doubt they'd have died in bed, but it wouldn't have been *us*! Someone from their own timeline would have been responsible, which means we created time paradoxes. You know what those are, right?>

<I read about them.> Defensive, this time. <But again, so what? I don't think it's possible! I might go back and kill my grandfather, but it wouldn't matter if my grandmother was already pregnant with my father or mother. Otherwise I *couldn't* have killed him, because I wouldn't have been born to go back and kill him.>

<Confusing, isn't it?>

<No, I'm certain that I'm right.> Determination again.

<I'm not, Libby! What about alternative timelines and parallel universes? How much do you know about those?>

<I've heard of them, but I don't believe it! They're just speculation, Uncle Ray. Mathematicians claim that time can be treated as a variable, but we didn't go into the future, did we? We got back to when you teleported to the past, and that was only because we were linked.>

<No, we didn't go into the future or at least I don't think we did, but that's proof; there *are* alternative timelines, and we can't go into the future because it hasn't *happened* yet on this one. There are too many branches.>

<*What* branches? You're trying to confuse me and I'm not buying it! I'm going!>

<Libby, just *think* before you decide. For every choice, there are two branches. It's like a fork in the road; in one, you killed that kidnapper but in the other, you didn't. He then had a choice of his own. In one, he killed you, in the other he decided to let you go.>

<Wait a minute! I killed him because I was scared, and I found out I could burn him where he stood. Why wouldn't I have done the same in every timeline?>

<You might have,> Ray agreed. <But again, you might not;

the *choice* is the only thing that matters. For every choice, there are two branches. Some choices have nothing to do with us. We don't control them, they just happen.

<We might be on a different time branch right now, but in this case it doesn't matter. Everything here is the way we remember. But we could come back next time and find that there's a different Libby and Ray who are *already* here. T might be back too; he might have figured out how to return just like I did.>

<You're guessing! You can't be sure about any of this!>

<Not yet. Suppose someone shows up a few minutes from now and swears she's the real Libby?>

 <I'm going! I was intending to go all along!>

<All right.> Ray, frustrated, gave up.

She was determined, there was no doubt about it. The bottom line was that he couldn't stop her, he could only go along to try to keep her out of trouble. <We need a plan. When are you coming up here?>

<Tonight. I'll wait until my parents are asleep.>

***

T wasn't the only soldier with anger issues.

Private Dolan simmered. He rubbed his still-swollen jaw and plotted.

Despite his bluster, he remembered clearly how the fight had gone. Drunk, yes; but drunk enough to forget, no. Next time, it wouldn't be a simple fight! Which, considering Tyler's speed, had never been a fair fight between strong men who used their fists to settle issues! But he would think it through before he did anything. And leave off the whiskey! Some claimed it slowed a man down, and maybe it did. If he'd been sober...

But Tyler was dangerous, too dangerous to face man to man. There was only one thing to do. And it could happen as early as the next patrol! Dolan felt a savage surge of joy at the thought; he'd done it before, after all. That goddamn stuck-up lieutenant in the Philippines! The Army thought the Moros had shot him, and maybe they had, but he'd already been stone dead by then, killed by a powerful rabbit punch to the back of his neck. No shot, no bullet, just a man using his natural strength and his good right fist to even up the score. But with Tyler...

A shot to his spine? Or maybe through his ugly skull? Yes, that would be best, and make sure with a head shot. An enemy was an enemy and better dead! It was the Irish way, and wasn't he Irish? Dolan half-smiled in satisfaction, then winced. The broken jaw still ached and the gums were tender, forcing him to chew carefully.

So he smoldered and plotted, unaware that someone had been sensing his thoughts.

***

Corporal O'Brien had been asleep when the voice began whispering in his mind. Subconsciously he'd tried to adapt as the dream evolved but that hadn't worked. Little by little, he'd drifted toward wakefulness.

Sitting up in bed, he yawned. Maybe a drink of water would help; his mouth was dry. He reached for his canteen, hanging from a peg on the wall, then paused as the words continued. Wide awake now, he listened. The voice was strange, but there was a sense that he'd heard it before. Not Tyler, the one he'd suspected when he first heard that faint whisper in his mind. But someone familiar.

Sergeant Mac? No, that didn't fit. Mac was a good man. He wouldn't have been thinking about Tyler, not in the way O'Brien had just heard. Smithers? No, Smithers was Tyler's friend and combat buddy. By process of elimination, he realized that it had to be Dolan. Stupid, bullying Dolan, a problem since he'd joined the company!

Should he try to contact Dolan? Perhaps make him realize that his scheming had been overheard?No; he'd sensed Dolan's thoughts this time, but suppose it was only a one-time thing? O'Brien had never experienced anything like this.

What if Dolan changed his plan? For that matter, was he still dreaming? Were the voices no more than artifacts of his dreams? Pinching didn't help. It was supposed to tell you if you were dreaming, but the sudden pain felt real.

Sighing, Corporal O'Brien rolled out of bed and got dressed. Picking up his rifle, he checked that the bolt was closed and the safety on. These were automatic actions. Finished, he headed for the hut that Tyler shared with Smithers. Tyler would be there now, asleep, which was a good thing. He needed to be warned before he left the hut.

Dolan was quartered in the barracks, so whatever he intended wouldn't happen before morning. For now, Tyler was with Smithers, hence out of Dolan's reach. But maybe it was time to do something permanent about Mister Dolan. O'Brien stopped, thinking it through. There might be a better way.

And he knew just the man to ask.

Chapter Ten

"So that's it. I don't know what to do about Dolan."

First Sergeant Mac leaned back and gave Corporal O'Brien a searching look. "How did you find this out?"

"I did a walk-through of the barracks. The men will smoke in bed if I'm not watching them close and we don't need another barracks fire. Dolan was muttering in his sleep and I heard him mention Tyler, so I stopped and listened. He's never been of much use, but up to now, I wouldn't have thought he'd shoot a fellow soldier! I don't trust him as far as I could throw him. He'd shoot you or *me* if he got the chance and thought he could get away with it!"

"But the real question is, are ye sure? You said he was sleeping; it might have been just a dream," countered Mac.

"Top, would you want him behind you in a fight? With a loaded rifle?"

"No, Lad. I wouldn't, for a fact. I need to think about this, because 'tis not a light thing we're discussing. Right now, you're sure his target is Tyler?"

"That's the only name I heard," said O'Brien. "But I couldn't stand there and wait around to see if he talked about anyone else."

"Aye. But a name mentioned in his sleep is not enough. This may blow over. It may have been no more than resentment for the beating Tyler gave him. Do ye this: keep an eye on him, and if he gives you trouble, do what you have to do. But not in camp, and not in front of witnesses, Lad. I'll cover for ye, but if an officer sees there's likely to be nowt I can do."

"Thanks, Top! I'll remember." Corporal O'Brien nodded and left the small office. It was unfortunate that he couldn't tell Mac the truth, that he'd listened to Dolan's thoughts, but at least he'd reported the problem and now the trick was to keep Tyler and Dolan apart as much as possible.

The opportunity rose by accident later that morning.

***

<I'm leaving now, Uncle Ray. I should reach the ranch in three hours, maybe sooner.>

<I'll be waiting. If you have a problem, comm me.>

<As if, Uncle Ray!> Libby's confidence came through clearly. Ray shook his head and smiled.

Bobby was looking at him, wondering why he'd stopped fitting the 6-ounce ingots into the vest's pockets. "Libby's on her way," Ray explained.

"We'll have plenty of time to finish up here and head down to the ranch," Bobby said. "Are you ready?"

"Almost. The raw gold was the last thing I needed. Now I just have to convince her that we're not just going to try to teleport straight to New York!"

"I can see how that might lead to problems! T intended to take it in short jumps. He thought it would be safer and more controllable."

"That's it," agreed Ray. "The stops will slow us down, and even if we hit our planned stopping point on the nose, we'll need to find out what year it is. But with luck, it won't take more than a day or two to get back to 1905 New York."

"Got an itinerary yet?"

"We'll take the southern route. The forecast for the next ten days is storms all across the Midwest, and I want to avoid those."

"No reason to take a chance," agreed Bobby. "I'm finished." He had been fitting coins into the belt Libby would wear. "I've got two more pockets to go before yours is ready. Bigger waist, more pockets. Ingots in the back, coins in the front."

"Works for me."

Ten minutes later, with Ray wearing his vest and carrying the belts, the two headed for the ranch to wait for Libby.

***

Corporal O'Brien found T helping Smithers clean his BAR. "Smithers can clean his own gun, Tyler. Get your rifle and come with me."

T shrugged and got to his feet. His ten-pouch Mills belt hung near the rifle; the corporal hadn't mentioned it, but the rifle wouldn't be much good without ammunition. He buckled the belt around his waist and adjusted the hang of the attached bayonet and pistol. As a next-to-last step, he checked the Springfield's safety and slung the rifle from his right shoulder. Donning his campaign hat, finally ready, he followed O'Brien toward the guard post.

"Keep your voice down. I heard something last night that you need to know about." O'Brien hesitated for a moment, then went on. "I niver expected something like this to happen." The corporal's brogue was more pronounced than usual, a sign of his stress. "'Tis Dolan. He means to kill you next time we're in action."

"You heard him, then?"

"Aye, like you. With my mind."

"I was afraid of that," T sighed. "Dolan may not be able to hear us yet, or at least understand what we're thinking; that's more difficult than just broadcasting his thoughts the way he's been doing. You picked it up fast!"

"I guess so. No idea how it happened, it just did. I'd been hearing something for more than a week, but I thought it was just the ringing in me ears."

"It could be that," T agreed, "but it might be that you're hearing more than one person. Dolan might not be the only one leaking thoughts! Or it could be that you're like my wife, a natural telepath and empath. It was always there, she just needed a push from a friend of mine, who was also a very strong telepath." *Technically they weren't married*, T thought, *but they might as well have been. The relationship was permanent.*

"Like hearing sounds when you're in the kitchen and everybody is talking at once?" asked Patrick.

"That's it," agreed T. "Don't worry about Mister Dolan. Right now, I'm more worried about you."

"Me? Is it a curse, this hearing of voices?"

"There are no curses, just abilities we call Talents. It's like anything else, some are better at it than others."

"So 'tis possible me sainted mither had this ability too? 'Twas said she had the sight, as did her mither before her. I never expected it, d'ye see, because me father was wise in the way of farming. He niver had the sight, just the farming. 'Twas no better man in Ireland for the growing of potatoes! Or was, until the blight hit. But in me family, 'twas only the women had the sight."

"Don't sell him short, Patrick. Nobody understood the blight. The problem in Ireland was that too many depended on the potato crop; people not only starved when it failed, whole families were forced off their land. Is that when you came to America?"

"Aye. I wuz but a boy at the time. Me father went to the railroad and me mither sewed dresses in New York, but she got the consumption and died. Me father...I just don't know. We'd not heard from him these twenty years and more. He sent money at first, but then it stopped.

"I wuz big for me age, so I went to work. The mines were hiring, but me mither wouldn't hear of it. 'Twas the coughing, d'ye see? The mines killed people faster even than the sewing. So I got a job workin' for a bricklayer. I was niver so big in the shoulders as some, but I was strong for the work. Then came the war. 'Twas between the French and the Kaiser at first, but then the English joined in and the Belgians too. 'Twas more work and better pay for a time, workin' in a factory, but the murderin' Boche were comin', I could tell. They drowned me aunt and two cousins, the dirty bastards, by torpedoing their ship. Me family had niver done aught to thim! And later on they blew up a cousin in the trenches. 'Twas no place for an Irishman or for that matter, a man, he wrote, but..." O'Brien shrugged.

"No. Your cousin was right."

"The sergeant came around with a poster, so he did, and it said that Uncle Sam wanted me to join the Army. There was already talk of the draft, d'ye see, and he said that if I joined up now I could fight against the murderin' Huns without havin' to go into the trenches. It sounded good at the time and he kept his word, so he did. I went to the Philippines, but not to fight the Hun. 'Twas the Moros, and as soon as we licked thim, the Army packed us off to Siberia."

"Nothing unusual in that," T said absently. He was still trying to come to terms with what had happened. The Talent was spreading. Was this the paradox he'd feared might happen? Or had it happened just this way in the past? What if there were others?

There had always been rumors regarding a few who had done things, known things, that others hadn't. People with insight, wisdom, who somehow always seemed to be a step ahead? Had those with Talent in the past done as his small group had done, avoided mixing with others as much as possible to contain the spread?

"I think you gained your ability by being around me. Dolan too. I've got a suggestion if you're interested."

"Have ye now? If ye plan to do away with Dolan, do it away from camp and make sure there are no witnesses. I got that advice from a very canny man, and 'tis the same for you."

"It may come to that, especially if he intends to make good on what he was thinking. But I've got something else in mind for you."

***

"I don't like this thing. It's uncomfortable!"

"But you need to wear it! It's for your own good. I hope we can find T and immediately return home, but we both have to be prepared for anything."

"What if I want to spend the gold?"

"That's what it's *for*. Spend it if you have to, but don't waste it. I've got a use for it."

"Oh?" asked Libby.

"It's time you started thinking about your future. The best use for whatever gold is left after the trip is to start a college fund for you. What do you think?"

"I haven't really thought about it. I could study history,

couldn't I?"

"You could, but you might have to put up with a lot of wrong ideas! You met people in the past, so did I, but the people who *write* history haven't gone back the way we did. Suppose you wrote a book about what you saw, but without mentioning that you actually met Sarah Winnemucca? Would people believe you? Especially if your book contradicted what they already believe?"

Libby frowned. "Why wouldn't they believe me?"

"Because you haven't studied history, haven't written learned papers on the period. You're not the authority, *they* are. Even if they're wrong. Could you do that, spend your life making things right?"

"I don't know. I don't know what I want to do yet, but there are worse ways to live, aren't there?"

"Yes, but you have to understand that Talent isn't enough; you have to work within the system. We work with cops, but only Captain Jay knows how we get things done. For that matter, he has to hide his own Talents. He *has* to work within the system, he can't just tell a judge he read a suspect's mind. That's what you've got to do. You could run for president one day, but ability isn't enough. You would have to work with people who are wrong, who are actually crooked! Could you do that?"

"I don't know." Libby's voice was soft. "Why would I need to work with evil people?"

"Because people aren't perfect, and because they get elected based on slick ad campaigns, and because they're rich and powerful. It doesn't matter what you do, you're going to have to work with people, and not all of them will be good people. College will give you the chance to find out where your interests lie and the gold will enable you to study at any college that will accept you. Which means keeping your grades up. Not three years from now, but starting next year. It means studying, taking tests fairly and not peeking into someone's mind for the answers."

"It's a lot to think about, isn't it?"

"Welcome to growing up, Libby. But it's time to plan our trip, and the only holdup now is waiting for your clothes. As soon as they're ready, we can go. Wear plain jeans, probably Levi's, they've been around for years. If you want to wear a hat, I suggest a plain Stetson. Cotton shirt, cotton underwear, and wear the money belt next to your skin. Ordinary boots, nothing fancy. We'll leave from the mine area; it's deserted, except for Bobby. From there, we teleport southeast to Albuquerque. I'm hoping that will put us twenty or thirty years in the past, but we'll have to check after we get there. No way of telling when we'll arrive or what season it will be. We'll have to check. Teleport in, but if it's winter teleport back to the mine. We'll need winter clothing."

"How about wearing a Levi's jacket? It's not all that heavy."

"Good idea. We might need to levitate without teleporting, and if we do the jacket will be more comfortable. Put a pair of goggles in the pocket too, just in case."

"I didn't do any of this before, Uncle Ray!"

"I didn't either. We were both very lucky."

***

"I'm going out tonight, alone," said T.

"You can't do that!" exploded Corporal O'Brien. "Mac I can talk to, but what if the lieutenant finds out?"

"I have to! I've done something like this before. I can't explain now, but it will keep me away from Dolan for a while."

"Tyler, I can't approve this! I don't have that kind of authority, neither does Mac."

"It won't matter, because I won't get caught. I only mention it because I might need help when I get back. Just don't make a big issue of it if I'm not back by tomorrow morning. I'll be all right."

"Where are you going?"

"Solo patrol. I'll look for bandits."

"What if you run into a large patrol?"

"What if I do?" T's voice was soft. "I'm not like other people."

"Tyler..." O'Brien started, then stopped.

"What are you?" he whispered.

Chapter Eleven

O'Brien, still protesting quietly, followed T to a dark area some 50 yards from the latrines. "Damnit, if you leave without permission, 'tis desertion!"

"It's only desertion if I don't come back! Relax, Patrick, I'll be back before morning."

T drifted slowly up, watching to make sure that O'Brien was the only one who could see him when he arrowed away toward the distant farmstead.

Would he insist on telling Sergeant Mac? Time would tell, but if they had kidnapped the young girl time was not on her side. Climbing as he flew, T blocked the worst of the cold wind with a clenched fist in front of his face.

His hand grew cold, despite his gloves. He switched, his other hand protecting his face while he warmed the chilled hand by placing it inside his woolen uniform.

Soon there was no choice; both hands were freezing. He slowed his flight, attempting to protect his numb face by extending his elbow in front. It helped, a little. But if he didn't find the bandits soon, he would have to stop somewhere and warm up.

Levitating was also growing difficult; Siberia was a near-endless sea of black. The trees, many of them evergreen, absorbed the moonlight. Occasionally a stream shown bright, and from time to time he spotted the dim glow from a chimney. Long practice allowed him to use such clues and whatever moon revealed. It was enough, considering his reduced speed.

Forty minutes into the flight, he spotted a flicker of yellow light. Five miles, perhaps? Slowing still more, T lost height and concentrated on the fire.

Flying was easier now; the glow provided enough detail for him to hover while he studied the scene below.

A man sat hunched over near the fire. A rifle lay beside him, the barrel resting against the log he was sitting on. Four mummy-like shapes lay stretched out near the fire, sleeping. A fifth was farther away, near a stunted tree.

Looking closely, T made out a line that had to be a rope of some kind. The girl was alive; he'd arrived in time. But what to do now?

Rescue the girl and kill the bandits, obviously. But what if someone found their bodies? Psychokinetics was a last resort. Gunshot wounds and stab marks, those would cause few questions, but four deaths with no obvious cause would cause talk. At the same time, a gunshot would wake the sleepers and they might decide to kill the girl.

There was only one thing to do. T eased the heavy trench knife out of its scabbard, avoiding the metal-on-metal sound as the blade cleared the throat. Knife in his left hand, boots a few inches above the ground, he paused above the sentry.

Clapping his right hand over the man's mouth, T yanked his head back and struck viciously. The razor-sharp knife sliced through coat and skin between the neck and the collarbone. Just below lay the aorta and the beating heart; the sentry died silently, never knowing what had killed him. He had felt a sudden, agonizing pain, mercifully short, then darkness. There had been no noise, other than the faint sound as the knife punched through cloth and flesh.

Easing the corpse to the ground, T listened. Faint snores came from two of the men and the one he'd identified as the girl. T grinned mirthlessly and floated toward one of the two silent shapes, knife now in his right hand.

In the end, it didn't matter. The noisy sleepers slipped as soundlessly into death as had the silent ones. But were there others?

T floated higher and as soon as he was ten feet above the ground he drifted away, spiraling outwards from the camp where only one person now lived.

Five minutes later, satisfied that no one was around, he sliced through the rope holding the girl. Some sort of braided material? Whatever it was, the knife handled it with ease.

She felt the slight tug, however. Eyes huge in the moonlight, she sat up, mouth opened to scream.

"Shhhh," he whispered. Despite his search, T decided it made sense to keep the noise down. She took a deep breath, understanding from the tone that this wasn't one of the men who'd beaten and raped her.

T followed the rope to where it was tied around her waist and cut it free. Lifting her, still inside her blankets, he carried her to the fire and eased her to the ground. For the first time, she saw his face. "Amerikansky?"

"Da, Amerikansky. Uh...you're safe now."

The girl didn't need to understand his words. Across the fire lay the huddled sentry, spilled blood a black pool beneath his head. She spared only a glance at the men in the bedrolls, understanding that they too had been dispatched.

"I'm going to get you out of here. Sit tight, I've still got a few things to do."

The girl's eyes followed him as he searched the bodies. He found a few knives, all small. Larger knives were attached to belts that held ammunition. T took the knives and ammo belts and stacked them by the coals.

Their clothing held a few coins, two of which were heavy enough to be gold. T slipped them into his pocket.

The girl whispered something and pointed. Off to the side was a pack and next to it, her family's samovar. Shrugging, T handed it to her. It appeared to be brass, not particularly expensive, but probably important because it had belonged to her family. She gathered the item in, hugging it tightly.

He collected the rifles, removed the bolts, then laid the weapons in the coals. Thin streams of smoke rose immediately; like most, the stocks had probably been oiled to protect the wood. Flames flared up as he added the larger knives to the fire. As a final step, he stacked the remaining firewood around the receivers and blades. The wood would catch fire in a few minutes and the heat would ruin the weapons.

He debated tossing the ammo into the fire and decided against it. Lifting the belts one at a time, he threw them as far as possible, aided by his PK ability. Maybe they wouldn't be found. It was time to go.

"I need to cover your face. Don't be afraid." She looked back at him, not understanding, but realizing that if he'd been like the others he'd never have cut her free. Gently, T folded the end of the blanket over her face and tucked it in her hand, then gently guided the hand inside the cocoon of blankets.

Well. If she peeked out, she would understand they were flying but no one would believe her. In any case, he'd done as much as he could. Now to get the girl to safety. <Corporal O'Brien?>

<Tyler?>

<Who's on guard tonight?>

<Linton, from Heintzelman's squad.>

<I need you to relieve him. Send him for coffee, tell him you felt sorry for him. Something, anything to get him away from the gate. I need you there, and no one else.>

<He won't believe me!>

<Probably not, but do it anyway. I'll be there in a little over half an hour and I need you on the gate when I get there.>

<*Goddamnit*, Tyler...> But there was no response.

Swearing, O'Brien picked up his rifle and headed for the gate.

***

T cradled the girl in his arms and levitated, using the flickering light of the campfire to form an image of the ground. As soon as he was some 30 feet above the treetops, moonlight revealed enough details that he was able to expand his focus.

Accelerating south, he headed for the camp. He was able to break the worst of the wind by ducking his face behind the girl's blanket-wrapped form.

He was ten minutes from the camp when O'Brien commed him.

<The gate guard won't leave. He said he'd have to check with Heintzelman first, and I knew that wasn't what you wanted. I told him to forget about it.>

<Don't worry about it. It means a change of plans, but I should still be able to make it before dawn. I'll explain everything when I see you tomorrow.>

<Okay.> With that, O'Brien dropped the connection.

Walking up to the gate was no longer an option, and if he tried to simply fly the girl over the wall and land in a dark corner he would have to explain the unexplainable. First Sergeant Mac, and probably the commanding officer as well, would soon be involved.

But the Russian village was only a few miles farther. He changed course slightly and flew on. Holding the girl had forced him to leave his hands exposed to the cold wind. They were now like blocks of ice with very little feeling, but time was growing critical. The moon was low in the sky and without the light, he wouldn't be able to levitate by pushing away from the ground. He sped up slightly, ignoring the pain in his hands.

Fifteen minutes later, he eased to the ground. He set the girl on her feet beside the dirt track leading into the village Even in the moonlight, he could see how wide her eyes were when he opened the flap of blanket. Had she realized they were flying?

There had been no help for it before and there was no help for it now. Getting her somewhere she would be safe was still the priority. Chances were she wouldn't be believed, but she would need money. He handed her the coins he'd taken from the bandits, folding her hands over them.

T walked with her into the village and loudly rattled the door of the largest house. Dogs began barking and moments later, a dim glow revealed that someone had turned up a lamp. T stepped back into the shadows and waited.

The door opened slowly, cautiously. Light shone dimly, revealing the girl. Russian words flowed back and forth rapidly and moments later, she stepped inside the house. T glanced around, making sure no one else had come out, then lifted off rapidly.

The moon was low on the horizon when he landed behind the hut he shared with Smithers. Going inside, he shrugged out of his ammunition belt and wrapped it around his pistol and trench knife before laying them at the end of the bunk. Exhausted, he managed to get his boots off before collapsing. He was asleep as soon as he lay down, hands tucked inside his armpits to warm.

***

Libby showed up dressed in jeans, a flannel shirt, and a pair of square-toed boots. Instead of a hat she wore a scarf. Ray raised his eyebrows questioningly, but she shrugged.

"A hat would be out of place in town and if I need one, I can always buy it."

"How's the money belt?"

"Heavy!" she acknowledged, "But I'm used to it now. Are we ready?"

"We are. First stop, Aztec ruins. They're just outside of Farmington, New Mexico. Take a look." Ray spread out the map and pointed to a spot. "It's a more direct route and the ruins have been around for centuries, so we're not likely to miss them even if our arrival time is off.

"From there, we levitate normally, no teleporting, until we get to Farmington. Stop long enough to find out what year it is, then decide where we want to go next."

"Are you sure? I don't want to end up way back in the past! Not again!"

Ray nodded. "I don't think we will. Distance and time are related; you went back more than a century and a half, but that was because you took one huge jump and didn't make it as far as you intended. It won't happen this time because we're going back one slow step at a time. If you're ready, follow me up; we'll teleport from a reasonable altitude to make sure we don't end up inside a tree. No mountains close to the ruins, but there are hills. You go first, I'll be right behind you. Form your bubble as soon as you arrive, just in case. When you can see the ground and know you're

108

safe, then and only then collapse the bubble. Don't hold it in close, it has to be large enough for oxygen to enter and carbon dioxide to escape."

"Well, duh!"

Doggedly Ray continued. "If something happens, stay where you are and I'll find you. If there's a problem, we won't go farther back in time until we figure out what went wrong. Understood?"

Libby nodded. "You might need my help. I won't leave without you."

Ray's amusement never showed. "Okay. So we meet up near Aztec Ruins and head for Farmington to find out how far back we went, assuming we did. I don't consider anything certain at this point. Look for a newspaper or a calendar, then decide whether we feel up to going on. It won't hurt to take rooms for the night if we have to. Even if we don't stay overnight, we'll probably need to eat. There's no hurry; we want to arrive in New York just before T does and 1905 will wait until we get there."

"You're right," Libby agreed. "So we follow that same slow process we used last trip and move on as soon as we find out where and when we are?"

"Yes. Time travel isn't a done deal, we're learning as we go. We've had too many mishaps and we're lucky nothing bad has happened, so far. Other than that you got lost in the past, *I* got lost, and T is *still* lost, so we take it slow and careful. We can always adjust our time of arrival by not going directly with or against the magnetic field. North or south should be neutral if I have it figured right, so teleporting a short distance and staying a few degrees off magnetic north or south should allow us to tweak our arrival date pretty close."

"Put that way, you're right. What if people try to talk to us? You're my uncle, right?"

"Right. I won't make a mistake, but you need to be very careful how you talk to people. Forget all the slang, the cute shortcuts. Stick to plain old standard English."

Libby dimpled at him. "Boring, but I'll try!"

"Ready?"

"Aztec Ruins, form my bubble until I know it's safe, and wait for you there?"

"That's it."

They had been rising slowly during the conversation. Ray used the shadows to orient himself and stopped. A few yards away, Libby did the same.

And vanished. One moment she was there, the next she was gone. Ray took a deep breath, focused on his mental image of the map, and teleported.

***

"Tyler, wake up! C'mon, man, shake a leg."

"What..." T sat up, realizing uneasily that it was daylight beyond the door. "I overslept?"

"I let you sleep as long as I could, but Mac wants to see us. The hetman of the village is here and he's complaining about something. Mac didn't explain, but I think he suspects you're involved and he wants me there because the Army thinks I'm responsible for you. You can leave your rifle, but wear your ammo belt and the pistol. I doubt you'll need it, but with Russians you never know. Smithers is already manning the wall and so are some of the other guys. Mac wanted him there with the BAR, just in case, but he didn't want to make it look like a general alert."

"Be right with you, I need to hit the latrine first. I hope Mac has coffee!"

"Hurry it up. I'll be at the office when you get there."

Ten minutes later, T knocked at the open door of Sergeant Mac's office.

A heavyset Russian, bearded as so many were, sat across the table from Mac, drinking tea. Sitting beside him was the girl T had rescued from the bandits. Between the two sat an interpreter.

Mac glanced at T and O'Brien, and interrupted the interpreter just long enough to tell O'Brien that he and Tyler were to wait outside until the conversation was finished.

110

Siberian Wizard

Chapter Twelve

"You have any idea what's going on?" asked Corporal O'Brien.

"Patrick, you don't want to know! Look surprised and I'll explain later."

"It better be good, Tyler!" he whispered. "Come to think on it, you've got a *lot* of explaining to do!"

"I'll tell you as much as I can, but not here; let's just see what happens. I promise, as soon as Mac is finished with us, we'll find a quiet place and I'll tell you everything that happened. For now, I'll tell you that I'm a veteran, I was before Mischa brought me here, and I mean absolutely no harm to any American. Well, except for Dolan; him I don't know about. He's trouble, more trouble than you know."

"No harm to any other soldier? Or any other American?"

"That's what I said. I'll explain...I may have to do more than that, but first I want to talk, okay? For now, I need you to trust me."

O'Brien nodded and turned his attention to the conversation going on in Mac's office.

Fifteen minutes later, the three Russians shook Mac's hand and filed out.

"In here, you two!" Mac growled.

T was calm, Patrick apprehensive. But Mac offered them coffee and indicated they should take the chairs recently occupied by the Russians. "You know anything about that girl, Tyler?"

"I saw her when Mischa brought me to their farm," T said carefully. "She went off to find his father."

"The village chief showed me a pair of gold coins. You have any idea where she got those?"

"I gave her parents a coin and I gave another pair to Mischa when he brought me here. But we've also been spending gold locally for supplies, haven't we? Her family may have gotten the coins from the Army."

"True enough, but these are different! Any idea of why?"

"No," T said warily.

"One is dated 1927. Now I wonder how that could have happened." Mac's tone was casual. "I don't know much about coins, but I read that misprinted stamps are worth a lot of money. Maybe this one was a proof that was stamped with the wrong date and then the rest of the run was dated 1917."

"I suppose that could be it, but this one has obviously been circulated. A fellow would think that in all that handling, someone would have noticed the date, now wouldn't you?"

But no one answered, so Mac moved on. "You can go, Tyler; I need a few minutes of the corporal's time."

"Okay, First Sergeant." T nodded to O'Brien and left.

<Be careful what you say! I'll explain later.>

Moments later, he got a brief, <All right.>

***

Teleporting was, as always, instantaneous so far as Ray could tell. One second, he was hovering far above the surface near the mine, the next he was--elsewhere, still above the ground, but falling. He formed his bubble and expanded it to the largest size he could control. He was still sinking, but slower now. He had time to examine his surroundings and realize he'd arrived precisely where he intended.

A full moon shown down through scattered clouds on the ghostly ruins. The stone enclosures that had given the site its name were clearly visible, now only about twenty feet below; early explorers thought that the stone construction meant they must be related to what the Conquistadores had found in Mexico. There was enough light for Ray to form a good image of the ground; he collapsed his bubble and levitated while he commed Libby.

There was no answer, but Ray wasn't worried. She was somewhere near in time. The trick was to use micro-jumps to find her. Fixing a point off to the east in his mind, he teleported.

Forming the bubble and sending out a comm took bare

moments. No answer, so he repeated the exercise. This time, she responded immediately.

<I'm not seeing a ruin, Uncle Ray. There's nothing here but hills and a lot of big rocks.>

<Don't panic; we're in the same time, we just need to find each other's location.>

<I'm not panicking! How can we do that?>

<First thing, form an image of the ground that you can push against. How high are you?>

<I'm just above the ground now, still in my bubble. That's what's holding me up.>

<Collapse the bubble, form a good image, and levitate. Rotate around as you rise and see if you can spot the ruins. I can't tell which direction you are or how far away, so you'll have to come to me.>

<Okay.>

Libby sent nothing for a full minute. <Still not seeing anything. I'm pretty high up, but I could be a hundred miles from you. I looked in every direction like you said.>

<We can find each other at daybreak by watching the sun rise, but I've got one more thing to try first. I'm seeing quite a bit of debris around here, some of it paper but some looks like tree branches. Give me a minute.>

Ray gathered wood and stuffed paper trash underneath the stack. Concentrating, he soon had a fire. Feeding it with more branches, he commed Libby. <Rotate again. This time, look for a fire. You're up pretty high, right?>

<Yes. I'm rotating now...nothing. I don't see a fire. There's a town, I think. I don't know what direction, just that it's a long way off.>

<One more thing to try, then. Rotate and keep watching.>

Ray lifted the largest of the burning sticks and turned it so that the flame was licking up along the unburned side. This would cause it to flame higher until the entire surface was ablaze. Slowly he levitated the makeshift torch, waiting to see if Libby spotted it.

It was barely visible, high above, when she finally responded. <I see a kind of spark. Is that what you mean?>

<Yes. Fly toward it. Don't try to match its elevation, just keep coming toward it. I'll lower it as you get closer and you'll soon be here.>

Fifteen minutes later, she drifted down and Ray dropped the smoldering torch in the fire.

"I saw two towns on the way, Uncle Ray! I was on the other side of a big lake and that's probably why I couldn't see your fire."

"There's a lake not far from here," Ray agreed. "We'll just wait a while before we head into town. We'll be less likely to attract attention if we arrive after sunrise, and we can get breakfast. I'm carrying a few older five-dollar bills and some Morgan silver dollars dated 1921. "I intend to save the gold coins if I can, and the ingots are for emergencies. With luck, we won't need them at all. As for having breakfast, restaurants often have calendars."

Libby nodded. "That makes sense. I was worried there for a minute! I thought I'd lost you!"

"That's why we're taking it slow. You go first, I'll adjust my time by taking short jumps until we find each other."

***

"Mac wants to talk to you again, but he's meeting with the lieutenant right now. You said you could explain what's going on?" said Patrick.

"I can, but we need someplace private. This is going to take a while," said T. "Grab your rifle and a bandoleer of cartridges. We'll head for the range; it's deserted and nobody will wonder what we're doing there. And I could use the practice if we have time. Just you and me, okay?"

O'Brien nodded. "Give me a few minutes and I'll find something for Smithers and Dolan to do. Wait for me at the gate."

T nodded and went off to collect his rifle and a bandoleer of ammunition. Fifteen minutes later, they were headed down the trail. "We're far enough now. Start talking," said Corporal O'Brien.

"Just talking, not mental communication," cautioned T. "There are reasons. The mental contact is only for emergencies. Dolan's already a problem, but so far he's the only one and I'm hoping we can keep it that way."

"You mean other people could learn to do this?"

"Yeah. This is fairly new stuff, even for me, but close association or just being around when someone is communicating seems to wake up latent Talents. That's what we call them and it's not only communicating and lifting things. I can do stuff you don't know about."

"So you're saying I can already--communicate, is that what you call it?"

"Comm for short, but yes," agreed T.

"I could learn how to do other things too?"

"Some of them, depending on your aptitude. It's like shooting or playing the piano, some take to it right away and some never do. It's like music in another way too, some become virtuosos, some can barely bang out a tune, and some are tone-deaf. Besides native Talent, practice has a lot to do with how far and how fast you progress."

"The only thing I can do right now is comm." O'Brien sounded disappointed. "I can hear Dolan, but I've never tried to answer him."

"Don't!" advised T. "Dolan's already a problem and one is enough. About that privacy I mentioned, we need to be where no one is going to walk up to us for the next hour or so. It probably won't take that long, but I won't take unnecessary chances. Turn left just beyond that big tree on the left. "

O'Brien turned and T followed. "Keep going. There's a big birch up ahead and we'll stop there. Hang onto your rifle."

"What? Why? Are you expecting..." O'Brien's voice trailed off as T lifted him above the scrub vegetation.

"Grab that limb and hang on."

Wordlessly, O'Brien did as he was told. Moments later, T settled on an adjacent branch.

O'Brien blinked. "Is that one of the things I could learn to do?"

"Yes, if you've got the raw ability." T sighed. "I don't like having to do what I'm about to do, but I don't have a choice. We have to stay up here, because we won't be conscious during the meld; anyone or anything could walk up and we'd never know. Not sure how long it will take, either, so take the sling off your rifle and lay it across a branch where it won't fall."

T began unclipping the frogs that held the sling on his own rifle. O'Brien was obviously puzzled, but did as T said. "Why wouldn't we be conscious?"

"There's something we have to do. You know too much, but at the same time not enough. You're about to learn the rest. Use your sling to tie yourself to the branch. You won't need to knot it, just slide the frog's hooks into the adjustment holes. You want one long loop around the branch and your waist so you don't fall off. Lean back against the tree when you're finished."

T waited until the corporal finished with his sling. As soon as he looked up, T reached out, searching for O'Brien's mind.

The link happened quickly. O'Brien froze, glassy eyed, but by then T was himself locked into the meld. The familiar feeling of being part of someone else's mind took over.

***

Dolan was resentful, and it was not the first time. O'Brien, damn him, glorying in those two stripes on his sleeve! *One day*, he promised himself, *all that would change. There is only so much a man can endure!* But here he was, stuck working with Smithers. Building new tables for the kitchen. Maybe, if he'd been allowed to go to the range with O'Brien and Tyler...

Beneath the resentment, he was uneasy. He had no idea why.

Lifting the heavy log, he laid it across the sawhorses and waited for Smithers to saw off an eighteen-inch baulk. Irritated, he swore. "Git yer lazy arse into it, Smithers! Or I'll be sticking that bow-saw where the sun don't shine!"

"Will you, then?"

Suddenly the saw was horizontal, held in front of Smithers. "Come and take it." The sharp teeth, each more than an inch long, glittered where they projected from the thin blade.

"Put that down and fight, damn ye!"

"Stuff it, Dolan! I've had enough of you! We're wise to you, all of us. Be warned, you're bigger, but it only takes a small bullet to settle your business quick as anything! Get back to work before I decide that now's the time! I'm wearing my pistol, in case you didn't notice, and you don't have one."

"Ye're a bloody coward, aye! Corporal's pet ye are, but ye'll not be awake all the time!"

"Not even you would be that stupid, Dolan." Smithers' voice wasn't excited. He might have been discussing the weather. "You had your chance at T, and now you think you can sneak into our hut? If he doesn't kill you, I will. I hear you don't like the blade. *I* do! It's second only to my BAR! If you give me more lip then you'd best never turn your back on me, not now, not ever again. Cossacks to the front, me and the rest of the company behind you. You've got one chance and one chance only, Dolan! If you expect to see the US again, you'll straighten up, do your work, and *soldier*! Otherwise, I wouldn't give a tinker's damn for your chances of ever leaving Siberia. Now hold that damned log in position while I cut!"

***

"Doesn't look all that different, does it?"

Farmington had just begun waking up. Ray waited on the sidewalk until the traffic passed, then walked across to the cafe. "Eggs, two sausage patties, hash browns and biscuits if you have them, otherwise toast. And coffee. Libby?"

"Same for me, but juice if you have it, milk if you don't."

"We've got both. I'll bring orange juice and your coffee. You folks aren't from around here, are you?"

"We live over west of here, and we don't get to town very often. Rough country, you know, and the roads aren't in good shape."

"I know what you mean! Not many live over there, a few
ranches and such. Be right back with your order." The waitress left
and Libby pointed across the room. "Newspapers, Uncle Ray."

"See what the headline says, Libby." Ray's tone was casual.
She nodded and walked over to look at the paper. When she
returned, her fingers moved on the tablecloth, spelling out 5-14-81.
Ray confirmed understanding by repeating the numbers and Libby
nodded very slightly. Satisfied, Ray casually rubbed at the
tablecloth, erasing any wrinkles they might have made. "Nothing
about beef prices, Uncle. Just local news." Libby's voice was
pitched to carry, in case anyone was listening.

The waitress soon returned with their food and they ate in
silence. When they were finished, the waitress brought the
coffeepot and laid the bill on the table before filling Ray's cup.

Hiding what he was doing beneath the tablecloth overhang,
Ray carefully sorted currency according to the date. Selecting a
ten-dollar bill, he handed it to the waitress. She showed no interest
in the bill as she rang up the charge. They left, Ray pocketing the
change as she called out cheerfully, "Come back next time you're
in town!"

"Weather's not a factor now," Ray said. "Southern or northern
route?"

"I don't think it matters," said Libby, "but when I went into the
past last time, I started in Houston. The towns along the southern
route aren't all that far apart."

"South it is," Ray agreed. "Let's look at the map." Tracing
their path, he used his finger as a comparison to judge how far
they'd come. While he was working out their next destination,
Libby sent out a call. <Uncle T? Can you hear me?> But there was
no answer.

"Too early," suggested Ray, "but it's not a bad idea. We don't
really know where or when he is. He might still be in New York,
but then again, he might be trying to get back to 2017. Here's what
I'm seeing; between here and New York, there are several

possibilities I like. I went roughly 450 miles on that first teleport, you went a bit farther. We went back in time about 40 years. For our next destination, I'm thinking this spot here, near Lawton, Oklahoma. It's not too far off the compass course we followed to get here, so if the Earth's magnetic field really does control how far back we travel in time, we should get to Lawton somewhere around 1935."

"That makes sense. Ready?"

"Not yet! First thing, I need to sort my remaining bills by date to make sure I can spend them. Private ownership of gold was banned during the 30s, something to do with the depression, and the bills were based on the price of silver. So we could theoretically swap gold for dollars here in 1987, but if we tried to do it in 1937 people would wonder."

Putting the bills away, Ray continued, "We've got a bit of walking to do first. As soon as we're far enough out of town that we're not likely to be seen, we'll levitate. We'll have to be pretty high up before our next teleport, because we don't know if there's a mountain between our departure and destination points. And we don't know if it makes a difference. Our heading is just about 100°, not quite a right angle from magnetic north. We're in a valley, elevation just over 5,000 feet, so I'm thinking we make two jumps to Lawton, and no need to check the date at the intermediate point. How about we go here first, just west of Las Vegas? Teleport from 8000 feet, which is about 3000 feet higher than we already are, and that should be enough to clear the peaks.

"Same drill as before, except we don't land; teleport, form our bubbles as soon as we get there, and make contact with each other. I'll adjust my arrival time by teleporting to here, about a hundred miles shorter than where you're going, and do small jumps to synchronize our time. Keep comming me until I answer, and you should also try comming T. We meet up and during our next jump, head almost due east to Oklahoma."

"Got it, Uncle Ray. No problem, but as soon as we think no one is watching, how about we levitate? My boots aren't broken in yet and my feet are hurting!"

Ray chuckled. "Something to remember next time."

The houses were farther apart as they approached the edge of town. Ray looked around and pointed off to the side. "If we stop after we're just high enough to clear the trees, that hilltop to the south will be private enough. And you won't blister your tender feet!"

Libby frowned at the joke, but followed Ray and halted beside him, floating just above the hill.

"Straight up from here. I want at least 3000 feet, and if we err, go higher rather than lower. You match my altitude." The two drifted straight up. Far off to the west, Ray spotted the glint of an airplane. Coming in to a local airport? Satisfied with their elevation, he pointed off to the southeast. "Las Vegas is that way. It's a short teleport; you want to just reach it. Start comming as soon as you arrive and I'll find you."

***

The sleepy cowtown of Las Vegas drowsed in the summer heat. Ray rotated slowly until he was facing east.

"Next stop, Lawton, Oklahoma. When you're ready, teleport. Same drill, form your bubble for protection and start comming. Try to comm me, I'll find you. While we're waiting to join up, see if T answers."

Libby nodded and moments later, vanished. Ray teleported. As soon as he materialized, he sensed her panic.

<Uncle Ray! Help!>

Chapter Thirteen

<Libby! Listen to me. Stop panicking.>

<I'm listening, Uncle Ray. But I don't know where I am and I can't see anything and I'm coughing from all that dust! All I did was take a breath; I didn't even have time to form my bubble!>

<Can you tell if you're right-side up?>

<I think so. Is it important?>

<Yes. Listen close, don't do anything until I finish, okay?>

<Okay, Uncle Ray. I'm listening.>

<You probably got some of the dust in when you formed your bubble. First step, we're going to get it out. Take a deep breath and hold it. Wait until you're right side up, then collapse your bubble. Don't do it yet, just think about what you're going to do.>

<Okay, but it doesn't make sense! I'll just get more dust in my nose!>

<That's why you're holding your breath. After you finish, snort the dust out of your nose and reform your bubble as close to your body as you can. Expand it until it's near the limit, where it's about to fail.>

<Got it. So I'm pushing the dust out but letting air go in and out, right?>

<That's it.>

<Okay. Oh, that's much better! I'm still coughing, but not as much. I think I'm all right now.>

<Good, but we're not done yet. Let's see if we can get above the dust cloud. This confirms that we're back in the 1930s. People called that decade the 'dirty thirties' for a reason!>

<So we go up as high as possible?>

<Right, if you can. If we can't clear the dust cloud, then we'll try to go with the wind or against it until we get clear. I won't kid you, this isn't going to be easy, but you can do it!>

<I just wish this wind would stop!>

Following his own advice, Ray tried to levitate but found no surface he could push against. Left with no other option, he rolled downhill and tried to keep from vomiting. Shaken, disoriented, he wondered briefly if he could return to the place and time he'd just left. But what of Libby? Could she go back? He couldn't abandon her...

The wind slowed.

Fifteen minutes later, the air was virtually still. Dusty, to be sure, but thinning now that the wind was no longer blowing. Could it be...?

<Can you see the ground now, Libby?>

<Yes. So much dust, but I can see it! You want to go up high now?>

<Yes. Don't collapse your bubble until you reach clean air.>

<Okay.> The pause while she sought cleaner air lasted a full five minutes. <Wow, that was *scary*!>

<Yeah, I was scared too. People died from the dust back then, or actually it's now I suppose. And a lot of others got sick, something called dust pneumonia. Babies and old people suffered the most.>

<Oh.>The tiny voice in his head sounded subdued. Maybe this was what Libby needed, something to shake her confidence.

Before overconfidence killed her.

***

"The first thing you have to understand is that your abilities can kill you," said T. "Not *get* you killed, *your abilities* can kill you. You experienced my memories, so you know what I mean. Two old men, levitating when the light was fading, that rammed head on into a granite bluff?"

"I can't believe...I mean, *you* believe it, but you have to be wrong! You *can't* be from the future!"

"Yeah, I sometimes find it hard to believe myself. Are you ready to quit sitting up in a tree like an overgrown buzzard?"

"I guess so. Should I try to levitate myself down?"

"Wait until I'm on the ground. If you fall, I'll catch you."

"Okay. But from the future! Hey, you know when we'll be

going home!"

"Nope, I haven't got a clue. I didn't even know the U.S. Army was here, I never heard of the Czech Legion, and as for the AEF in 1919, the only thing I remember is that the allies won."

"It didn't end war after all, did it?" O'Brien's voice was soft, sad.

"Not even close! It's been one war after another ever since, and the next world war will be worse even than this one."

"My god, all those men! Millions, dead for nothing! I've seen the reports from the Western Front. Hundreds of thousands killed in a single attack, an entire country laid waste..."

"Yeah, and we never seem to learn. Just more greed, more men sent off to die a long way from home..."

"Wait a minute, you're a deserter! You left the Army without permission!"

"Technically, I'm not; I won't join the future army for almost a century. The only Army I've joined so far is this one, and I'm still here. But since you got that far, keep searching my memories. There's more to it than that."

"They were trying to *kill you*? Your own people?"

"Yeah. They had already killed everyone like me except for Surfer. The control they'd implanted eventually got him too. It didn't stop the Talent, though. They didn't understand it any better than we did. Or for that matter, do."

"So what do I do now?"

"Nothing, not until I've had a chance to see what you can do. Remember what I said, the Talents aren't just a parlor trick or sleight of hand, they're dangerous. I was lucky, but you might not be, so don't try to use them until you've had the chance to practice! Don't worry, I'll help you. I showed you all this stuff, remember? So don't try to go too fast."

"What if I try those exercises like you did, start by lifting small objects?" asked Patrick.

"And what if Dolan picks up on what you're doing? He's already a problem, let's not make it worse!"

"Yeah, Dolan." Patrick was thoughtful. "I forgot about him. I'm scheduled to take out a patrol tomorrow morning, but I can't take you and him both." O'Brien paused, thinking it through. "I'll leave you in camp and just take Smithers and Dolan. Three people should be enough, we haven't had enemy contact since you rescued that girl. I wish I'd been there!"

"You're eager, I understand that, but we still need a place far away from everyone where you can practice. I've got an idea, it fits with something I did before in that future army. I'll talk to Mac when we get back and you play along."

***

Mac was waiting when they returned to camp, but T didn't get a chance to talk to him. Instead, he was sent away while Mac conferred with Corporal O'Brien. "And did you slay the targets, young Corporal?"

"No." O'Brien suddenly understood why Mac was asking. There had been no firing; the reports would have been heard in camp. "I had a problem with my rifle. The first round fed in crooked and so did the second one I tried. I checked the feed ramp, there was nothing wrong there, so I'm thinking I need to take the bolt apart and see what's wrong."

"Might be the extractor spring," agreed Mac. "It gets rusty in all this humidity and if it weakens enough, the extractor won't grab onto the cartridge rim. I thought that problem was fixed, but maybe not. It only affected a few rifles so maybe you got one of the defective ones."

"That was my idea. I'll see the armorer about replacing the spring. Meantime, I'll do a careful cleaning. That might help. If it doesn't, I'll swap mine for one of the extras here in camp. A couple of the guys won't be coming back from the hospital."

"Aye. Well, I wondered, is all. I was about to take a few of the lads and go find you."

"'Twas just a rifle malfunction. I didn't think we should continue, being there were two of us with only one usable rifle between us, and we were far enough from camp that an enemy patrol might find us."

"But you'll have it fixed or replaced by tomorrow, won't you?" asked Mac.

"Oh, aye; never fear, I'll be taking the patrol. But as we talked about, I can't have Dolan and Tyler together, so I'll leave Tyler here and take Dolan. He can use the exercise and I'm sure you've got things Tyler can do."

"Aye, I do. Tell Tyler to report to me tomorrow; I've got a question or two for him, and after that I'll find work for his idle hands."

"I'll do that, Sergeant Mac. Well, I should get to work on this rifle..."

Mac nodded and went on his way.

O'Brien found T, waiting. "Your hut, I'm thinking. I need to take my rifle apart and we can talk. There are still a few things I don't understand."

"Okay," agreed T. "But just so you know, there are things I don't understand either."

"You didn't even remember your name?"

"The only thing I knew was that I was in the middle of the biggest forest I had ever seen! I had no idea who I was, how I got there, or what to do next. But then I heard chopping noises and you know the rest. I remembered who I was a few weeks ago."

"So why didn't you leave? You're not really part of the AEF-S," said Patrick.

"And go where? Do you have any idea how big Siberia is?"

"Kind of, but just from the big map at battalion headquarters. I saw it once. We sailed from the Philippines, and they sent us here when we disembarked in Vladivostok. I didn't exactly get a chance to tour the country."

"Neither did I, but I remember seeing Russia on a globe. It's huge, the biggest country in the world if I remember correctly, and most of the eastern part is Siberia. You could drop the entire US of A into Siberia and have room left over."

"That big?"

"Bigger. And that's not the only problem. From what I've seen, the country is mostly forest and I don't speak the local language. I've started to pick up a few thoughts, but not enough. I'm lucky to understand one word out of ten. I also can't levitate, fly you would call it, far enough to make a difference; I'd have to stop to rest, and I don't dare try to teleport. There's no way of telling where or when I might end up."

"But what about crossing to America? Vladivostok isn't that far, right?"

"Wrong. Farther north, where eastern Siberia gets closer to Alaska, then maybe. A hop from Siberia to one of the islands might be doable, but that area has really harsh weather and I get as cold as the next man. As for crossing the ocean, think waves; I need something steady that I can push against. Trying to form an image of a ten or twenty foot wave that's constantly changing? Forget it. And waves off Alaska can be much bigger."

"So what are you going to do?"

"I don't have a lot of options. Believe me, I've thought about it. I can't cross the ocean and going west is out too. I'd have to go almost all the way around the Earth to get back to the US. That's what, about 25,000 miles or so? So I'd have to levitate, always staying within my limits, and travel at least 10,000 miles? And even if I somehow got to France, I'd still need to cross the Atlantic. For now, I'm stuck here. I'm staying in the Army and hoping that will get me to the USA. Actually, I'm *counting* on it! It's that or steal a boat, because I don't have enough money to buy one that's big enough. I can't just take passage on a ship either; the only place I could board is Vladivostok, which is under US control. I'm stuck."

"You know more about geography than I do! I just go where the Army sends me. But I'm sure the Army will ship you back with the rest of us."

"Anyway, I'm here for now so I might as well make the best of it. It might be possible for us to go together after we get back to the states, to the future I mean. I was already thinking that before I decided to meld with your mind."

"Wait a minute, I'm a career soldier! I can retire after another twenty years or so and have a good pension for the rest of me days!" O'Brien's brogue was back.

"Do you really need a pension, now that you understand at least some of what I can do? What *you* may be able to do? You can already read minds, not well but some, that much we know. And now that you know something of the future, do you want to stay back here in 1919?"

"I hadn't thought of it! Here is all I know."

"You also mentioned that I deserted. Suppose the Army finds out you can do things, or that you know something about the future. What will happen to you then?"

Patrick elected not to answer that one. "People really fly in airplanes without a propeller? And the planes have only one wing?"

"That they do, and a lot more. Men have flown to the moon! Walked around on the surface and brought back rock samples. Wouldn't the government love to know about that?"

"Yeah, they would." T waited, allowing O'Brien to think his way through the problem. "They'd lock me away, wouldn't they? Pick my brain until they'd wrung me dry, then toss me aside. Or kill me so no one else would know what they found out."

"They would. An agency of the U.S. Government certainly tried to kill me! Are you beginning to understand, Corporal? You may have to do the same thing I did, just take off and get lost. Change your name and find a place to live where you won't come into contact with many people. Never try to contact friends or family again, because if you do the government may try to use them to get to you."

"You're saying I may have to desert too, like you did."

"Maybe not. I can tell it bothers you, but you're not the man you were an hour ago. Here's another possible solution for you; sooner or later, the government will transfer us home. We'll be demobbed, same as so many others have already been, but I don't think I should be on board when the ship arrives. Once the Army starts checking files, they'll know I couldn't possibly be Tyler. They'll ask questions and people will remember him. And when that happens, they'll wonder who I really am. They'll still wonder if I'm not there, but there won't be any proof unless the real Tyler shows up or someone identifies his remains. Assuming that doesn't happen, and knowing how clerks think, they'll forget about me."

"So what will you do?" asked O'Brien.

"Disappear, just before the ship reaches port. I'll need your help, but it won't be difficult. Stack my duffle bag on the rail somewhere that no one will see what happens. I'll levitate by pushing off from the ship, I should be able to do that, and as soon as I'm gone you push my bag over the side. For that matter, I could do it myself. You yell 'man overboard'. If they even bother to lower a boat, they'll find the floating bag. No body, Tyler's gone, lost at sea. Stamp the file closed, body not recovered. If I'm within sight of land when I leave the ship, I can levitate the rest of the way there. Easy."

"That's so strange! Us going home hasn't happened yet, but to you it already has."

"Time travel is funny that way. Get used to it. When the ship docks, you'll be discharged. We meet up and head for my home. My partner Ray and I own a ranch and we're not hurting for money. Even if I end up stuck in the past, I know where there's at least one gold deposit and I'm sure I could find more. You can help and we'll share what we find."

"I've got to think about it. 'Twas the army or the mines, or maybe work on the bridges and the great buildings in New York. But what you're talking about...'tis not the same, is it?"

"No. But the first thing is to find out what you can do and give you a chance to practice. With me watching you, for safety. You think about it, and when you get back from the patrol we'll talk.

***

"It's really dirty, isn't it?" Libby was almost whispering. A few people were stirring, but not all; some simply stood or sat, staring emptily at the thick layer of brown dust that covered almost everything.

"I've seen pictures of houses and cars buried by the dust," Ray agreed. !A whole state just packed up and left because of it, most of them. You've heard of the Okies, haven't you?"

"I heard the term in history class, but it didn't mean anything until now. Why doesn't it rain?"

"Lots of reasons. Eventually, it will. As soon as a few areas got rain and the grass reseeded, the dust stopped. There was still wind, probably always will be, but without the loose dust it was bearable. No one knows exactly what happened, it just did."

"I wish it would rain now! These poor people! But what should we do?"

"We go on. There's nothing we can do and nothing we *should* do. It's that time paradox thing I mentioned. I'm thinking Chicago for our next destination, or a better option would be somewhere just outside the city. It's a long trip, but you did a longer one.

"It's also not that far in terms of the magnetic field. From here to there, it's about 750 miles. But in terms of how far east we're going, it's only about five hundred miles. So 750 miles following a course of around 44 or 45 degrees should take us back to...somewhere around 1925. Depending on the date here, which we still don't know."

"So find out the date, then go northeast?"

"Right. Want to stay here tonight? You've got to be tired."

"No. I can make it if you can and I don't like this place! It's *dirty*!"

"It's not their fault, Libby." Ray's voice was gentle. "There was so much dust that it just overwhelmed people. Old people and babies died. People got lost, and some were never found. They were just buried by the blowing dust."

"But what bothers me is that we can't do anything about it, Uncle Ray! I understand, we can't take a chance on disturbing history because of that paradox thing, but that doesn't mean I like it. I don't even care what day it is; why can't we just go on to Chicago now?"

"We can. Did you try to call T?"

"I did, but there was no answer. Please, can we just go?"

"We'll have to walk until we're out of town, but no one will pay attention. A lot of people found themselves walking back then." Ray's voice was grim.

"I'm ready."

"Let's go."

Libby reached for Ray's hand, needing the reassurance. Ray said nothing; it was little enough to do. And he pitied the people caught up in the disaster as much as Libby did.

Thirty minutes later, when they were barely out of town, clouds rolled up and obscured the sun.

"More dust, Uncle Ray?"

"Not this time, Libby. They look like rain clouds to me."

"Oh, I hope so! Maybe it will lay the dust!"

Ray suppressed the thought, not without difficulty, until Libby had teleported away. Had *she* caused the rain? Could this the end of the dust bowl? Surely not...she couldn't really be that powerful, could she? He was still wondering when he faced northeast.

The first few drops left muddy spots on his skin as he teleported.

Chapter Fourteen

"Fifteen minutes, Dolan. I'll be outside with Smithers."

"Damn it, why me? Why aren't ye taking Tyler?"

"Because I'm the corporal," O'Brien explained patiently, "and *I* say *you're* going, and Tyler is staying back to work for Sergeant Mac. Fourteen minutes, and if yer late, you'll wish you weren't!"

Grumbling, Dolan rolled out of his pallet and reached for his trousers. Corporal O'Brien joined Smithers outside the bunkhouse.

"Coffee, Corporal? You'll need your own cup, I've only got mine."

"Mine's in my pack. Give me a minute." The coffee was hot, black, and strong. The two men sipped appreciatively while instinctively avoiding burning their lips. The folding government-issue metal cups were handy, but they did have a drawback where hot liquids were concerned! The heat even penetrated their leather gloves.

"Dolan give you a hard time? I heard some of it."

"The usual. He's a lazy bastard, is our Dolan."

"Not to be telling you your business, Corporal, but I'd feel better if you'd left him behind and brought Tyler along. T's everything Dolan is not."

"That he is! But gripe though he may, Dolan's going to do his share. We're few enough as 'tis, what with so many still in the hospital. I can handle Dolan."

Smithers said nothing. He poured the rest of the coffee into his cup, then set the pitcher by the door. O'Brien watched, amused; there would be no coffee for Dolan!

Minutes later, Dolan leading, Smithers following and O'Brien trailing, they left the gate and headed for the railroad tracks. Dolan was muttering under his breath, just loud enough to be overheard. "Not even breakfast, and me starvin'. I'm a big man, I am, and I need my vittles! There's bacon in me meat can, but nothing to eat this morning and just water for me drink! While his pet Tyler is loafing in camp! 'Tis a shame, it is, and no way to treat a proper soldier!"

"Shut yer gob, Dolan! If the damned Cossacks don't do for you, I will!" said Patrick angrily.

The muttering continued, but so soft as to be barely audible. O'Brien fumed; the stupid bastard would get them all killed with his griping!

But the noise stopped when they reached the tracks. They turned north, heading into disputed territory, and even Dolan was watchful now, alert for any threat. O'Brien wondered for a moment; would that magical protective bubble work for him as it worked for T? He felt a sudden urge to try, but suppressed it. The scarlet flash would be unmistakable.

Well, nothing would probably happen anyway so he wouldn't need it, now that the Cossacks appeared to have pulled back. Maybe, as Mac had explained, they were recruiting now, using the money from their new paymaster. The British had finally had enough of Semenoff, but the Japanese had stepped in.

The Japanese had their eye on Siberia, China too. They were allies for the moment, but few believed that would last. But it wasn't his problem; sooner or later, the US Army would pull out and after that, let the Russians, Chinese, British, and Japanese fight it out amongst themselves.

During the time of no pay, when the British had stopped paying Semenoff, many of his guerrillas might have deserted. But they wouldn't have gone away; they would simply have turned bandit and raided the local farmers.

***

"Take a walk with me, Bucko." Sergeant Mac settled his campaign hat on his head and headed out to inspect the camp. T was half a step behind.

"I've got a few questions for ye, so I have. Now who do you suppose it was that rescued the Russian girl and dropped her off at the village headman's house?"

"Why are you asking me, Sarge?" T was careful not to directly answer the question. Mac was suspicious, no doubt about it.

"Couple of reasons, me Boy! For one, I know that you had met the girl before. For another, she told the headman that the man who rescued her had been 'the Amerikansky'. She said that he'd killed the men who'd murdered her family and brought her back, although I have to tell ye she didn't make a lot of sense in the telling. Which is why the headman brought her to me."

"But I was right outside the door when you were talking to her and she didn't say anything," T argued. "She had the chance to point the finger at me and say I was the one, but she didn't. And if she wasn't making sense, as you said, then the rest of her story can't be relied on either! I'm guessing she really was taken prisoner and rescued, but it could have been anyone! It might not have been an American at all! She could have been hallucinating. Young girl, taken by bandits and thinking some sort of one-man army had swooped in to save her? And then somehow managed to take her to the village? I have to say, she sounds nuts."

"Ah, but she's no shrinking violet! She told us what they'd done to her, and how glad she was when her rescuer got there. She also said as how she wished she'd had the chance to knife them herself. You do have a combat knife, don't you?"

"Sure; it's just a standard trench knife. I got it after we stole those weapons. You've got one too, I think."

"That I do! And do ye have yours with you, Lad?"

"It's back at our hut, Sergeant."

"And I would imagine it's clean, now wouldn't I?"

"All my weapons are clean, Top!"

"Well, 'twas only a thought. I hear as how ye're strong, me boy. Corporal Brennan himself told me that ye did quite the job repairing the wall. 'Tis too bad."

"Oh? "T's voice showed none of the tension he was feeling.

"Aye. We'll only have to tear it down, I'm thinking. We'll be pulling back soon, or so sez my contact at battalion. The Czech Legion has begun arriving at Vladivostok, d'ye see, and when they're accounted for we'll be withdrawn. 'Tis a matter of time, it is, and we'll be heading for home."

"That's great, Top! Will you be staying in the Army?"

"Oh, aye. 'Tis home for me, the Army, but most of my lads will be discharged. 'Tis always the way when the shooting's done. And with yer memory problems, they'll not be keeping you. What will ye do after ye're mustered out, Private Tyler?"

"I suppose I'll just have to see, won't I? But I'm sure I'll find something."

***

Ray had been lucky the first jump, and even luckier the second.

It had taken only seconds to move himself farther back in time until he heard Libby answer, and the second time they'd arrived close enough together that their arrivals were synchronized. But *next* time it might be a lot more difficult, especially since they were going farther in distance and hence further back in time.

But there was a better way, something he'd learned the hard way during a map exercise. Rather than attempt to go directly to an objective, a bridge for example, he'd learned to offset slightly. Deliberately aiming for a point off to one side made it easy to correct when he reached the stream. Knowing the direction made things much simpler. Time travel should work the same way; deliberately teleport a shorter distance, arrive a few minutes later in time, then work his way back in time by making short jumps while comming Libby. Mind firmly fixed on his objective, he teleported.

And found himself floating above a thick woods. Forming his bubble, he called Libby but there was no answer.

Well, he hadn't expected one. Consulting the map, he picked a spot five miles farther east and teleported. Three tries later, she responded. "I was beginning to worry. I've been here almost half an hour! I think next time we should do what we did before, link our minds before we teleport. Or at least hold hands!"

"I don't have any secrets, Libby, but if we link our minds you won't have any either. A link is a link; are you sure you want to do that?"

Libby flushed. "I trust you. You won't tell anyone!"

"No, but I'll know."

"I'll know your secrets too! No response from Uncle T, by the way, but I'm ready to go on to Chicago. I need a bath and a good night's sleep! How far back do you think we've come?"

"I can't be sure, probably somewhere around 1925 or perhaps as early as 1920. No way we can be certain until we find something with a date. But from now on, we take shorter jumps to be sure we don't go back too far. If this is 1925, then we only need to go back another twenty years."

Ray glanced at the small compass to orient himself. Finding east was simple, just put the sun behind them. Midafternoon, then. And Chicago was farther to the east.

"Ready?" At Libby's nod, Ray lifted above the trees. Far off to the east he spotted a trail of smoke puffs.

"Is that a *train*, Uncle Ray? All that smoke?"

"I think so. Why don't we take a look? I'm sure it's going toward Chicago. We'll just follow the tracks!"

Moments later, Ray smiled. Libby's hand had found its way into his. For all her outward assurance, she was in many ways still a child.

***

A cold rain was falling. The gusting wind blew the rain into their faces and inevitably into the open collars of their uniform blouses. Plodding along, trying to watch both sides of the trail, Corporal O'Brien almost walked into Dolan.

"You see something?" O'Brien swung the Springfield up as he whispered. He'd been carrying it muzzle-down to keep rain out of the barrel.

"No, nor even the saints could see a bloody thing in all this rain! How are we supposed to find the bastard Semenoff's Cossacks in this, I ask ye? I'm freezing my arse off for no good reason, I am!"

"Keep moving, Dolan," O'Brien grated. "Our objective, that small hill across the bridge, is only about a half mile ahead."

"And there's not so much as a tree there to shelter us! I'm tellin' ye, we should be avoidin' the rain before we catch our death! I can feel a cold comin' on, I can!"

"Shut yer gob and keep moving!"

Smithers had heard the whispered exchange. Glancing apprehensively at the dripping trees on both sides, he whispered, "We're standing out in the open! We need to keep moving!"

"I'm damned if I do!" Dolan was no longer whispering.

"Shut yer mouth, you idiot!" O'Brien's whisper showed his anger.

"And if I don't, what are ye goin' ter do? Will ye face me man to man?"

"Last chance, Dolan. Shut your mouth and move ahead!"

"I'll not!" said Dolan. "Put up yer maulies and face me like a man!" Suiting action to words, he dropped his rifle. It landed on the tracks with a clatter as Dolan balled up his fists. Drawing back his right hand, he unleashed a mighty punch at O'Brien's face.

Which would have ended the fight had it landed.

But Dolan froze in mid-swing, mouth open and gasping. A stream of blood gouted from his mouth, black in the dimness, accompanied by a coppery smell that was soon carried away by the wind. The gout of blood pulsed twice, then slowed to a trickle as he collapsed.

"Grab his rifle and head for the trees," whispered O'Brien harshly. "Move, move, move!"

"But what about Dolan?" Smithers asked, looking around. "Somebody had to have heard that noise. Is he dead?"

"Dead as mutton! You carry his rifle to the treeline, I'll deal with the body and join you. Move out now!"

"He's heavy. Give me a moment, I'll help you. Drag it over to the bank and dump it into the ravine?"

"Aye. The rain will wash away the blood and our tracks, but

I'll not be needing your help. You understand that he died during an attack, right? And that we were under fire, so we couldn't recover the body?"

"I understand. Don't forget to take his bandoleer before you dump the body, he was carrying my spare ammo. I'll wait in the woods."

"I'll find you."

Smithers slung Dolan's rifle over his shoulder; with the BAR he was already carrying, it made a heavy and awkward load. Partially concealed, he stopped with his back against the trunk of a large tree...some sort of evergreen, he thought. Whatever it was, it did a fair job of shedding the rain.

Fifteen minutes later, Corporal O'Brien slipped up beside him.

"You have any problems with Dolan getting killed by the Cossacks, Smithers?"

"Hell, no! I saw it clearly. He got stabbed with one of those big swords they carry. It was a stab, right?"

"Aye, that's what it was. I was just making sure that's what ye saw. Which reminds me, I need to wash the blood off. I wiped me knife on his uniform, but I doubt I got it clean."

O'Brien found a spot were the drops were falling faster off the branches above. He held the pig-sticker out and let the water drip over it for a few minutes.

"You sure you want to keep it with you? Shouldn't you get rid of it? What if someone asks questions?"

"They won't, and anyway, this one is mine. I've even got me name on it. See?" O'Brien held out the weapon, showing where 'O'Brien' had been crudely scratched into the thick brass knuckle-guard.

"Do we go ahead with the patrol?" asked Smithers.

"No, this one's blown. I don't know if the Cossacks were here, but if they were there's no way we're going to surprise them now. And now that there's just the two of us, we need to be getting back."

"Right, then. Cover your ears." Smithers flipped off the BAR's safety while pointing it to the sky. At O'Brien's nod, he squeezed off two three-round bursts, then a succession of single shots.

"In case someone is close enough to hear the battle. But I think we need to get moving now. What about Dolan's rifle?"

"We'll have to leave it," O'Brien said regretfully. "I'll take the bolt so that in case it's found, it can't be used. I'll just toss the larger parts into the creek on the way back, and the smaller items into the forest. Nobody will ever find them. But to be sure, go ahead and give the barrel a hard whack against a rail. Try to bend it. 'Tis the best we can do, I think; the Cossacks won't be able to use it and if we took it back, someone would wonder why we recovered the rifle but not Dolan's body."

Neither looked back as they headed for the camp, this time moving just inside the treeline. Ten minutes later, the rain stopped. Their uniforms steamed gently as they slogged on through the mud.

Three hours later they walked through the camp's entrance. "Get yerself into a dry uniform," said Corporal O'Brien tiredly. "I'll report to Mac; if he wants you, he'll send for you. Make sure you clean and oil your piece before you crap out."

Smithers almost smiled; the incident with Dolan was behind them. O'Brien was back to being the corporal in charge.

Chapter Fifteen

"So Corporal O'Brien did for Dolan, did he? What will he tell First Sergeant Mac?" T aske.

"That the Cossacks ambushed us. We were too few to fight them off, so we had to withdraw. By then, Dolan was cut off and they were after him with those swords. He didn't stand a chance."

"That should work, but maybe we should go join O'Brien. Mac may have questions. One tip, don't try to match O'Brien's story exactly. A few minor differences, say the number of Cossacks you saw, makes it more believable."

"Thanks, I'll remember that," said Smithers. The two arrived outside Sergeant Mac's office just as O'Brien was finishing his story.

"Well, I can't say as how it's a surprise," Mac said. "The only surprise is that Dolan lasted as long as he did! Aye, he was always too impulsive for his own good. But that leaves me with a problem, so it does. I need Smithers available to man the wall with his BAR for the time being, what with us being shorthanded. Three more men came down with the flu while ye were gone. The which leaves you with only Tyler, at least until some begin returning from hospital. 'Tis not a real squad with only two men, so I don't know what I'm going to do with you. And since you're so short-handed, that's going to put more of a burden on the other squads."

"I've been meaning to talk to you, Top," said T. "You remember that patrol two weeks ago where I killed those four Cossacks? I didn't really need any help. I can hear better when I'm by myself, and if I run into something that's too big for me to handle, I'll just hide until they're gone."

"Did you know about this, Corporal?"

"News to me, First Sergeant, but he's right. We were there to back him up, but he didn't need us. We never fired a shot."

"I'm not about to be sending one soldier out alone!" Mac said decisively, "and there's an end to it! But I need Smithers here, so that means if I approve this you'll have to go with Tyler. What say ye, young Corporal?"

"If you're looking for a volunteer, aye, I'll go. Two is better than one, and maybe I can keep Tyler from doing something foolish."

"And ye'll not be doing foolishness yerself, now will ye?" Mac asked.

"Not me, Top! I've heard the rumors; we'll be going home soon, and I haven't seen America in more than three years. Ye may call me Cautious Patrick, so ye may."

"'Tis not official yet, ye know. And ye're sure you want to do this? Because I'm not at all sure *I'm* doing the right thing, that I'm not. I wouldn't even consider it if I had more men. But at the same time, we can't be about doing our job if we hide behind the walls, so we can't."

"We can do this, Top. We'll leave tomorrow morning before daylight and be in position before the guerrillas begin moving about."

Mac sighed. "Needs must, lad. Do ye yer jobs, and be careful."

***

"It's not what I expected." Libby wrinkled her nose. "It stinks!"

"That's the smell of money. Chicago is still a center for meat packing at this time and it's not exactly a clean industry; a man named Upton Sinclair even wrote a book about it. Most of it will be gone a few years from now, but until that happens this side of Chicago is a center for stinks!"

"If this is what Chicago is like I'd rather go on to New York!"

"I think it will be better when we reach the city center, and I'd rather be rested before we start the final leg. We should be getting close now. T didn't answer your comm?"

"No, but I sensed something different. Not a contact and definitely not Uncle T, but I felt something."

"You might have sensed a wild Talent, someone who *could* become a telepath one day but probably won't," suggested Ray.

"It could be that, I suppose. It's something I should expect from now on; I'm a much better telepath than anyone I know, so it seems reasonable that I'll pick up random thoughts from almost everyone."

"You can pick up the thoughts of strangers, people who aren't telepaths?"

"Most of the time," Libby said. "I have to be nearby and concentrating, but sure. The difficulty is sorting through what I hear, but even then it's not perfect. I keep practicing, but I'm not yet able to do a complete read of what they're thinking."

"T thought Surfer could do that," Ray mused, "but he never admitted it. Paranoia, probably. He kept his secrets, even with us; he knew that if Henderson's people found him they'd kill him."

"I wish I'd known him. So what will we do now?"

"We'll stay for at least a day. This could be important for you later, if you do decide to study history. I think a taxi might be in order, and an overnight stay in a good hotel."

"Okay, as long as it doesn't stink!"

***

T met Corporal O'Brien at the kitchen for an early-morning breakfast.

"First thing after we leave, I'll do a fast survey of the area. As soon as I'm sure no one is around, you'll start learning what you can and can't do. We'll still do the patrol, but not until you can reliably use your abilities, and when you're ready to use your Talents, we'll start ranging farther out. There's no reason why we can't check out anything suspicious looking anywhere within 20 miles of the camp."

"That far? And what if the Cossacks are mixed in with people in the towns?" O'Brien asked.

"They won't be. The Cossacks aren't guerrillas, they're the core of his army, and he wouldn't have time to concentrate them if they were spread out. The bandit faction, maybe. Oh, there might be a few small Cossack detachments in towns along the railroad, but that's it. And even if there are, most will be farther west of here."

"Makes sense. So what do we do first?"

"Find a place you can be comfortable while I snoop around. And *don't* try anything until I get back!"

"Well, I already used a Talent, I think."

"Just don't do it again until you've had a chance to practice! I'm not sensing anyone nearby, so let's find you a hiding place. We'll talk when I get back."

***

Lieutenant Thornton called First Sergeant MacAuliffe into his office. "You've probably heard that we're going to be leaving Siberia soon. This news is for your NCOs only; expect to leave before winter sets in. We're the detachment that's farthest away from Vladivostok, so I anticipate we'll be pulled back first, or at least be part of the first group. But until then, our job is to keep the pressure on. Listening posts, patrols near the camp, and longer-range patrols to inspect the bridge and the railway."

"I'll be doin' that, Sir. We're in good shape now, except for the shortage of men. The palisade is complete, and the abatis line is anchored in position. Horses won't be jumping it, that they won't, no matter how much the Cossacks try. As for Semenoff's people, intelligence says they're mostly on foot now except for his personal guard. Pretty fancy bunch, got uniforms and everything. They're brave enough when they're waving the swords around, so they are, but I wonder if they still remember how to fight?"

"I know what you mean! I saw them showing off in Vladivostok, all shiny and polished, although Semenoff wasn't there at the time. They had come in to pick up a draft of horses from Ireland. Supposedly the horses were for breeding, but I spotted several geldings."

"Aye, 'tis remounts, I'm thinking."

"The colonel said for us not to expect any new replacements. That's why we've not seen any up to now; the War Department knows we'll be withdrawn soon. The men currently in the hospital may come back, most of them, but the closer we get to pulling out, the less likely it is that we'll see them again. Just make the best arrangements you can, First Sergeant."

"Aye, Lieutenant. I'll be doing just that, so I will." Reassured, Mac left. The lieutenant's order was vague enough to cover the two-man team he'd sent out. But was there anything else he could do, now that they'd be leaving soon? Maybe do something about the wall? It really was longer than necessary, now that their numbers had been reduced. Not to mention that he didn't have the troops to man the longer wall. If he had a few of the outlying huts torn down, and a new section of wall built across the interior to shorten the line? Salvage timbers from the original perimeter to strengthen the rest? And just to be sure, a central redoubt in case the enemy did manage to breach the wall?

Well. 'Twas busy work, perhaps, but it would keep the men from thinking about how few they were, and how far away help was if Semenoff did attack. And did not the Army have a tradition of finding work for idle hands?

***

T landed soundlessly, surprising Corporal O'Brien. "You can put the safety back on, Patrick. There's no one within a mile of us. Not even a bear, although there's a big one just about a mile and a half to the north. He's heading away."

"You're sure?"

"I'm certain. I not only looked for people, I listened for thoughts. Nothing. I can't understand more than a few words or concepts unless they're close, but I can detect their thoughts. Not sure that makes sense, but I know they're thinking even if I can't understand them. As for the bear, I saw him. You said something earlier about using your new abilities?"

"Aye, it was Dolan. Not with putting him down, I did that on me own, but with disposing of his body later on. Faith, I don't think I could have dragged him that far without help, but I remembered something from when you joined your mind with mine. Actually, 'twas my memory of your memory if that makes sense. So I lifted him as you would have done and when I got to the edge of the ravine, I threw his body as far as I could. It fell into the trees below and I lost sight of it. I doubt it will ever be found, and 'tis good riddance, I'm thinking."

"Okay," said T. "Psychokinetics...some call it telekinetics, but I prefer PK...is actually one of the easiest Talents to use. It's also the easiest to improve, along with telepathy. Some of the other Talents seem to be related to PK, levitation for example. Instead of lifting an object, you lift yourself by pushing against a fixed surface. The ground works best, of course, but you can also do it indoors. Unload your rifle, please."

"What, unload my rifle? Out here? Ye're crazy!"

"I told you I checked the area! I mean, I *really checked out* the area. There's nothing larger than a fox except for that bear, and I can handle a bear."

"You can?" O'Brien was skeptical.

"A bear can't walk, much less run, if his feet aren't touching the ground. I could easily kill a bear by breaking his neck, but I wouldn't need to. Just pick him up, turn him around, and give him a swift psychokinetic boot in the rear. After you practice, you can do it too. How hard was it to throw Dolan's body away?"

"Well...'twas not difficult at all. It felt like he weighed less than a pound by the time I got to the ravine's edge. I probably could have done it without even using me hands."

"I've handled much heavier weights. I've yanked full-grown trees out by the roots, and along with my partner Ray kept a cliffside from falling until people got past it. We weren't lifting it, of course, just pushing, but even so it was a huge weight. I had an awful headache afterwards and so did Ray. I'm guessing we stretched our Talents to the limit. Not because of the weight, but because we had to sense the full scope of the rock. Maybe it's like eyestrain after you read too much?"

"I remember that," confessed O'Brien. "I wouldn't have believed it, but I got it from your memories. Can't say I've ever had eyestrain. Reading does not come easy to me, d'ye see. And ye can sense buried treasure too?"

"I can sense gold with reasonable reliability, silver too as long as I have a sample to work with. I don't think Ray ever learned how, or maybe he doesn't have that Talent. Some things I can do better, some things he does better. But back to emptying the rifle; you're going to use it to practice lifting using psychokinetics, and it's safer if it's not loaded. Later on, after you learn how to use the bubble, it probably won't matter."

"Okay." Patrick pointed the barrel up and operated the bolt, ejected the rounds. T caught them as they flew out of the action, floating them to where Patrick could easily retrieve them. The corporal grinned as he picked up the cartridges. "I could have done that too, couldn't I?"

"Sure, with practice. But until you know what you're doing, it would be far too easy to set off a round. Let's start with something easy. Lay your rifle on the ground, then step back and pick it up using only your Talent."

O'Brien's first effort was clumsy. He lifted the rifle, which wavered in the air before turning muzzle-down. "What am I doing wrong?" he asked.

"You're not concentrating on the center of balance. You're trying to pick the whole thing up at once, and you don't have a good sense of how it feels. Balance the rifle on your hand and sense it," advised T. "I don't need to worry about that now, but I did at first. Now I just form a total image, what you just did, and work with that. You shouldn't expect to do it right away because it takes a lot of practice. You're training your brain, not your muscles."

"Can I see how you do it?" asked O'Brien.

Wordlessly, T lifted the rifle. It floated in front of Patrick, rock steady. Moments later, it began to spin. After three revolutions, now with the barrel pointed up, he lowered the weapon until the butt was resting on the ground. "It took me months to develop that level of control and even now I wouldn't try spinning anything really heavy, but a rifle makes a good practice item. Do it right and it looks like you're practicing the manual of arms."

"Okay, let me try." This time, the rifle was much steadier. Not as motionless as when T had demonstrated his control, but it no longer looked as if it was about to fall any second.

"Next step, stand at attention with the rifle by your side. You're going to go through the manual of arms, but little by little let your PK take over. Keep your hand on the rifle for the time being."

An observer, had there been one, would have wondered why two men who were ostensibly patrolling for enemies would bother with parade movements. But by the end of the first hour, O'Brien was much more assured. His hand was still touching the wood of the forearm, but practically speaking the movements were being carried out using PK.

"What next?"

"Now we'll work on using the bubble. It has to become a part of you, something that's there without thinking.

"The easiest way to learn how is to link your mind with mine. Not a full meld, just a link so that you can follow along while I do it."

"I'm ready," said O'Brien. Moments later, there was a dim red flash surrounding T. There was no sign that anything was different, except that T was now floating a few inches above the ground and slowly tipping over to his right.

"Is something wrong?" asked O'Brien.

"No, it's just that I no longer have contact with the ground. I'm not worried about falling; as you're about to see, no part of me will touch the ground."

"And this protects you from gunfire?" asked O'Brien.

"It protected me from shrapnel and I'm sure it would deflect a bullet, but I don't know what would happen if someone shot at me with a large artillery projectile. The projectile wouldn't penetrate the bubble, but the kinetic energy would slam me around. It's not magic; I was blown aside by an explosive device once and it slammed me against a wall. I was shook up, even though none of the shrapnel penetrated. But a direct hit by an incoming artillery shell? The sudden acceleration might kill me."

"Yeah, I've heard of guys who were killed when a shell passed nearby. Not a mark on them, but they were stone dead," O'Brien agreed.

"I'm not sure it's the same thing, but it's not important. The bubble's a good safety factor and you need to make sure it will work for you before you try levitation. If you lose your concentration, the ground will reach up and smack you. When you're ready, try to link your mind with mine."

Moments later, T felt the first tentative efforts. He completed the link and sent, <Pay close attention. I'm going to form my bubble, expand it, then collapse it. Follow through and try to do what I do.>

Fifteen minutes later, O'Brien was able to form and collapse the bubble for himself.

"Graduation exercise. I'm going to lift you to treetop height. Be ready." Moments later, with no warning, T dropped O'Brien. The first effort was a failure; O'Brien panicked.

"We'll try it again. This time, don't think of anything but forming the bubble. You've got to learn to trust it." An hour later, with O'Brien showing his newfound confidence, T resumed the mental link and taught him to levitate.

O'Brien led when they flew off together, T followed. Training complete, it was time to resume the patrol.

<We need to follow a spiral course to make sure we find everything. Try to fly about half a mile farther out from where you were before; we want to be almost twenty miles from camp before we finish. Think you can do that, or should I take the lead?>

<I think I can handle it. You just tell me if I'm off course.>

Late that afternoon, just before sundown, they came up on a small body of armed men.

Chapter Sixteen

<That's no ordinary recon patrol,> sent O'Brien. <Could be a combat patrol, but why they would be here? What are they expecting to find? They could be Kolchak's people or Bolsheviks, but this area is claimed by Semenoff and they don't have enough men to threaten his bunch, not even the bandits. We've never seen more than a dozen working together and most are half that size.>

<I make it twenty-four men, fifteen in uniform,> sent T. <Japanese? There's an officer with a long sword and another that may be a noncom. They aren't marching in column with the others in uniform, they're slightly off to the side. As for the rest, they look like guerrillas or simple bandits. Same old rifles with the welded-on bayonets. I need a closer look. You wait here, I'll see what I can find out. No offense, but your Talents aren't as reliable as mine and if they see me, I'll be better off not worrying about you.>

O'Brien obediently slowed, hovering, and waited. From his elevation, roughly three times the height of a tall Siberian pine, the patrol was easily seen. It was indeed strange; why would a Japanese half-platoon be traveling with such a scruffy bunch? And why the cart? Rations? Ammo? Probably not water, there were plenty of streams around. Strange.

T soon returned and motioned to O'Brien to join him. The two flew south until they were far enough away to be out of sight. Hovering next to Patrick, T explained. "Japanese paymaster; he's the one carrying the sword. That's why the soldiers in uniform are along, and I'm guessing the others are from Semenoff's band. The Japanese are along to make sure the money gets to Semenoff, the guerrillas are along in case there are problems with Semenoff's people along the way."

"You're sure they're carrying money?"

"No question about it. I had a feeling we should look in this direction, but I didn't understand why. I have hunches from time to time. It's a Talent, even if it's not reliable, and I've learned to pay attention when I get one of those feelings."

"I remember that from your memories. So what do we do now? Can we take on that many?"

"We could. If we waited until dark, maybe as late as midnight, we could wipe them out. But maybe there's a better way."

"They're *enemies*, T. The Japanese are supposed to be allies, but they're paying our enemies!"

"Yeah. No question, we need to stop that payroll; that will hurt Semenoff more than the loss of a few men. But suppose we could take the money *without* killing them? Then what?"

"Well...the Japanese would probably think their people stole the money. Semenoff would too. They'd do the killing for us, so they would."

"They might. But suppose all of them told the same foolish story? Even under torture, which Semenoff would probably try. Not sure about the Japanese, but they might torture their people too."

"What kind of foolish story?" asked Patrick.

"Suppose they said the money was taken by a flying man that bullets bounced off of? The Cossacks are probably superstitious. I'm not sure about the Japanese, but they probably are too. Here's the thing; they're likely to believe that if the patrol had stolen the money, they'd have come up with a reasonable explanation. The flying man excuse is just too preposterous. Unless, of course, it was a demon."

"Oh, *hell*! You think they'd fall for that? And are ye sure the bubble will protect ye?"

"I'm sure, but just in case, you're my safety measure. We're going to land and do a few exercises first. When we're ready, I'll put you ahead of the patrol and you remain hidden while I do my demonic imitation. In case I'm wrong, you'll lift me out of danger."

"I'm glad ye're letting me do something! I don't like being the little kid tagging along with big brother."

"You won't always be," said T. "Would you feel better if you were the one hanging in the air while they shoot at you?"

"No, you're right about that much, but just sitting there and watching doesn't feel right! Ye be the one taking all the chances."

"How about if you take the money from the cart? I could do it, but it's not easy. I'll be holding my bubble tight enough to stop bullets, but I also have to let air in and out. That's going to take some adjusting.

"The money is in the four satchels just behind the board at the cart's front. They're not easy to see from ground level, but you should be able to make out the handles. The other packs, the ones behind them, are probably rations or the soldiers personal packs, so leave them alone. No gold or silver; I would know. The cart's being pulled by two Japanese soldiers, the others are walking behind. So they can keep an eye on the satchels? The officer and what appears to be an NCO are where they can watch their men.

"You'll be hidden, so if you do it right they won't even notice when you lift the satchels off the cart. They'll be watching me. And to make *sure* they're watching, I'm going to be making faces and waving my arms. Thumbs in my mouth, pulling out, and flapping my fingers at them. Go slow so the soldiers holding the drawbars don't notice. Maybe rock the cart a time or two first, using psychokinetics, so they won't realize what's happening when you lift the money. It'll be fun!"

"Your idea of fun isn't the same as mine!" Patrick observed dryly. "You're right, practice won't hurt. You want me to move you someplace safe if a bullet gets through?"

"That's it, and you'll be doing it from five hundred yards away. If it's necessary, I mean, but that's why we're practicing. The trick is not to worry about the weight, just visualize the relationship between me and the ground. Concentrate on increasing the separation, and you'll do the same thing with the satchels. Pick one, bring it to you, then do it again. Don't raise them high enough to be noticed. They'll be watching the sky, so it shouldn't be a problem.

"When you've got them all, I'll fly high enough to distract them. I'll be on the side away from you, probably flapping my arms and dancing in the air like a marionette. I want them watching me, not the satchels. You lift the money and head south, I'll find you. Don't expect me to get there for half an hour or so, and make sure you don't leave tracks. You'll have to levitate while carrying the weight of all four, but that should be doable since you won't be in your bubble."

O'Brien agreed. They spent more than an hour practicing before T decided they were as ready as they were going to get. By then, the sun was almost touching the horizon.

The actual theft went off like clockwork. There was considerable shouting, dozens of gunshots, and much waving of his sword by the Japanese officer. Eventually the shooting slowed as they gawked at T. By then, O'Brien and the money were floating just above the trees, several miles south of the patrol and moving rapidly, when T decided he'd done enough. With a final grimace and wave of his arms, T ostentatiously turned away from the patrol and vanished. Half an hour later, he overtook O'Brien.

"Getting tired?"

"They're heavy, and holding all four is awkward," admitted O'Brien.

"There's a clearing up ahead. Land there, take a break, and when we move on I'll carry the money. I estimate we're less than an hour away from where we hid our rifles and packs."

"We're going back to camp tomorrow, right?"

"I think so. After we find a place to hide the money, of course!"

"You're not going to turn it in?"

"Certainly not! For one, how would we explain where we got it? Two men, taking a money shipment from two dozen without killing them? No; and besides, you're going to need the money."

"Me?" asked O'Brien.

"Mostly you. I'll need some too, but you're going to need money after you leave the army. Easiest way would be if you take your discharge and vanish; that's where the money comes in. As for me, I've still got a few coins in a money belt which might be enough to last me until I get home. But since we've got this windfall, I might as well refill the belt pouches. I remember having a lot more in a vest, but when I woke up here in Siberia the vest was gone. If you still want to join me in Nevada, you'll want land of your own."

"I niver had money," mused Patrick. "Just the few dollars the army paid me. Me family was poor; all we had was what we earned from our sweat, and I niver expected to have a place of me own. I hoped, d'ye see, but I never believed it could happen. There might be enough to support a wife, d'ye think?"

"I think so. Get used to the feeling! You'll never have to worry about money again. The only thing you need do is remember not to take advantage of people who can't do what you can. *Dolan* wouldn't have spared a thought for anyone else, but you're not Dolan. There's no *reason* to take unfair advantage, because you don't need to."

"'Tis a lot to think about!" O'Brien's brogue was back. T smiled; most of the time, the accent was barely noticeable but under stress the speech patterns of his childhood returned.

***

"Could we go for a ride after breakfast, Uncle Ray?"

"A ride? You mean the streetcar?"

"No, horses. We could rent horses, couldn't we? And after lunch, we could ride the streetcar and go shopping, couldn't we? And I really would like to stay another night in Chicago. It's not like what I saw when I went back in time before. Sarah was wonderful and her people were interesting, but this is so different!"

"Sure, why not? Time really does wait for us. I'll ask at the desk; they'll know of a place we can ride. I miss my horses too."

No question, Libby was enjoying herself. Ray had been worried after the mishap when she'd teleported into the dust storm, but she'd recovered rapidly. As for Ray himself, he had been an only child and might never have children of his own. He was enjoying Libby's company.

They found the stables with no trouble by following the

bellman's directions and rented horses from an old man with a long, drooping mustache. "Rode before, I take it?"

"I've done a lot of riding, my niece not so much. I'm not worried about her."

"Wal, good. I've a couple of nags, but I don't like renting them nowadays; they're getting pretty old. If you think you can handle horses with more spirit, I've got a pair of geldings. One's a chestnut half-Arabian that's about fourteen hands tall, and the other is about fifteen and a half hands."

"Another Arab?"

"Naw, but I'm pretty sure he's all horse! No cow at all in his bloodlines." The two shared a chuckle. "Anyway, he's big enough to carry you and if you're experienced, he won't give you much trouble. No spurs, though. I've had problems with tenderfeet and spurs. Reckon you can ride without them?"

"We can; I don't use spurs with my horses either. If you know how to use your knees, you don't need spurs for a pleasure ride on a well-trained horse."

The old man nodded approval. "My horses are trained. They'll neck-rein or answer to the bit, depending on whether you prefer western or eastern style."

"Libby prefers eastern; that's what she rides when she visits me, either an eastern saddle with no horn or my Australian saddle. As for me, I like a good western trail saddle."

"Don't reckon I ever saw an Australian saddle! Come to think on it, I never heard of one and I never saw an eastern saddle until I came to Chicago. But I've got several now and one should suit her."

"Where are you from?" asked Ray. The old man reminded him of someone, maybe the wrangler who helped Ray care for his horses.

"Texas. Growed up in east Texas, headed west when I got old enough to saddle a horse for myself. I hated farming but cowboying was already about done by then. Railroads was pushing down into Texas and trail drivin' was over. But I got a job working on a ranch down in south Texas. Worked there ten years until I got hurt. I was breaking a big steeldust at the time and he fell on me. After I healed up, my last paycheck and what I'd saved was almost enough to get started here. That was about fifteen years ago. My breaking days were done, so I drove a wagon for a year after I got to Chicago and saved my money. When that job played out, I bought the stables. My savings were enough for the down payment, and I paid off the bank two years ago. Now it's mine."

"You've done well," agreed Ray.

"Well enough," said the man. "I'm George Milton."

"Ray Wilson."

"Good to meet you, Ray. Wal, let me finish tacking up and you folks can go enjoy your ride."

Fifteen minutes later, directions on following the trails fixed in their minds, they headed out. "I was surprised," Ray commented. "I knew you could ride, you rode with us when you visited, but I didn't realize you enjoyed it so much. Maybe when we get back we can find you a horse of your own. You could keep it at the ranch and ride when you came out to visit."

"I like riding, but this time I just wanted to get away from people! Stop talking and listen for a comm, see what you hear."

Ray did as she said. They rode silently, horses at a walk.

"I'm not hearing anything," Ray said.

"I'm not sure I am either. But when I woke up, there was something. I can't say I heard a voice, just a feeling that I was missing something. Does that make sense?"

"Not to me. You think we're getting close to T? Maybe a year away or less?"

"I don't know. It could be." Libby's frustration showed. "It could be someone else, but why can't I *hear* it?"

"You're much more sensitive than I am. But to hear T when we're not in the same time? That doesn't make sense."

"I don't know if that's what it is, but we don't really understand how the Talents work, do we?"

"No. T thought telepathy had to do with resonance, allowing

155

his mind to resonate with someone else's, but we're just guessing. If you're right and it's T you're sensing, you're doing something the rest of us can't do."

"I want to wait for at least a day, just to be sure," Libby said. "That will give me time to decide whether I'm hearing a voice or whether I'm picking up thoughts from someone I don't know. But it doesn't sound like that and anyway it feels like more than one voice. Two people, maybe. I can't explain it."

"We could try going farther back just a few days at a time. It should work if you're almost close enough to hear T. Pick a spot only ten or twenty miles east...but no, we can't do that. That would put us in the middle of Lake Michigan. We could try it if we headed south, maybe to Saint Louis or Memphis. From there, we could go east in 20-mile jumps until he responds. We wouldn't even have to go as far as New York; just teleport, levitate back, and repeat."

"Can we wait until tomorrow? I may know more by then."

"Sure, and like you said before, you want to go shopping. Just don't buy more than we can carry!"

Chapter Seventeen

"How much?" O'Brien's mouth sagged.

"I'm guessing that each satchel contains about $5,000 if the coins were converted to American money. I can't be sure, of course; some of the coins are Russian, but the others look like they're Chinese or Japanese. There are quite a few silver coins too. It's not easy coming up with an accurate value, but figure there's between $3,000 and $5,000 per satchel. Meaning the total is somewhere between $12,000 and $20,000."

"I niver thought to see such a fortune, niver!"

"It's not really all that much," said T absently. "But it's enough to hold you over while you adjust to the future. Assuming I'm right about the value, of course. Figuring that the Russian coins are about the size of a U.S. double eagle, a hundred would be worth about $2,000. The Japanese gold coins are about the size of eagles and half eagles. The silver ones are probably about as valuable as US silver dollars. My guess should be pretty close. As for the coins, they're useful now, but people don't use gold or silver money in the 21st Century; it's all greenbacks or plastic. There are coins, but they're made of cheaper metals."

"And this plastic ye remember; I don't understand that at all, I don't." Patrick shook his head. "And I don't like what ye're talking about, us taking the money for ourselves. A pistol, aye, that's a war trophy, so 'tis. But all this money? 'Tis *looting*!"

T sighed. "Think it through, Corporal. Say you handed it in. Say also that you report that we attacked this paymaster and the soldiers ran away. Then what?"

"Why, the lieutenant would turn it over to the colonel. 'Tis the law, I'm thinking. Eventually it would go to the general and he would turn it in to the government."

"Tell me more about the government."

O'Brien floundered. "'Tis the government! 'Tis President Wilson and the Congress and the Secretary of War."

"The people who sent you here, in other words. The people

who sent an army to France without enough artillery, machine guns or ammunition. American troops, people just like you, had to beg, buy, or borrow everything from British ships to machine guns and cannons. You may also have noticed that we're outnumbered out here. Why do you suppose that is?"

"I don't understand you, T. I wonder about your loyalty!"

"Oh, I'm loyal, just not the way you think of it. I would never betray you or First Sergeant Mac. My loyalty is to the guys who are loyal to me."

"But that includes the government. Does it not?"

"Ask yourself first whether they're loyal to you. Are they? Or are they willing to sacrifice you and every other soldier in the name of political advantage? Why *didn't* the troops have machine guns or airplanes or artillery pieces? The Germans certainly did! The French had them too, more than we had, and so did the British. But *our* people flew borrowed French airplanes, fired *French* cannons and machine guns, sailed in *British* ships, and fought in borrowed tanks. They used the same kind of French machine guns, the Chauchats, that we swapped for BARs."

"And 'twas it because of the money, ye think?"

"There was plenty of money, if the government had been willing to spend it! Remember when you first got here? Where was the cold weather gear? Sending troops without winter clothing to *Siberia*? Smithers told me about it; he said he nearly froze to death. Somewhere, probably at the cabinet level or maybe it was in Congress, someone in government, *our* government, decided that lives were cheaper. It's the same in every war, and I don't owe *that* guy a damned thing! It's the same for every soldier, Boche, French, British, Italian, American, Japanese, Russian. Governments make war on the cheap. They sent us here to make sure the Czech legion got out, but up north there's a detachment of Americans that's there to recover U.S. supplies. The Bolsheviks won't pay, so the U.S. government wants them back! If a few soldiers die, the government thinks that supplies for lives is a good bargain.

"But not enough troops to make a *real* difference over here, because that would cost too much money! Sure, I have a lot more knowledge than you do because I read a lot of history while I was in Afghanistan, but it's been that way from the beginning. Soldiers die. Back home, some rich guy gets richer."

"But what about the colonel? You're loyal to him, aren't you? He's over here with us, the general too."

"Absolutely not, not in the sense you mean. Oh, I wouldn't sell him out any more than I would sell *you* out, but he doesn't deserve this money. If *he* turned it in, he'd get a medal and maybe a promotion. You and I, we'd get a handshake and a 'thank you'. If that. I want you to think about where I got that rifle I'm using."

"You stole it from the colonel!"

"I did. And why?"

"Because it had been specially accurized?"

"So why did the colonel have this special rifle that he never bothered to use? Why did I have to bribe the armorer so that I could use it to kill the enemy?"

"Ye're making my head hurt!"

"I'm forcing you to *think*! I had a harsh lesson; my own people were willing to betray me, to murder me and the others like me. Not because I had done something wrong, but simply because I had done what they wanted. After the course, I had become too dangerous, and the people in charge understood they had no means of controlling us. I wasn't the first, I won't be the last. Soldiers, people like us, don't fight for a government or even a country. We fight for the guy who's laying there in the mud beside us, the guy who's out front leading and taking the same chances we are. We fight because we're afraid of letting our friends down. *Not* for the government, and not for some senior officer giving the orders from way behind the lines. For the guy *next* to us, the guy who would have done the same for *us* if our positions had been reversed!"

"So we keep the money?"

"We do, and you'll get most of it. I'll probably restock my money belt, but that's all. I won't need money after I get to America. And even if I can't get back to my own time, there are ways I can make a living. If it comes to that, I can do more work in a day than a dozen men, and you can too.

"You mentioned the mines at one time, but if you ever do take up mining you won't need to work for someone else. You also won't need to take advantage of someone unless they're trying to cheat you. I wouldn't *have* to read a cheat's mind, I would know. You would too, with a little more practice."

"I niver thought of that! But if I search through your memories, I could learn to do what you do. Couldn't I?"

"Some of it. That's why we call it Talent, some have more of it than others. We don't know *what* you can do, not yet."

"But we can't be takin' all this money back to camp! People would see us, so they would."

"No, you're right, we'll have to hide it. Mischa's farm would work, at least for now; it's not too far away from the camp--half an hour by levitation if we're in a hurry--and the girl couldn't live there by herself, so it's likely deserted. That'll give us time to find a better location closer to the camp, maybe somewhere near the rifle range. As soon as we get orders to pull out, we recover the money and take it with us.

"The satchels aren't full, so we should be able to parcel out the money from at least one among the others. Maybe two. Considering the mix of money, I would guess the Japanese paymaster wanted the satchels to be equal in value. That's not an issue for us. Anyway, keep a few coins out for yourself before we bury the rest, and I'll do the same. But no more than one or two in your pockets; sew the rest into the linings of your uniform blouse and greatcoat. This late in the year, we won't be turning in our winter gear even if we get orders within the next month or two. Hiding money by sewing it into the linings should be safe enough."

"And anyway, 'tis stolen money," said O'Brien. "'Tis not as if we *worked* for it."

"You're a stubborn man, Patrick! If it makes you feel better, think of it as just another war trophy."

***

Ray explained his thinking to Libby.

"We don't need to go as far as Saint Louis, and anyway, that's heading back west. There's a town about fifty miles south called Kankakee. Base ourselves in Kankakee, teleport east fifty miles to...let's see..."

Ray tapped the map again. "I don't see a town where we want to go, but I don't think we need one. Suppose I just pick a spot? We're not teleporting very far, so I doubt we'll get separated. Try to comm T as soon as you arrive and if you don't get an answer, we levitate back to Kankakee and do it all again. Say a fifty-mile bubbled-up teleport due east, then back to where we started but without using the bubble. Take it easy so we don't get chilled, an hour and a half to two hours for a round trip? Figure four or five complete cycles and if we get tired, find a place to stay in Kankakee or head back to Chicago. Doable, I think."

"Less than a day, I'm thinking," said Libby confidently. "I'm not sure what I was sensing, but I think it has to be Uncle T. He may not be there now...I might have picked up some sort of trace from when he was there before...but I'm sure we're getting close."

"I hope you're right. I was worried about him," confessed Ray. "That article, the one that said a man named Tagliaferro died? It scared me! I'm still concerned, and I will be until T answers you. And after we get back to our own time, I think we should never do this again."

"I don't understand, Uncle Ray. It's the best way to really learn about the past."

"It is, but every time we go into the past we take the chance of causing a paradox. Maybe even a time loop, where we go into the past because we *went* into the past. We can't take the chance that will happen."

"I don't see how it's possible," said Libby stubbornly. "We would have had to start the loop, so that means we could stop it."

"Maybe. But we're traveling back in time without really

understanding it, that's what worries me."

"But we do! Uncle T went back to find me, you did too. Then you found me and we went home!"

"We did, but why? Time displacement and distance displacement must be related, but they also have to be related to the Earth. We *think* it has to do with the magnetic field, but that changes all the time. Magnetic north moves around in a big circle. We think we're going due east because that's what the map shows, but in a year, east will have shifted a tiny amount. And then there's Earth and the sun. Earth is constantly moving, so is the sun. If we had simply gone nowhere, just kept the same position and gone back in time, we'd have found ourselves floating in empty space."

"Oh." Libby packed a lot of meaning in that soft utterance.

"But that's not what happened. We moved, so distance and time *on the Earth* have to be related in a fundamental way. I know there are mathematical relationships, but they always depend on units of measurement, and we don't really know what time is. We try to relate it to other concepts, but that doesn't tell us what it *is*! We're doing what we do because we first spotted a small echo when we commed, something like what you were sensing before. But we're..." Ray paused, searching for the words. "We're like handing gunpowder to someone who just discovered how to make fire. And we're playing around with something much more dangerous than fire. We're playing with our past, and that means we're endangering our future."

***

"Ready?" T asked. "Know what you're going to tell Mac?"

"That we had no contact. The only sign of the enemy was tracks of a large patrol that passed off to the east a few days ago. We checked the railroad tracks and the bridge, but it didn't look like anyone had been there in the past week. And in case he asks, there was no sign of Dolan's body. What about the coins?"

"*What* coins?"

"That's it," agreed T. "We don't know anything about a

paymaster or satchels, and we're not carrying anything. We'll head for the rifle range tomorrow or next day and dig up the handful you kept out. Mine are in my money belt and you'll hide yours in the linings of your uniform as soon as possible. Mac already knows I had a belt and gold, so if someone spots it no questions will be asked. But you can't be seen with one; people would wonder why a corporal needed such a thing. And one Dolan was enough! No more comming unless we leave the camp again or it's an emergency. No practicing either, unless you're absolutely sure no one is around. I would say no practicing at all, but I remember how I felt that first week after I discovered I could move things by mind power alone. Just...be very careful."

"Got it. For the tenth time, I've got it."

"Now you wouldn't exaggerate, would you Corporal?" T's attempt at Patrick's brogue showed his amusement.

"I'm the very soul of truth, I am!" Patrick took a deep breath. "I'm ready. But 'tis not the same as it was before, now is it?"

"No. It's not, because you're not the same man you were. "

Chapter Eighteen

Mac met them as soon as they passed through the gate. The sentry had called his corporal, who had passed the word to the First Sergeant.

"I expected you back before now," Mac said. "I was thinking of sending Corporal Heintzelman out to look for you. Aye, and with a full squad, the which I can't be sparing!"

"We went farther than I intended," O'Brien explained. "It seemed safe enough, and I think they've given up on trying to sabotage the railroad. We inspected the tracks as far as that side-track ten miles to the north, and there was no sign of any damage. Maybe Semenoff got tired of losing people with nothing to show for it?"

"Or maybe his troops decided raiding farms was easier. It wouldn't be the first time that irregulars like his were sent out to do a job and decided they'd rather not. Were there other signs of activity?"

"A large party had crossed the tracks some time ago, headed northeast. Could have been bandits, but they could also have been farmers heading for the next town. We spotted footprints and cart tracks, but no sign of horses."

"Doesn't sound like Cossacks," agreed Mac. "The cart sounds like farmers and we know they band together now when they travel. Too dangerous to go alone. But they were moving away from us, ye think?"

"Aye. We followed the tracks long enough to be sure before turning back. That's another reason we were out as long as we were."

"'Tis probably a good thing. We're to be pulled out in less than a month, and the major wants no more casualties. He was not happy when the lieutenant told him two men were overdue, so he wasn't."

"Back to Vladivostok?"

"Aye, and then to California. Some of our people volunteered out of the 8th Division, but they won't be going back. Most will be demobilized. If yer interested in staying in the Army, I'll see what I can do."

"I don't think so, Mac. I've had enough soldiering. California, ye say?"

"'Tis the rumor. You might get a job in the movies; I hear they're always hiring."

"I just might. I..." O'Brien grabbed at his head and sank to the ground. Crouching, he held his hands over his ears.

"What was that? Did you hear something?"

***

O'Brien had indeed heard something, and so loud that it stunned him momentarily.

<Uncle T! You're alive!>

<Easy, Libby! It's not necessary to shout!>

<I'm sorry.> The mental voice was much quieter. <But we were so worried! Are you in New York?>

<Not now. It's a long story, but the short answer is no. I'm in Siberia.>

<Siberia?> sent Ray. <How did you get *there*?>

<I don't know. One minute I was in New York, the next I was...somewhere else. When I woke up, I didn't remember who I was and I was in Siberia. It's good to hear from both of you! Are you at the ranch?>

<No. I found Libby; she was in Nevada, back in the past. I was never sure of the date, somewhere around 1850, but I figured out a way we could get back to our future. Lots to tell you when we have time. But when you didn't return, I got worried and we decided to see if I could find you. We thought you might have been killed in New York. We intended to bring you out of the past before it happened. Anyway, Libby insisted on coming with me, so here we are. The trick is to use controllable short-distance teleports to get back to our time, working with or against the magnetic field. You'll have to experiment to find out which way works for you.

I'm not sure why that is, but that's the way it works. When you have a direction, magnetic east or west, just bubble-up and teleport in the direction that takes you toward the future, and keep on until you're home. If you want to stay in the same general location on the ground, alternate teleports with levitating back to where you teleported from.>

<Sounds simple enough. Except that I can't do that, not yet; I'm too far from America and I don't have reliable maps or any idea of where I want to go. First thing, get myself out of Siberia. If I did manage to reach the 21st Century in Siberia, I'd have to deal with ID cards and a tightly controlled society, so I'll wait. Second thing, get discharged from the Army, not that I expect a problem with that. But there's something else to consider; say hello to Corporal Patrick O'Brien. He learned telepathy on his own. There was another man, too, something of a bad actor, but he's not a problem now.>

<Corporal O'Brien?>

<I'm here! By all the saints, I thought that first shout was going to take me head off! Ye're Ray, I take it?>

<I'm Ray, and the shout was Libby. Say hello, Libby. Or maybe an apology would work better.>

<I'm sorry, Corporal Patrick! But I heard Uncle T, and I was so surprised...>

<You mentioned another man, T?>

<He was killed during a patrol. But I can't leave Patrick in the past, not now. Levitating, psychokinetics, and telepathy he's got.>

<And just by being around him, other Talents would begin to develop,> agreed Ray. <It's what I was afraid of, causing dormant Talents to become active. It's why I came back for you. But I don't think he can go into the future, because he's never been into the past. His future hasn't happened yet and he's already a time paradox by virtue of existing in the past with active Talents.>

<*Damn*! You're sure?>

<Reasonably sure. We got back to the time when we went into the past, but that was it. Libby returned to when she teleported that

first time, which was several weeks before I did. After I reached the 21st Century, I avoided her and refused to answer any comms until she'd caught up to when I went back. For a while, there were two of me. So I'm guessing you can return to when you teleported that first time, but no farther, and Patrick can't go into the future at all.>

<That's a problem! Now I don't know what to do about Patrick.>

<Bring him to the states. He will need to never be around anyone for very long to avoid creating a paradox, which means avoiding people and probably traveling instead of settling down. That's what Bobby intends to do. Which won't be easy for Patrick, because he'll need money. How much gold is left from what you took back?>

T's chuckle was clear, even through the telepathic connection. <That's not a problem for us either. I hope I didn't leave *you* short; I pretty much cleaned out one of the caches on the ranch.>

<Money is not a problem. You've got a lot to catch up on too!
>

<The mine?> T guessed.

<Oh, yeah! Bobby has been a busy boy. There's more than enough to support all of us as long as necessary. Again, assuming Patrick can get here. Which I doubt.>

<That's good to know. So all I need to do is get back to the ranch about the time I left! I'm starting to get anxious, but my best chance is still to catch the troopship back to the states.>

<You mentioned the Army? In Siberia? Is that another paradox?>

<No. Not many remember it now, but the Army sent a couple of detachments to Siberia just before the end of World War I. One is up near Murmansk; they're under British command, and from what we hear they've had it much worse than we have. The unit I'm with is west of Vladivostok, not far from the Mongolian border. I just heard that we'll be pulling out soon. We were sent to guard the railroad until the Czech Legion got out, and the other mission was

to recover as many American-owned supplies as possible. Most are up north, or were; they were shipped through the port of Murmansk before the Russian Revolution.

<The idea was to up-arm the Russians so that they could keep pressure on the Germans. They tied up a lot of German divisions on the Eastern Front. But during the revolution the Tsar was deposed and the government, such as it is, is refusing to pay. As for the supplies, I'm guessing they were either shipped back by now or destroyed. Or maybe the government just got tired of having us here and is cutting their losses. We're not accomplishing much, that's for sure, and as far as I'm concerned let the Bolsheviks and Cossacks and White Russians fight it out. Anyway, we'll be leaving soon.>

<Fascinating. But what's that got to do with you? Why are you in the Army?>

<I had amnesia when I first got here and the Army took me in. They thought at the time that I was one of their soldiers, a man named Tyler. But just in case I wasn't, they offered to enlist me and I took them up on it. I've got most of my memory back now, but there's another issue; I'm not willing to just leave the guys. We're shorthanded, what with the epidemics. For a while it was typhus, then the flu. Probably half the detachment got sick and a dozen or so died. The survivors are finally being released from the hospital, but we're still shorthanded.

<Hetman Semenoff's Cossacks were sniffing around...I hear he's calling himself general now...for a while, but I think we finally convinced them to stay away. Or maybe one of the other factions is threatening them, I just don't know. We were guarding the Trans-Siberian Railway so that the Czech legion could escape. I think they're gone by now, most of them. Our being here has made a difference.>

<Aye, it has,> chimed in O'Brien.

<But they took me in and now they need me, so I'll stay until we pull out. I'm stationed at a small outpost, one of the most distant from the main base at Vladivostok. There's another post, almost twenty miles away, that's supposed to support us, but they're short handed too. The battalion headquarters is closer, but they're mostly admin and logistics types and disease hit pretty much everyone this past summer.>

<Okay,> sent Ray. <It's not a problem. I'll find out when your ship will dock, and I'll be waiting when you get there.>

<Libby too?> asked T.

<I don't know. Libby?>

<No; now that I know Uncle T is okay and that he knows how to return, I'm going home. I want real hot running water and computers and my smartphone and...>

T chuckled, his mirth obvious.

<And you'll not spend the gold foolishly? It's okay to cash it in when you get back, but you'll deposit it in an education account?> asked Ray.

<Oh, sure. I've been listening to you and Uncle T. Do you really think I forgot the things I learned when our minds were joined? Including how to earn as much money as I'll ever need? I may go prospecting when I get back! Bye.>

The feeling of resonance from Libby's voice vanished.

<Will she be all right? I get the impression that's she's young,> Patrick sent.

<Corporal, she may be young, but trust me, Libby can take care of herself. I'm leaving too; I need to research a few things, such as when and where your ship will land. Expect me to comm you just before you dock,> Ray sent.

<Be good to see you and having someone ashore will probably turn out to be useful. We'll be all right,> sent T.

<Then I'm gone. Nice to have met you, Corporal.> Ray's voice vanished as abruptly as Libby's had.

***

"O'Brien! Wake up, Lad!" Sergeant Mac lightly slapped O'Brien's face, something he'd apparently already done.

"I'm awake, Mac! What happened?"

"I'm not to be knowing, Lad. One minute we were talking about the patrol, the next you just stopped. Be you epileptic?"

"Not that I know of, Mac. I didn't fall down, did I?"

"No, but could be 'twas another kind of seizure. I'll be wanting you to see the doctor, so I will, and to make sure you get there I'll send Tyler with you. But 'twill have to be tomorrow," Mac decided. "The train's not due to pass until then."

"Top, I'm all right. I don't need to see the doctor!"

"But you will, my boy, because I insist! 'Tis not for you to decide! And while you forget to call me by my rank from time to time, I'm still the First Sergeant and you're still one of my corporals. Tyler, I'll be holding ye responsible to see he gets there."

"I'll see to it, Top."

"Then 'tis dismissed ye are. I'll be talking to the sawbones when ye get back."

,

The two were sitting outside O'Brien's hut.

"That could have gone better," said Patrick glumly.

"Maybe not. I'll see you to the hospital and while you're there, I'll have a look around. I'll find a suitable spot and hide the satchels near Vladivostok. We may not have time later on; knowing the Army, it wouldn't surprise me to get orders to drop everything but our packs and rifles and get on the train."

"Aye, 'tis what happened in the Philippines. We pulled back to the barracks and the next morning they marched us onto the ship. We barely had time for breakfast, and even then, 'twas cold. The cooks were packing up too."

"But we do have a problem. If Ray is right, I can't take you to the future with me. You understand why you'll need to keep on the move, and when you decide to stop, make sure it's the most deserted area you can find?"

"Aye, we don't want another Dolan! Or for that matter, another me. Before the time when there was you and the others, I mean," agreed Patrick.

"That's it. There may have been Espers before us, but if so, nobody knew. Not many knew about Rhine's investigations or the ones going on in California, and the ones who did thought they were crackpots looking for grant money. The CIA's school was more hope than plan."

"But you've been hiding out since then, so maybe others did too," argued Patrick.

"I can't rule it out. I suppose we'll never know, unless someone shows up and tells us," said T.

"So let's say that I'm left in San Francisco, and you head off for the future. The money's a fortune, if we can but get it there!"

"If Ray's there to meet us, it won't be a problem at all. All we'll have to do, just before we reach the dock, is levitate the satchels. He brings them ashore and waits for us."

"So no need for the man-overboard plan?"

"Not for you. But I'm not Tyler, and if I'm not very careful the Army will find that out. As soon as we reach Vladivostok, we'll have hundreds and maybe thousands of men milling around. Some of them almost certainly knew Tyler, and when they hear the name they'll start looking for him. No, I'm still going to have to disappear, but you can go ashore with the rest, take your discharge, and resume your normal life. If you're careful, you've got more than enough money to give you a good start."

"About this depression that's going to hit, where so many lose their jobs; will that affect me, d'ye think?"

"My advice is to hang on to as much gold as you can, and when the Depression hits you might turn it to advantage. People will be looking to sell property. But be careful; a lot of things happened between the wars, including civil unrest. I remember reading about veterans marching on Washington. And then there was the Dust Bowl. You're better off keeping well away from all that. Find a small town somewhere and buy a farm or ranch. Change your name too. You want to avoid being noticed."

"'Tis strange, so 'tis. I've niver been rich before!"

"Don't let it go to your head. Rich is like poor, except with money, and that only matters if you use it intelligently. You also know where thousands of dollars worth of gold is located, but you can't spend a one of them!"

Chapter Nineteen

The two left camp the next morning and caught the train for Vladivostok.

"'Tis funny," said Corporal O'Brien. "I used to think that traveling on the train was fast! I was always a little afraid to be going that fast, I was, but now? We could have flown to Vladivostok in half the time, so we could!"

"But we wouldn't have been able to fly into the town! We would have landed somewhere in the woods and walked the rest of the way. Instead, an Army truck will pick us up and take us right to the hospital. It's easier and probably faster. If we were traveling after dark?" T shrugged. "Different. Assuming, of course that we had enough moonlight. It should be possible to levitate in total darkness, but I haven't figured out how."

"T'would be a problem, so it would. But I agree, it might be possible. Can you not remember the images?"

"No. The new image immediately wipes away the previous one. It's probably better that way. I've wondered why air or water won't work, but they don't. Air pushes against us, so why can't we push against it?"

"Because it's like the water, it keeps changin'?" guessed O'Brien.

"Yeah. Well, maybe someday. We know how to use our Talents, but we really don't understand them."

"In your memory, I found that Ray took on a powerful Talent and defeated him. Is he stronger than you?"

"I don't know. We're both strong PKs, but we've never tried to arm wrestle. Too much chance we'd injure each other! As for strength, Libby may be off the scale. I have no idea what her limits are, and I don't think she knows herself."

"Be ye serious? That young girl?"

"Don't underestimate her! That little girl fried a kidnapper to a crisp. We've taught her a few things since and learned pyrokinetics ourselves, but there are things about her I simply don't understand.

If they're even real, I mean. Were you synchronized with Ray's mind while I was comming him?"

"Nay. I did not know I could."

"I did, briefly. I needed to know as much as possible about how he returned from the past. But part of what I picked up had to do with how he got back to this time. We can't be sure, but it appears that she can influence the weather just by wishing it."

"Saints presaerve us! The weather?"

"That's what it looks like. I don't know that she could make it snow in summer, but clouds and rain...Ray thinks she stopped a howling dust storm in less than half an hour. She just said she wished the wind wasn't blowing and a short time later it wasn't."

"'Tis said of Saint Patrick that he could do fey things. But of course, he had the help of God, so people say, so 'tis not to be wondered at. Yet did Libby stun me with the power of her voice when she commed you! Aye, 'tis strong she is. I had not thought of it in that way."

T nodded. "If we're right, Libby could turn out to be the strongest of us all. Not in everything, maybe, but we won't know until she grows up. There'll be changes because she's just now entering puberty, but we don't know what they'll be."

"You remembered living in Nevada on a ranch," said Patrick. "Are there other ranches nearby? Do ye farm, or only raise the cattle?"

"No cattle, but Ray has horses. We bought the ranch so we could launder the gold bars I found. As part of the deception, I did some work on an old mine and located a deposit of gold ore. Our friend Bobby mined that one out, but he found others. If you can reach the future...we won't know until you try...there'll be money for your own place."

"I cannot be takin' your money, so I can't! I've always made me own way and I'll be a-keepin' on with it! Now more than iver!"

"Relax, Patrick. Or should I address you as Corporal? If you're going to be difficult, maybe I should go back to the formal style."

"'Tis Patrick. Or Pat, for 'tis what me friends call me."

"We're unique, Pat. Fewer than a dozen people can do what we do. Some can do one thing, a few can do more, but only three of us so far have ever gone back in time. You may be the fourth, but I'd rather you didn't try. Too much chance you'll cause a time paradox. Trying to go to the future is different, because if you succeed you'll just be another like us."

"Then I'll not be a-going back. Lifting of things, with no need of me muscles? Flying like a bird? And this comming thing we did? 'Tis enough! What more can a man wish for, I ask ye?"

"You'd be surprised! But even if you can't *go* there, you might be able to sense the future before it happens; I almost can, it's just not very reliable. I've long thought that there were others who could do more. And I can sense where gold or silver is to be found, which may be one of your Talents."

"'Twould be useful, aye, and me gran had the sight. But I felt nothing when I lifted those satchels. They might have contained bricks, so they might."

"It may just take practice, but it also may not work for you. Shezzie has an enormous sense of empathy, so much that she could tell when a paralyzed patient wasn't completely under the anesthetic. I can't do that."

"I'm not so sure," said Patrick. "I joined with you, perhaps not completely, but I felt what you were feeling. I felt your guilt, wrong though 'tis. A man without the sense of others could not be feelin' that, I'm thinkin'. 'Tis as you said, it may be that you need practice."

"You might be right," said T, surprised. There were unexpected depths to Patrick! "But we're pulling into the depot, and there's the truck. You get to ride up front, I'll make do in the back."

"But will ye not be uncomfortable? We could both fit by the driver."

"Patrick, think about it. If the seats in back are hard, I'll simple take some of the weight off. For that matter, I might float and hang onto the truck's side panels."

"Oh. I niver thought o' that!"

"You'll learn to, after a while. Right now, you have to think too much about what you're doing. Later on, it will just happen."

***

T returned the following day and was allowed in for a short visit.

"Any results yet?"

"I haven't even seen a doctor, but the nurse said that if they decide it's epilepsy I'll be discharged. The gold could be a problem if they send me home early."

"It's not our only problem, but as for the gold, I found a place to hide the satchels. There's a big warehouse near the waterfront. The entrances are locked, but there are windows up near the roof. I was able to see the latch and unlocking it was easy. Removing enough old paint around the frame was a chore, but I did it. I marked the window by flaking off the pain on the lower corners, so you'll know which one. Just levitate, open the latch and you'll find the satchels hidden inside where the rafters overhang the wall. Just watch out for the pigeons; there were screens over the openings, but they've rusted away."

"I'll not forget. You mentioned another problem?"

"Ekaterina. She's got two other names, but Ekaterina will do. She's a telepath.

"She heard Dolan...she says the world is better for not having him in it...but also you and me. You've met her; she was with the village chief when he came to talk to Mac."

"Mischa's sister? Ye're saying she's a Talent?"

"She's a telepath at least. I'm not sure about anything else."

"How..."

"It was Dolan, at first. He was broadcasting and she picked it up the same as you did. She sort of speaks English now, but with an Irish accent and it's mixed up with Russian. Her ability may also have to do with my rescuing her. Anyway, she was at the farm when I showed up. Talk about a surprise! She was angry because she'd been trying to call me and I didn't respond. All I heard was a mutter of Russian!"

"By all the saints! What are we to do? She's done nothing wrong; we'll not be killing her, we'll not, even if it creates this time paradox you're so fearful of." Patrick's tone left no doubt of his determination.

"No, I'm not about to kill off a kid! I have no idea what to do now. I don't see how we can take her with us."

"We'll have to." O'Brien decided. "We'll just have to find a way. Do ye have a spare uniform?"

"Sure, I was issued two. Why?"

"I have me housewife...you know what that is, right?"

"Haven't got a clue. There are no women in the camp."

"'Tis a *sewing kit*, along with buttons and a few other things to repair me uniform. I can't be giving her *my* uniform, because even if she removed the stripes the darker area would show. You'll have to give her your uniform and my kit. She'll know how to sew, I'm thinking, so have her tailor your uniform to fit her. We'll just have to smuggle her on board the ship."

"And what if you wind up being shipped back early?"

"There's no hospital ship here, just the regular troop transport, and I'll be smuggling her on board, so I will. Not sure how, but I'll find a way because I must. She's a child yet, and skinny enough to pass as a man. 'Tis cut her hair we must, but that's not an issue. Keeping her hidden is what's important."

"I'm tempted to steal a ship or buy one! A fisherman would sell if I offered him gold," T said.

"And do you know the way of sailing? I confess I don't, despite having lived in Ireland. We're seafaring folk, we are, but I was too young when we left the old country. I do remember watching the crews setting and taking in the sails, and I couldn't begin to. Not even with a small ship, and if it's too small it would never swim among the great waves you spoke of."

"It's still an option," said T stubbornly. "I might not be able to fly across an ocean, but I could push a boat along."

"Aye, 'tis possible, but you don't know that and what would we do if the weather got up? No, the first plan is still best. Aye, and maybe this is an advantage. The ships sail with cargo, so they do, but they're not full with passengers at all. Later on, when all the boys are going home, 'twill be different."

"I grant your expertise; you crossed the sea on a troopship," said T. "As for what you remember, it's not an easy thing to believe the navy crammed men in like sardines back then."

"'Tis easy enough after you're there. The worst of all is the lasting of it, day after day for months," said Patrick.

"Better you than me!" T said. "But maybe you're right about smuggling her out. I left Afghanistan disguised as a casualty. We might be able to use bandages, so that her face is at least partly hidden?"

"'Tis a thought. But ye must understand, your friend Ray won't be waiting if we arrive early."

"Having help on shore is a convenience. You can still do it."

"But ye must also join yer mind with hers in the way that you did with mine. 'Tis needing her help, we are. 'Twill help her understanding of English for one, and if she can simply fly away from prying eyes on shipboard and carry herself to the shore, why, 'twill be a simple matter to leave the ship when we arrive."

"I grant your point, but this is getting complicated!"

"'Tis what it is."

Chapter Twenty

"Two things," insisted Corporal O'Brien. "You've got to bring her here as soon as possible, and then you're going to have to meld your mind with hers as ye did with me."

"I can understand bringing her here," T agreed. "Semenoff's guerrillas pass through the area and for that matter, they're not the only raiders around. But melding with her? I'm trying to avoid that! You're one too many, but I didn't really have a choice."

"Ye still don't," argued Pat. "No matter which ship we sail on, we'll always have a heavy load to carry ashore, and 'twill be over water."

"Probably not. The ship won't come to anchor; it will tie up to the dock in San Francisco, same as here in Vladivostok. That's as good as dry land as far as levitating goes."

"I hadn't thought of that, but ye're right. That's how we boarded and disembarked when we left the states, and on our way here from the Philippines. Still, there's still the weight of our bags and the young lady herself. I'll help, but 'twill be best if she can do her share, I'm thinking."

"I suppose," said T reluctantly, "and at this point I don't suppose it matters. I'll fetch her here to Vladivostok tonight and get her settled before I do the meld. But after that I'll need to get back to camp. I know what Top said about staying with you, but I don't think he would be happy if I kept hanging around the hospital with nothing to do."

"Aye. If he asks, you can tell him I kept you here because I expected the hospital to return me to duty. We both know there's nothing wrong with me, but I can't explain what happened. We shall have to make new plans, I'm thinking. I don't think it matters whether they discharge me early or after we get to America. I don't like the thought of letting the First Sergeant down, so I don't, but they'll not be needing me. Things have been quiet lately. Semenoff's got his hands full, what with the Bolsheviks pushing down from the northwest and Kolchak's people nipping at him from the northeast. His army, such as it is, may be already falling apart. He didn't get the guns he expected and that Japanese payroll niver showed up, thanks to us. 'Tis finished, he is."

***

Semenoff himself had been wondering what to do next. Even a few of his prized Cossack cavalrymen had vanished without warning! Had they given up, or perhaps even gone over to Kolchak? He rubbed at his neck, an unconscious gesture. Events were closing in around him. Was this truly the end? Should he think of saving himself, or perhaps trying a last roll of the dice?

No! The opportunity was still here, he needed but to seize it with both hands! Galvanized, he slammed open the door and bellowed for his chief aide.

***

T returned to the hospital the following afternoon as soon as visiting hours opened. "I don't have much time. I've got less than an hour to catch the train, assuming it leaves on time."

"But Ekaterina is here? And she has a place she can stay?"

"Yes to both, and I got her a uniform. Not mine; I bought it from a Russian who got it from a soldier who was on his way home. She'll be coming by to visit, but I told her I needed to talk to you first. The meld didn't go as well as I had hoped."

"You weren't able to?"

"Not at first. I had to hypnotize her, or at least relax her before I could make contact."

"But she's a telepath, you said."

"Oh, is she ever! She felt it when I tried to make contact and slammed the door. I've never experienced anything like it, not since Surfer died! I told her she would need money and laid the coins on a table, thinking she would conceal them wherever she thought best. But she was watching the coins while I was talking...I'm guessing she had never seen that much money at one time...and that gave me an idea. I started flipping one of the gold pieces with my thumb. You know what I mean, right?"

"Aye," said Patrick. "Spinning it over and over in the air."

"That's it, and I held it in the air, spinning, so she would keep watching. While she was concentrating on the flash, I started explaining why the mind meld was necessary. I kept my voice low and repetitive. I'm pretty sure she understood the English word for 'sleep' and that helped relax her. Took about five minutes, but the next time I tried joining minds I managed at least a partial contact. I think she was in control by then, not me. I understand a lot more Russian now and I'm sure she picked up more English, but both of us will need to practice before it sounds natural. But after that, nothing. I don't know what else she got from the meld."

"'Tis a problem," agreed Patrick. "What if she can't levitate? Or use the psychokinetics? One of us would have to carry her *and* the gold when we board the ship. 'Twill be the same when we reach America."

"Talk to her when she gets here. Maybe *you* can get her to open up. You're only about ten years older than she is. It could be that she caught more than I realized and understands what I was attempting. If you have to, comm me. I need to know how successful it was. She's a strong telepath, so we have to take her with us, but if that's all she can do it will complicate getting her to America."

"Is this your first failure?" asked Patrick.

"I don't know. I'm wondering now if Shezzie made the difference. Her particular Talent is empathy, a sense of what the other person is feeling. Let me ask you a question: what did you feel when I linked my mind to yours?"

"Well, I felt your thoughts when it happened. I knew some of what you remembered, but I don't think I caught everything. But 'twas more than just the hearing of your voice."

"But there was no sense of losing your identity? You were always aware of who you are?"

"Aye, I was, and I understood who you were. I know a lot more about ye now, and 'tis better I feel. Ye're a man who would risk his life for others without a thought. Ye take far too much responsibility onto yerself, I'm thinking, that ye do."

T shrugged off the implied compliment. "It was different when I joined with Shezzie," he said. "I couldn't tell where I left off and she began. It was like that with Ana Maria and Ray too. But now that I think about it, not with Shorty and Bobby. The connection was stronger than when I tried with Kat, but not the same as when Shezzie was involved. The full melding may have been her doing. Now it sounds like I never melded fully with you, and I have no idea how well it went with Kat. See what you can find out and then we'll decided how we're to get her to the states."

***

The train was its usual bumpy, slow, and dirty self. The cars rocked and the wheels clacked over the gaps where rail section met rail section. Coal smoke blew in whenever a window was cracked open and between times, the potbellied stove near the car's center added its own stink.

T was happy to step off at the stop, which was only a handful of miles from the camp. But there would be no levitating. Corporal Heintzelman and two returning privates also left the train; he had picked them up at the hospital.

So T hiked with the others, and by the corporal's order carried his rifle, loaded and safed, at the ready position. Enemy scouts had been spotted by a patrol, less than two miles from the camp.

First Sergeant Mac was happy to see him. "I can use you, Lad. Corporal Heintzelman brought two back from the hospital, but we're still overextended. What can ye tell me of Corporal O'Brien?"

"No idea what's going to happen, Top. The nurse says he may be discharged from the service."

"The devil ye say! Be ye sure, Lad?"

"No. I don't think there's been a diagnosis, but Patrick believes they're discharging people as fast as they can, now that the European war has ended."

"So the major says too." Mac shook his head in disappointment. "I had hopes for young Patrick, so I did. Tis a problem. I could make do with fewer men, not easily but could be done, but I'm down to just three active corporals and one in hospital who's no help to me. Aye, and the damned Cossacks are sneakin' about, looking for mischief. But could be yer right and the hospital will be sendin' him home. Which leaves me in the meantime with too much perimeter to defend, and too few corporals.

"Ye've acquitted yerself well since you arrived, takin' of responsibility in a manner not expected of a newly-recruited private. Now I canna say what the lieutenant will do, or for that matter what the major will say, but I've a mind to recommend you for acting corporal. 'Tis only in case Corporal O'Brien is taken away from us and 'tis temporary in any case until the colonel confirms it. Ye'll have PFC Smithers to start and I'll get ye more help when I can. The lieutenant says we'll be getting the last of the sick men back in but a day or two, and ye shall have them in yer squad. Think ye that ye can handle the responsibility?"

"I can, but..."

"We'll say no more about it then. Don't thank me, for the truth is I need ye, Lad. I'll be getting the lieutenant's permission first, and if he approves 'tis stripes for yer arm. Ye'll not be paid as a corporal yet, but 'tis no small thing to lead men in wartime. Most find it the most satisfying thing they can ever do with their lives. For the men depend on ye, d' ye see, and ye must have a care for them as well as see to carryin' out your tasks. With luck, and ye want it, I'll put in a good word for ye. 'Tis possible the stripes may become permanent. 'Twas in that way that I gained my first promotion, and 'tis a compliment to you. There's many a man remains a private soldier until retirement."

***

Patrick O'Brien was sitting outside, enjoying the crisp air. The temperature was just short of unpleasant, despite his thick uniform, but the stink inside the hospital made going back in something to put off as long as possible. Three books lay beside him; he'd selected two he thought he might want to read, and the nurse had added another. For the first time in his life, he was reading poetry-- and *such* poetry!

He might have passed over it, despite the nurse's recommendation, but a landowner, as such he would be when he returned to America, should be an educated man. Not to mention that with his new abilities would come responsibilities an unschooled man would not be able to comprehend. And so, for the first time in his life, Patrick O'Brien was not only reading but thanks to what he'd plucked from T's mind, enjoying the process.

Many of the words were strange, but he could puzzle through them based on their context. He marveled at the ability of the Englishman who'd lived so long ago, a man named Shakespeare, to cram so much meaning into so few words! Clearly 'twas a talent of a different sort and not to be looked down upon! He was following the words with his finger, lips moving slowly, when Kat found him.

He glanced up, then gawked at her; she looked like a young soldier! The uniform was loose on her slim body and the shoes appeared to have been acquired locally, but the long hair was gone and the campaign hat was tilted slightly forward as was customary.

"Ye be the corporal."

"Aye, and ye be Kat. Private Kat! Ye look like a soldier, so ye do. Do ye find yerself well, Lass?"

"I not..." she paused, rethinking what she wanted to say. T had been right; she would need all the practice she could get. "I do not know. 'Tis strange. I never...I have never worn such clothing nor had so much gold in me hands! I not know T, but he give me gold! The trousers are different, but I like the way they feel. They are not so warm as good Russian clothes, but 'twill do."

"Ye'll need to have a care with the gold, Lass. For 'tis a fact that many will try to take yer money if they know ye have it. Change a coin or two into silver and copper and spend those wisely. 'Tis safer for ye." Patrick chuckled. "Ye look a proper soldier, but ye sound like a true daughter of Ireland, so ye do!"

He understood only a single word of the torrent of Russian she replied with, 'Rus'. Despite the accent, she knew very well who she was and wasn't happy with what he implied!

"But what else did ye learn from our friend T?"

"Too much, I'm thinking! Am I a witch now? For in all Russia, only witches can do the things I can!"

"No, Lass. T believes there are no witches, nor shamans either. 'Tis only knowledge, but of a different sort. How old be ye?"

She laboriously started to count on her fingers, then stopped and put her hands at her side. Had she also picked up simple arithmetic from T? Face showing intense concentration, she said, "I am fifteen years."

"I would have thought less, so I would."

She was becoming more familiar with English. Her reply this time was barely delayed. "Life has been very hard for us. T thinks I will grow taller. My new landlady is very good. She has chicken and potatoes, as well as very good borscht. I am allowed to have seconds!"

Patrick's smile never reached his lips, but it was a struggle. 'Twas clear that Russians in their way had suffered almost as much as had the Irish, and for the same reason: rapacious men, who took what they wanted and cared nowt for others. "Ye learned much from our friend T, 'tis clear. Ye mentioned witches; can ye move things?"

"Like this?" The book of poetry, lying open and forgotten on his lap, snapped closed. Patrick blinked. "Useful, to be sure. And is there more?"

She appeared to straighten her back, but then he realized she was actually floating, feet barely touching the floor.

"'Tis enough! We're not to do such things, especially here in town!"

"I was not here in town. I left after breakfast this morning. I went home to visit the graves of my family. 'Tis...it is...a sad thing to leave behind yer...*your*...home."

"Aye. So ye made a fast trip there and back?"

"I did other things too. I dug plants from the forest and placed them at the ends of their graves. It was not so much, but I felt better. The flowers will bloom in the spring, and if my family looks down upon their resting place they will know I have not forgotten them. Even when I am in America, I will remember."

"So ye...you will be well cared for here in the town. You have a place to live and a landlady who feeds you well.

"T has gone back to the camp, but I am not allowed to leave. Did he tell ye...you...that there is more gold?"

"Yes. He said you know of it."

"Aye, I know where it is. We'll be needing your help when we leave, for some of the gold will be yours, I'm thinking. I'll be finding you when the hospital releases me, and if 'tis to be discharged from the Army I am, we'll find a way to take you to America with us."

Chapter Twenty-one

T had barely gotten to sleep. Exhausted, he'd sent his three men to dinner while he kept working on the wall. Finally, he'd decided there was nothing more he could do without making it obvious that he was shortening the perimeter in an unusual manner, and had gone to bed. And then this.

<T, wake up!>

<Patrick? What's the matter?>

<They're shipping me out tomorrow morning! I can't leave the hospital, there's a sergeant here watching us get ready. We're boarding in half an hour and the ship sails on the morning tide.>

T sat up, now fully awake. How to handle this? But maybe it was what he needed. After all, the objective was to get O'Brien-- and Kat!--back to the states, then see whether they could go into the future. T could take care of himself. But... <You couldn't get the gold?>

<I didn't have time! There was no warning, the sergeant just showed up and told us to get ready. My barracks bag is already packed and my bedding turned in. As for the gold, all I've got is what's sewn into my linings! Should I try to take Kat with me?>

<If you can, yes. Comm her, see what she thinks. Even if she decides to wait, ask her if she pick up at least one of the satchels. More if she can handle the weight. If she can't get the gold, don't worry about it, I'll bring it with me. You should have enough to last until I get there, even with two of you. Or Ray may get there before I do, and he'll help.>

<Can't you come with us? I'm sure there's to be plenty of room on the ship, and 'tis not as if you had to walk up the boarding ramp like we do!>

<I can't! Here's the thing, Mac made me a corporal--the lieutenant confirmed it late yesterday--and I'm needed here. Semenoff's people are sniffing around, Corporal Heintzelman's squad spotted two of them, but they were too far away to take under fire. I doubt he'd send common bandits this time. It's one

thing for them to sabotage deserted railroad tracks, but as for attacking a fortified camp? I can't see it happening. So he sent soldiers, real soldiers. He's planning something, no idea what just yet, but he may have found out that we're about to evacuate Siberia. He needs the rest of those weapons, which gives him plenty of motive to hit us before we leave. For all he knows, we may intend to take them with us.

<Anyway, I'm in charge of the squad now, PFC Smithers is my assistant, and we'll get two more men late this afternoon, back from the hospital. They've lost a lot of weight and they're weak, thanks to the flu, but they're better than nothing. Everybody is shorthanded! We don't have enough men to man the walls, so we've been shortening the perimeter by rebuilding the palisade. That's what I'll be doing after breakfast.

<Comm Kat, ask her if she can collect at least some of the money, and get it and herself on board. It shouldn't be a problem if things are like you say, no one to watch out for but the crew, and they'll be busy getting you guys settled. But let me know what happens. If she can't get on the ship, don't worry about it, I'll find a way. But it would be a real help if she can put at least one of the satchels on board.

<The priority right now is to get yourself to the states. Kat and the gold are secondary. I'll find a way. When Ray shows up, work with him and in the meantime keep me updated, okay?>

<Aye, I'll get back to you after I comm Kat,> Patrick sent. <Her English is improving, but this might take a while.>

T dropped the connection, realizing there was nothing more he could do. His leaving now might endanger his comrades in the camp, and that was a nonstarter. Patrick would have to do what T himself would have done, do the best he could.

Moments later, he was once again asleep.

***

Patrick finally managed to calm Kat down; her initial response had been in Russian. He'd been able to pick out a word from time to time, enough to realize that she was scolding him for waking her up. <Quiet! There's no time for this! I need your help. I'm being shipped to America tomorrow morning and the ship leaves early! You remember how to levitate?>

<Da! I will help!>

<Okay. You're going to the big warehouse near the docks and fly up to the roof. When you're there, look for a window. There's a row of them that stick out. Okay so far?>

<Da, I know the building! But there may be a watchman.>

<So fly over him! He'll be watching the ground, not the roof. Look for a dormer window that has lost the paint on the two lower corners. Can you do that?>

<I do not understand this dormer.>

<It's an extension from the upper roof. The window is up and down and swings open for ventilation in the summer.>

<I will look for this.>

<Comm me if you have trouble. Think you can do it?>

<Da...ah, yes.>

<Okay, this is the hard part. Find the window's latch and open it. Use your PK; there's no reason to break the window. The paint has been removed from around the sides, so the window should swing open easily. The gold is in satchels that are hidden among the second floor rafters where they meet the wall. I suggest you lift the satchels one at a time and set them outside on the roof. Go outside and move them to the ground, then come down yourself. Don't forget to close and lock the window before you leave.>

<Why can't I do everything at the same time?>

<Can you?>

<I think so. But if not, I will do as you say.>

<I'm to take the gold to America and wait for T. Do you want to go on the ship with me?>

<*Yes.* I will go now, I want see America! Is true, no more Cossacks? No filthy Mongolian raiders?>

<It's true. Wear your uniform when you go out; you may not have time to go back for your other clothes. We'll buy you new

clothes when we get to America. The sergeant will stay with us until we board the ship. They want to make sure we don't miss it, I guess, but as soon as we're aboard, he'll leave us alone. When he does, I'll head for the rear of the ship and comm you as soon as I can; I can help transfer the satchels to the ship.>

<I will do this!>

***

T was still groggy when he woke up, but the added sleep had helped. Glancing at the door, he realized it was after dawn. The men had probably eaten by now, but maybe he could talk the cook into feeding him breakfast. Settling the ammo belt around his waist, he picked up his Springfield. The belt held five-round clips, 125 cartridges in all, plus two pouches that held four pistol magazines. A bayonet in its scabbard was on the left side and the holstered M1911 pistol hung from the right. Altogether, the belt weighed more than twenty pounds. By now, T was used to the weight and the new orders required each man to be fully armed at all times.

Mac was already at work, supervising men digging the mortar pit and positioning the machine guns. T paused with him while Mac brought him up to date.

Intelligence had spies of their own who reported that Semenoff's 'army' had left their camps two days before and headed southeast. Based on this, the lieutenant expected an attack within the next two days, but Mac believed attack might be imminent. Regimental intelligence wasn't necessarily accurate, and Semenoff had two armored trains for mobility, so he concentrated on improving the position in the camp's center, the final line of defense should the perimeter be breached.

Other men were deepening the trench around the outside of the new wall. It wouldn't stop the attackers, but it would slow them and might cause them to take cover. If so, thanks to advice from T, Mac had an unpleasant surprise in store for them. The undelivered shipment had contained several boxes of Mills grenades, and the

190

trench was an easy throw from the walls.

***

Keeping his voice low, Patrick asked, "Did you have any trouble?"

"No, everything went almost as planned. There were no guards, and I found the window and the satchels where you said. It took less than an hour and that was only because of the birds."

"Oh, the pigeons."

"Yes. I formed the bubble, because I was frightened! But I realized they were only birds and as frightened as I was, so I did not wish to kill them. They bounced off my bubble and flew away. When they had gone, I brought out the satchels, although they were heavy. I locked the window behind me as you said, though nothing of ours is there now."

"And boarding the ship?"

"'Twas—it was--also easy! I put the satchels of gold on top of a small building on the upper deck, then flew on board. There was no one around, although I could hear voices from the front of the ship."

"'Tis called the bow, but I understand what you mean. The crewmen are getting ready to take in the mooring lines. Then what?"

"I found a place I could hide right away, but 'tis not comfortable. There is a steel platform just above the steering board behind the ship. It is hidden by the curve of the ship's outside. I took some rope that was by one of the stairways and tied the satchels to the angled supports that are welded to the ship's side. If I have to hide, that is where I will go. It will be cold, but I brought my warm Russian fur coat. It makes the bag that holds my possessions very full and heavy, but that is not a problem."

"You're talking about a platform above the rudder post. If we run into stormy weather, *do not* go there! Waves will wash the satchels away, and if you're there they will wash you away too!"

"But I have the psy--cho--kin--etics. I will be safe, and there is

191

always the bubble!"

"Not good enough! You can die from drowning and if it's cold enough, you'll lose consciousness. It's not worth it, we can always get more money."

"But I do not want to lose the gold! I have never been rich before!"

"You've never been dead before either! You will do as I say!"

She slipped away in the gloom, and Patrick was forced to hope she had gotten the message. Moments later, the after guard showed up and told him to return to his berth while the ship got underway. He heard the commands to single up the lines, accompanied by the hiss of escaping steam, as he went down the ladder.

The ship shivered slightly, then rocked as the last lines were cast off. They were headed for San Francisco.

***

As soon as he found a quiet spot, he commed T.

<We're moving, sailing in half an hour as soon as the pilot gives the order. As soon as we reach San Francisco, Kat will go ashore. People will be moving around, lots of confusion, so it should be easy enough. I will then transfer the satchels to her. She and the money should be safe enough, and as soon as I can I'll join her and we'll find a place to stay until you get there.>

<I won't be long,> T replied. <We're abandoning the camp tomorrow, if possible, but we may have to put it off a day if Semenoff's army gets here before we leave. Mac says the lieutenant intends to play it by ear. The Czechs are in Vladivostok and some have probably shipped out by now, so that part of our mission is accomplished. As for us, Semenoff has two armored trains and about a thousand men. We could probably hold off a battalion, but if he brings his entire force we'll be overrun. Our best chance is to get out, but if we can't we'll fight it out right here.>

<Will you be all right?>

<Yeah. If he gets here before we leave, he'll get a bloody nose. Thanks to that shipment he never got, we now have several full-up

machine guns around the perimeter and BARs in between to cover any gaps. We could have gotten more, but we don't have enough trained crewmen and no time to train more. Mac has three or four mortars too, and they're dug in as part of the redoubt he's building in the middle of the camp. Not much ammo, we only had time for one trip to the explosives bunker. I could have brought more, but-- not with others around. The major told him to take whatever he could use, because he'd rather shoot the ammo at Semenoff than let him get his hands on it. Although he may get at least some of what's left over after we're gone, since we didn't manage to take everything. Him or the Bolsheviks, I don't suppose it matters, but we can't take the weapons with us so the plan is to blow up whatever we don't use before we move out. If we have time!>

<The armored trains are bad news,> sent Patrick. <but the last I heard he had only light artillery. Not enough range to shell the camp, but they may have mortars. His irregulars are afoot, but the Cossacks are mounted so watch out for them.>

<Against machine guns and automatic rifles? I hope they do come! We've got a line of abatis out front, trees with the limbs chopped off at a sharp angle, and no cavalry is going to get through those! And I'll have a surprise waiting if Semenoff's men try to move them.>

<Aye, I'll bet you will! But they may not attack; those scouts may have been checking to make sure you're still there, now that you're no longer doing the long-range patrols. Intelligence has been wrong before! They've avoided direct assaults, at least this year, although they did wipe out a platoon sized post last October.>

<I heard about that,> sent T, <but they're definitely showing interest and a couple of the listening posts heard movement last night. Could have been a bear, I suppose, but the sentries said it sounded like whispers. I might have picked up something telepathically, but I was asleep. Anyway, you understand why I can't leave now. Machine guns can jam, and even if they don't, they have to be allowed to cool between bursts to keep from

burning out the barrels.

<We're demolishing the buildings, the few that are left, so I'll be sleeping in a slit trench tonight. Most buildings are already gone. Mac's guys will need clear fields of fire if they get past the parapet. Good luck on the trip, remember to keep me advised, and I'll see you when I get there.>

***

Patrick commed T an hour later.

<We're on our way. Kat and the satchels are aboard. No bunk for her, but I stole a couple of blankets and she's bedded down on the roof over the control room. What's happening at the camp?>

<We're not under attack yet, but the firing step around the wall is manned around the clock. The lieutenant thinks they're coming.>

<But you'll get away before they get there, won't you? And they won't have a reason to follow.>

<Intelligence telephoned an update. Semenoff definitely knows now that the colonel won't be handing over the remaining weapons. I don't think we can leave, not without a fight. We'd be caught, strung out along the road, and wiped out.

<Semenoff picked up part of the shipment in Vladivostok a month ago, so he's better armed than we hoped; I guess the politicians decided it was more important to keep their promise to a damned *bandit* than to worry about the lives of a few soldiers! But we're still sitting on at least half of what they promised, including most of the ammunition. The major wanted to blow everything immediately, but the colonel isn't ready so here we sit, twiddling our thumbs! Semenoff's on his way and we'll have a fight on our hands when he gets here.>

<But what about you?>

<I've been in tougher spots. You worry about Kat and yourself, I'll see you in San Francisco, and don't forget to comm Ray when you get there. He'll help you.>

<I shall worry about you until you arrive!>

<Don't! I can take care of myself. It's my guys that I'm

concerned about, and that will last until they're on the train out of here. If anything, Semenoff should be worried!>

<T...?>

But there was no reply. T had broken the connection.

Chapter Twenty-two

That last time jump into the past took us too far back, Ray mused; *had we arrived in 1918 instead of 1919, T might have already returned to the US.*

After two subjective weeks away, Ray found sitting in front of the computer strange. But by the time the computer finished booting up, the old familiarity had returned. He began his search by scanning back-issues of the New York Times. It was slow going. Wouldn't the return of the Siberian expedition have made the news? But his efforts to narrow down the time to the period immediately after 1919 proved fruitless. Articles there were, some about Siberia, but the search engine was clumsy.

He scanned past a late-WWII article that mentioned that General Pershing was 'in spirit, again Over There' with the generals he'd helped train. Another time, perhaps...

He tapped the screen, scrolling down the newspaper pages. The search was frustrating. When would T get to the states? He narrowed his search to 'Doughboys Siberia' and the articles finally began appearing. One, dated Dec 22, 1919, was about 'Reds'. Some 249 of them, communists all, were being exiled to Soviet Russia on a ship called the Buford. Had the turmoil been settled by that time? But what of the soldiers of the AEF-Siberia? Perhaps if he researched the enemy general, Semenoff?

But the Cossack leader getting the headlines in 1919, at least in the Times, was named Deniken. Moments later he found mention of Semenoff, who had been arrested in April, 1922. Charged with looting half a million dollars during the Siberian campaign? Interesting! T had been right. Semenoff was more bandit than 'general'. Following it was another article. Semenov, as the name was now spelled, testified during his trial in Moscow that he had worked in close collaboration with Japanese generals during WWII. The old Cossack had survived that long?

Ray had better results from the Library of Congress, in particular the *Chronicling America* files. An article in the

Harrisburg, Pa Telegraph, November 14, 1919, was about a shipload of Christmas gifts for the doughboys in Siberia. So some at least were still there at that time. Frustrated, he closed the file and considered what he knew. It might be necessary to return to 1919, say in late December, and simply wait until T and his new friends arrived. But unlike his previous trips to the past, this time he would be better prepared. He'd given Libby the remaining coins, keeping the currency for himself, but that wouldn't be a problem. Instead of sorting through the caches to see what remained, simply pause long enough in the past to exchange some of the gold ingots for coins. Collectors often specialized, didn't they? He could pass as a collector of early double eagles and eagles.

Now that he knew more about time travel, a single time jump could take him back to 1925 Chicago. The city had any number of people who would accept gold; he could convert some of his raw gold there, then take the train to California. And after he arrived in California, go back in short, controlled jumps until he arrived in 1919. He could rent a hotel room then, even a house if that seemed best at the time, and simply wait. Why not? Exploring the past, especially in such a dynamic city as San Francisco, was the best possible tourist trip! What better way to use the gold?

But too *much* gold was better than too little, so he would refill the vest's pouches before heading into the past, and while he waited for T he could shop around and convert the rest to spendable coins. And not just gold; silver dollars or currency would be better for most minor purchases. For that matter, why not establish a reserve safe haven?

Ray leaned back, thinking. Suppose he bought land somewhere in California? He could build on the property, even buy land with a suitable house already there! It would need to be of stone or possibly adobe, and as earthquake-proof as possible. There had been a number of quakes since the great San Francisco quake, but perhaps if he avoided the fault zones near the coast? And set up a trust account to pay the taxes?

Doable, he decided. *The property would be there, waiting, and if by chance the authorities started sniffing around again in present-day Nevada, no one would suspect that the fugitives had gone into the past to hide!* Ray smiled at the thought. T would be pleased!

He almost overlooked the small article mentioning that a ship from Vladivostok had brought casualties from the AEF's Siberia contingent. It had docked in San Francisco on December 16th, 1919, but probably not what he was looking for; T had not been injured and it was very unlikely that he would have gotten sick, but did Corporal O'Brien have the body-protection Talent? Ray studied the reports, then made his decision. He would go back to that time and be there when the ship arrived. Easiest way, teleport east until he'd reached, say, 1920, then travel west.

Levitate, or take the train? Well, why not? People nowadays rode the old steam trains for the fun of it! How bad could they be?

***

"Go find Sergeant Mac. Ask him to come here," said T.

"Okay, Corporal. But what should I say if he's busy?" asked Private Salazar.

"Tell him I hear voices!"

"*Shit*, I don't hear anything! Are you sure?"

"On your way, Private!"

"Jeezus, Corporal. What if you're making a mistake?" asked Johnson. He was one of the new arrivals from the hospital.

"Don't worry about it, that's between First Sergeant Mac and me! But I didn't make a mistake; they're here! Smithers, your job is to kill as many as possible before they reach the ditch. The bodies will slow the follow-on attackers. As for you guys with the Mills grenades, just make sure you're careful! Mister Grenade is *not* your buddy after the pin is pulled, so make sure it falls in the ditch! And wait until they're *in* there before you pull that pin! They'll crowd together toward the front wall, and as soon as the first ones start to climb out, *that's* when you pull the pin and throw the grenades.

And *keep* throwing until they're all gone! The ditch's rear wall is sloped, so you've got some leeway; the bomb will roll downhill before it blows.

"Don't get excited, just do your job. Smithers will kill a few, so will the machine gunners, and I'll pick off the ones they miss." T motioned to the other men of his squad. "Poindexter, you're assistant gunner. If Smithers can't continue, you take over and Reynolds becomes your assistant. That BAR *has* to stay in action. The rest of you, wait for my signal. They'll have to clear the abatis first, and unless they brought fascines to fill in the ditch, that's where the real killing will happen."

"What about the mortar guys? Shouldn't they be told?"

"That's why I wanted Mac to come up. He'll see to the mortars and the redoubt's machine guns. The movement I hear is on this side, but I'm sure they're all around us."

"Damn, I wish I had your ears!" whispered Smithers.

Puffing, Mac arrived a few moments later. "What do you have, me young Corporal?"

"Movement, Top. They're being quiet now, but take a look at that bush over by the treeline. There's no wind, but watch closely. Someone's behind it. See him?"

"I'm not seeing...by all the saints!" A man stumbled into view, the astonished expression on his face clear to the watchers. He immediately scrabbled back behind the concealing shrub.

"Don't fire yet," whispered Mac. "Wait until they rush the wall. Can you hold them here? I'll be with the heavy weapons in the second line of defense, but 'twould make my day much more pleasant if not a one of the bastards reached the top! I'll be about alerting the lieutenant, and he may want to come up so do ye watch for him."

"What *about* your machine guns and mortars?" T asked.

"I wish we had more ammunition, so I do, but I'll be seeing that what we have isn't wasted. Do ye suppose I should be thanking General Semenoff? For 'tis rightly his weapons and ammunition that we're to be using!"

"He won't be with the ones rushing the wall, Top, even if he's here. But he *might* be back in the trees, and if he is I hope we can take him out. Meantime, I've got two cases of Mills bombs right here and Smithers is ready with his BAR. It's too bad there were no mines or barbed wire in that shipment, but the abatis and the ditch should slow them enough."

"Take care of yerself, Lad. I'll be speaking to ye when it's over. I'll...what in the world be they doin'?"

Across the open area, men had left the cover of the trees.

"Damned if I know! I wonder if they're drunk? Maybe they are, but drunk or sober, we will need those mortars. What about the guys on the other side of the perimeter?"

"Don't be teaching yer grandfather new tricks, me Boy! I sent a runner to alert the other corporals before I came here. And do ye try not to let Lieutenant Thornton do anything stupid when he comes up! He's a good officer, or will be if he lives long enough. I'll be getting back to the redoubt now, Lad. Hold them off as long as ye can."

"I'll do my best, Mac. Good luck."

"Soldier's luck to ye, Lad." Mac slipped quietly away, heading toward the final defensive position in the center of the camp. The lieutenant would roam around, but the redoubt was Mac's post during the attack.

T peered out between two logs and studied the cleared area. The trench, not as deep as he would have wished, surrounded the parapet. It would have to do. The cleared areas were covered by either a Lewis gun or one of the newer Brownings. The weapons could swivel in a wide arc, providing interlocking coverage all the way out to the woodline.

Inside the perimeter, the huts were gone, torn down, and even the firepits had been filled in. The mortars were in a pit behind the redoubt's trench, facing out, but the shipping canisters had held only two dozen bombs, meaning that each gun was limited to a maximum of eight. When they were gone the crewmen would move into the trench and serve as riflemen.

There was nothing more to be done. Now they waited. Tense, the men fingered the safety levers on their weapons.

Out beyond the treeline, the noises grew louder. The men they'd seen before milled around at the edge of the clearing. Had they been sent out to draw fire? It didn't make sense, but...

A hollow thump from back in the trees signaled that Semenoff's men had mortars of their own. Machine guns opened up from the woodline, the bullets thumping into the palisade. None of the bullets that hit in front of T's squad penetrated, but dust puffed out from the logs. Some sort of *heavy* machine gun, then. Russian?

The thick double-layered palisade soaked up most of the bullets, but occasional cries from wounded men meant that some had found chinks between the logs. Mortar rounds impacted the cleared area outside the camp, the ear-shattering crashes rendering the defenders temporarily deaf. T's men huddled close to the wall as the explosions walked toward the palisade. He glanced out just as the first round landed among the abatis, blowing a hole in the line. Moments later, a man wearing a greatcoat and swinging a sword ran into view, and the ones who'd left cover before joined him. T realized they held no rifles, only coiled ropes. But they had swords of their own, hence potentially dangerous. If they got inside...

But they headed immediately for the damaged abatis and began tying the ropes around the shattered trunks, intending to drag them away and widen a breach for the assault force that would be coming next.

"Wait for it...not yet!" T yelled, his voice carrying beyond his small detachment. "Hold the grenades in your hand, finger through the ring! They're still working on the abatis, so let the BARs and machine guns stop them. *Your* job is to kill the ones that get into the trench!"

BARs chattered, distinct because they cycled slightly faster than the machine guns, and the men working on the abatis began falling. The fire was answered by a storm of shots from the treeline. Concealed machine guns rattled out there, paused to let the barrels cool slightly, then tac-tac-tacked again.

There were openings now where the abatis line had been. But so far, there was no sign of cavalry. Were the Cossacks waiting for the breaches to widen? The firing spread and soon every weapon on the wall was in action.

Infantry charged from the treeline, shooting as they came. Guerrillas, not Cossacks! They wore ordinary peasant clothing, not uniforms, and were virtually identical to the bandits that kidnapped Kat.

The sword-swinging Cossack had gone down first, only a few feet from the treeline.

Realizing the unarmed ones were no immediate threat, PFC Smithers' shifted his fire. The bullets pecked busily at the charging men, dropping one or two, then moved on to the others. Around the wall, machine guns paused briefly as assistants fed in new belts, then picked up again.

The sound of mortars firing from inside the redoubt had stopped. But judging by the smoke above the trees, they had done their job.

"Good shooting, Smithers! Keep your head down—that heavy machine gun over there is back in action!" But the warning came too late. Poindexter rolled Smithers' body aside and slid behind the BAR, waiting. Seeing no immediate target, he changed the partially-depleted magazine and looked at T. "Just like that! Stay close to the wall. Our mortars have stopped but there's no telling about theirs."

Out in the treeline, the heavy machine gun had gone quiet again. "That machine gun has either been knocked out or they're moving it to concentrate on other targets! See if you can knock down the rest of those men with the ropes!"

Poindexter nodded, tin hat sliding. T grinned and Poindexter grinned back. The BAR chattered, a long burst that emptied the new magazine. Well, he would get the hang of it; after all, he'd only had two days to practice. But if he didn't keep on shooting, an overheated barrel was the least of their worries. "Grenade crews, get ready! Here they come!"

The ditch was too wide to jump. The enemy soldiers, those that had survived the trip across the cleared zone, huddled against the front wall, sheltering from the defensive fires. "Grenades now!" T yelled. "Pull the pin and throw!"

The first grenades exploded and soon there were others. The drunken cries and battle yells changed to screams as shrapnel tore into the men sheltering in the ditch. "Jones, you're in charge here! Keep the grenades going and make sure the BAR stays in action," T yelled.

"Got it! Where you going, Corporal?"

"Right over there, to Corporal Heintzelman's area! They're coming over the wall!"

Jones nodded, but T had no time to notice. Firing his rifle as he advanced, he shot two men off the wall before his firing pin snapped on an empty chamber. Drawing his bayonet, he snapped it into the barrel lug and raced ahead. Three other attackers were inside the wall now, but their weapons were also empty. Dropping the rifles, they drew their swords as he approached. Behind them others were climbing over to join the first three.

"Now ye'll not be having them all for yerself, me boy!" Mac had drawn his pistol and was firing left-handed. His right hand hung awkwardly at his side, blood running down his arm.

"Stay behind me, Mac! You watch for any trying to get around us, I've got this!"

Chapter Twenty-three

Tired men sat behind their guns, looking at nothing.

Lieutenant Thornton limped away from the perimeter and found Sergeant Mac. "Tell you the truth, Lieutenant, I've niver seen anything like it! 'Twas the *madness* came upon him! He had a pistol, but niver used it. I asked him why and he said he just forgot he had one! He had been thinking about using his rifle since he joined up, d'ye see, and when it went empty, he charged that bunch with the bayonet." Mac shook his head in wonder. "*Niver* did I see the like!"

"I understand you accounted for at least two of them," said Lieutenant Thornton.

"Aye, three I'm thinking before my pistol went empty. I saw them fall after I fired, so I did, and 'twas but a pace or two away. I dropped the pistol and took out me trench knife, but by then 'twas over. 'Twas a flashing of swords...I *niver* thought to see anything like that!—and then Corporal Tyler's bayonet. A *marvel*, it was. He did not stab, he chopped through necks! 'Tis possible, I own, but 'tis not the way men are taught!"

"You didn't drop your pistol, Mac. Private Johnson said you threw it at them. And our men are taught to use the bayonet on one enemy at a time."

"Well, I may have done," Mac admitted. "D'ye know that Tyler killed eight of them? There was another, had his leg over the parapet he did, but when he saw what was happening he ran away. Niver heard such screaming! 'Twas if he'd seen the very angel of death! 'Twas after that when the rest of thim outside the parapet ran away too. I'm thinkin' that action broke the attack. Tis recommending Tyler for the Medal of Honor I'll be! Did ye see it?"

"No, I was down by then. I caught a bullet in my leg. You were wounded too," Lieutenant Thornton pointed out.

"Ah, 'twas nothing. I've cut meself worse *shavin'*, so I have." Mac glanced at the bloody cloth wrapped around his forearm. "Broke the small bone, but 'twill heal fast enough, I'm thinking."

"It wasn't only Tyler," Thornton said. "They were starting to pull back, but he might well have been the final straw. I didn't expect them to press as hard as they did! According to what I read, mercenaries won't do that! But they did, so maybe Asians are different. Write up your report, First Sergeant. If that's your writing arm that got shot, get one of the men to help. I'll be writing my own report later this afternoon. Casualties among our people?"

"Nine men killed, two that probably won't make it to the hospital. One of them is Corporal Heintzelman."

"Damn! You're sure?"

"He'll not last until the morrow, Sir. Shot through the right lung, he is, but he got to be a corporal before it happened, so that's something."

"I suppose so. I'll have to write the families. And the enemy dead?"

"At least a company, I'm thinking, but we don't have a count yet. There are more back in the woods, d'ye see? 'Twas a good idea, putting that trench out ahead of the parapet to slow them up, and Tyler's idea of throwing grenades into it paid off."

"Busy man, our Corporal Tyler! Be sure and mention his role in your report, then see how many witnessed his bayonet charge." Lieutenant Thornton leaned back in his chair. "He won't get the Medal of Honor, Mac, or even the new Distinguished Service Cross. It's a shame, but this was a minor action at best compared with the Western Front, and anyway we're pulling out tomorrow. The general may never hear what happened here, and I can't see the War Department approving a medal even if he does. Right now, they're concentrating on getting us out with the fewest casualties. It's politics and I'm sorry, but that's the way it is. The colonel has the authority to award a Silver Star, so I'll see about getting Tyler decorated as soon as we get to Vladivostok.

"The important thing is that Semenoff's bandits won't get that shipment. What's left will be blown up when the battalion headquarters detachment pulls out. Should make a fine big bang, and it will probably destroy the camp too, what with all that

205

dynamite in the bunker. Assign a detail—not Tyler's squad—to collect the enemy weapons and bury the bodies. Put the ones from the open area in the trench with the rest. Have the men throw a few shovels of dirt over them and that should be enough. The ones in the woods? You might as well leave them, but try to get a count. By the time they get ripe, we'll be out of here. Get an accurate count of enemy weapons and then destroy them. The major will want to know the numbers, and for that matter, so will the colonel. Ready for a refill?"

"Aye, Sir. And thanks! The coffee was good, and the sweetener was better!"

Lieutenant Thornton topped off both cups, then divided the remaining brandy equally before adding it.

"'Tis a shame that we lost good men defending a place that we're handing back to the enemy," observed Mac.

"Semenoff won't occupy it," Thornton said. "He wanted the weapons. He hit us because he couldn't afford to leave us in his rear when he attacked battalion headquarters. But the upshot is that not only won't he get the weapons, we've crippled him at least for a while. We won't have a problem pulling out tomorrow morning."

"Aye, Sir, I expect you're right. Form up the men at 8 ack emma?"

"Yes. Tell me about the demolition plan."

"Tyler is in charge of that, and I've given him the men from Corporal Heintzelman's squad to help. They'll set the explosives right after breakfast and he'll light the fuses as soon as we're far enough away to be safe. He'll rejoin his squad and they'll act as rear guard until we board the train."

"I won't be sorry to see the last of this place!" said Lieutenant Thornton. "We'll load the walking wounded first, then board the train by squads. You'll board with me after the other wounded; your 'scratch' is bleeding again. Tyler's squad will board last. I would, or you would, but since we're wounded he's earned the honor."

"Aye, Sir. I'll be folding Corporal Heintzelman's people in

with Tyler's squad permanently when we get to Vladivostok. 'Tis not long for this world he is; will ye see him before he dies, Sir?"

"Yes, and from the sound of it I'd better hurry. He did well too."

"Aye. Bronze Star, I'm thinking?"

"Write it up, Mac. I'll endorse your recommendations and I'm sure the colonel will approve the awards."

***

Ray reexamined his plan, looking for flaws.

Nothing for it; he would need to spend time in San Francisco, waiting, or try more hit-or-miss comms and see if he got a response. T would hear as soon as their time synchronized, and for that matter, so would Corporal O'Brien and the girl. Ray shook his head, an unconscious gesture. T had reacted as expected; he was death on mistreatment of children, particularly girls, a hangover from his service in Afghanistan. Still thinking about what he would do, Ray rejected the idea of attempting a contact after every teleport. There had been too much paranormal activity already, and probably they were fortunate it hadn't caused more of a paradox! But there was no mention in any of the articles he'd scanned of unusual activities, so maybe this time they'd gotten away with it, and at the cost of only two new Talents that had survived. The third, Dolan, was apparently no loss to anyone. Like Solaris and his gang, some Talents didn't deserve to live.

He could take a hotel room in San Francisco. It was a town accustomed to transients, after all. He might even look at property nearby, not just watch for arrivals from Vladivostok. Thinking more about property, he realized they'd overlooked something. But to do what he intended, he would need more gold. Donning his vest, he headed for the mine.

There was no sign of Bobby when he landed, and the place felt deserted. Ray frowned; had Bobby simply gone away without even saying goodbye? Or had he been unable to contact him while he and Libby were in the past? Objectively he'd been gone a relatively short time, but traveling through time was tricky. Even so, the gold should be here...

Ray drifted down the side tunnel, looking for the apparently-collapsed roof. He found it, but it was obvious that Bobby had done more work since the last time Ray had been here; there was a pile of old shoring with several broken pieces dumped near the cave-in. Even if someone did get this far, they would see that and back away.

Lifting higher to clear the broken rock, Ray's flashlight played across the broken wood, returning a faint greenish glint. The anomaly slipped his mind moments later, as soon as the lamp illuminated the gold beyond the fallen rock.

How much had Bobby taken? He had intended to take his share, but the small chamber was stacked nearly half-full of ingots! If any had been taken since he'd seen it last, it didn't show; Bobby must have cleaned out another pocket, a rich one.

Ray eased through the small space above the broken rock and landed atop the gold. He spotted a paper and picked it up; unsigned, but it had clearly been written by Bobby. *I couldn't contact you when I was ready to leave. I cleaned out the second pocket I mentioned. There's at least one more pocket deeper in the mountain. I got other twinges past that, but I couldn't get a precise location. I'm sure T can locate it if you want to mine it.*

There's a souvenir in the broken timber, something left by the original owner I'm guessing. I'll be back one day. Meantime, enjoy the gold. You'll never have to mine another day unless you want to.

What was that about a souvenir? The gold ingots were souvenir enough! Ray laid the note aside, intending to show it to T when he got back. Filling the empty pockets in his vest took only a few minutes, and there were so many ingots that he could barely tell he'd taken any. Gold...it was only important if you didn't have it, and clearly they had more than they would ever need!

He returned to the ranch and consulted his map. They'd gone back a total of how many miles, before they'd started the short trips to narrow in their destination? Maybe this time, one jump to

Chicago? Then exchange some of his raw gold and take the train to San Francisco? San Francisco was still the west in 1925, the estimated arrival year after the Chicago time jump, so jeans, his old black Stetson, and a thick sheepskin coat and gloves should work.

No longer worried about Libby, Ray intended to teleport east from an altitude where he'd be sure of clearing the mountains. He wouldn't be at that altitude long, but—.

He tucked the small oxygen bottle inside his vest so that it was making contact with his skin. Pulling the mask into place, he levitated. The GPS unit that he was using to determine his altitude here in Nevada would, with the mask and oxygen canister, be dumped somewhere it wouldn't be found for years. Lake Michigan would work. Fifteen thousand feet, maybe a bit more?

Ray rotated until he was facing due east, checked the compass a final time, and teleported.

***

Corporal O'Brien joined Kat on the ship's fantail. Behind them, the bubbles that had trailed them across the northern Pacific had diminished as the ship slowed. The stern was deserted, except for the two of them; the starboard bow was crammed with soldiers, those who could walk, all anxious to catch sight of the city.

"I brought as much food as I could," Patrick said. "I'm sorry I couldn't get more, but the cooks are watching me now. It should be enough until we leave the ship and as soon as we're away, we'll find a place to get a real dinner. Ready?"

"Aye!" said Kat. "'Tis anxious I am!"

"Don't overdo the accent. There are Irish around, railroad workers and such, and one may ask ye which town in County Cork ye hail from!"

"Okay. Are we nearly there?"

"An hour, two at the most, before we dock. 'Tis a slow process, easing into the wharf. 'Twill be after sunset before we're tied up, although perhaps not yet dark. I'm thinking they may not allow us to leave the ship until tomorrow."

"I would like to go tonight!" said Kat. "I have had problems with a soldier. I think he knows I am a girl."

"It will be dark by the time we arrive," said O'Brien thoughtfully. "But can ye make the shore by levitating? Ye'll have to go quite high, so make sure ye have a large base under you, enough for the trip. At the same time, ye'll need light on the shore to land."

"I think I can do it. I have not, not yet, but..."

"The most important thing is that ye not fall into the bay. Let me think." Moments later, he continued. "I could lift ye to the wharf when we dock, so I could, and that way, ye'll not need to go so high. I can pass ye the duffle bags with the gold too, but getting off the wharf is a problem. I think I'll have to come with ye."

"I would feel better if you did!"

"Well, I intended to ask for a discharge anyway, even if the Army doesn't decide I'm medically unfit. 'Tis no great matter to hurry things along a bit, I'm thinking. We'll go in two trips. I'll help ye reach the wharf, pass the duffle bags to ye, then join ye. We'll look for a deserted place on the shore. I'll be bringing me duffle bag up from the hold now. Is yours still up in the crosstrees?"

"No; I moved it again. It's on the roof atop the steps, what the sailors call a ladder. A sailor started up the ladder to that high platform when we sailed into the bay. He would have been below the crosstrees, but I thought 'twas better the bags not be above him, but he's gone now."

"I'll only be a few minutes. Bring your bag to where we are, and as soon as we've docked, we'll leave from here."

***

But departing from the fantail proved impossible. The visible locations were busy. They would have to find a higher place, high enough to see past the activity.

Kat reminded Patrick that the lookout's post on the forward mast was deserted, now that the ship was being pushed by the tugboat. They landed there moments later and took stock of the view from what would have been the crow's nest on a sailing ship. "'Tis dim over there, past the first two lighted areas. I'll set ye down on that spot between the lights 'Tis dark enough, I'm thinking, and deserted. Ye'll remain until I arrive, but they're unlikely to look there anyway. Are ye ready?"

She nodded and Patrick lifted her until she vanished in the darkness above the deck. Concentrating, transferred her the hundred yards or so until she was over the wharf, he lowered her into the patch of darkness. Moments later, the two duffle bags eased onto the wharf by where she was standing. Patrick glanced around, a last look at the ship that represented all that was left of his military service, and levitated.

Chapter Twenty-four

<We're in San Francisco, T. Kat had to leave the ship, so I went with her. We brought the gold with us,> Patrick sent.

<Good luck, then, and you'd better be thinking of new names for yourselves! As for us, we'll be leaving the camp soon. I thought today, but we've heard nothing so far. There was a fight, and it was a close thing for a while, but we broke the attack. The enemy are gone now, the live ones anyway; they lost somewhere between two hundred and three hundred men! There were more farther back in the woods where most of the mortar shells hit, and the lieutenant said to just leave them. The rest are probably still running. We've been told we're to go to Vladivostok first, but I don't suppose the order matters. The whole AEF-S is being withdrawn. I expect the last of us to reach the US within a month.

<Ray doesn't think you can teleport to the future, and he's the guy with experience. You may want to give it a try, just to be sure, but I would suggest you only try to go a few seconds ahead if you do. Leave yourself a way to return to where you are now, and if you can't, it won't cause much of a disruption. You should probably have Kat with you, just in case something happens and you end up on a different timeline. Maybe link her mind with yours before you teleport?>

<Aye, I'll do that. And if it doesn't work, we'll make our way east and find someplace to live where there are only a few people. Or go to Alaska, if the east doesn't work out. We're both accustomed to the weather!>

<That's probably best. Good luck, and if I don't see you before you go, I was glad to have had the chance to know both of you.> With that, T dropped the connection.

"Well. I promised you a proper dinner, Lass, so I did," said Patrick. "Would ye prefer fish or a steak?"

They walked along the street, two anonymous soldiers carrying duffle bags over their shoulders, in appearance much like the many others in uniform, soldiers and sailors both. Patrick realized that the criminal element, always present, wouldn't hesitate to accost them, but if they did, it might even be fun! He unconsciously touched the pigsticker beneath his uniform blouse, on the left side with the brass knuckle guard facing forward and resting just above his belt.

***

Kat had devoured the huge steak and a baked potato, then asked for a slice of pie. The steak had been overcooked and tough, but it was far better than the necessarily-skimpy meals Patrick had smuggled out of the troopship's mess. Patrick contented himself with the mesquite-broiled filet of a yellowtail caught only that morning, accompanied by a baked potato. The server had frowned at his choice—most preferred rice with fish—but if the Irish corporal wanted a potato, he would have a potato.

"I think we should have a look about, Lass. There's bound to be a seller of clothing this close to the waterfront. Ye...you!...will need proper clothing and so will I. The uniforms will attract attention later, and if something goes wrong when we try to teleport, 'tis best if we do it in ordinary civilian clothing."

"Yes," agreed Kat. "I'll be glad to change out of the uniform, but I do like the trousers. Women wear them here, do they not?"

"Some do, I'm thinking, and 'tis more practical if the teleport fails."

"I've been thinking about that," Kat said. "Why should we try to go into the future? I agree that both of us owe a great deal to Soldier T, but the things he remembered! Flying in a great metal machine? Levitation is quite bad enough, but at least I am in control! I am fearful of this future, where people are crushed to death in automobiles. Compared with Siberia, this land is wonderful just as it is. I wish more spoke Russian, but that seems a small price to pay."

"And do ye think that living where there are few people would disappoint ye, Lass? What of schooling?"

"I would like to go to a school," Kat agreed, "but what I need most is practice. I have many of T's memories now, and it but remains to make them my own through practice. Can we not buy a book for me to read? And one about ciphering? I understand some of what I found in his mind, but this al-ge-bra is very strange! I wonder why people bother to learn it?"

Patrick nodded. "Trigonometry is also strange, lass, but I can see that it would be very useful. Maybe we can get several books. I too would like to use what I found when T joined his mind with mine. But what about living away from cities?"

"I have always lived on a farm. 'Twas only for a short time I lived in the town, and I did not like it! I would rather live on a farm."

"My family lived on a farm when I was but a child," mused Patrick. "Then the potato crop failed, and we were expelled from the land. I will not rent land again, but at the same time a man without land is not complete. I will buy a farm, or perhaps a ranch, with the gold. I will have a place where I can grow me own food and call no man master! The army was good to me in some ways, but I always intended to retire someday and buy land of me own."

"We have the money," agreed Kat. "And did not T say that we could use it? And that he could always find more for himself? We could live together on this farm or ranch."

"Aye, he did. So ye're saying we should not try for the future at all? 'Tis a fearful place, I own, with uncounted numbers of motorcars and huge trucks going thither and yon. The important thing, I'm thinking, is that we do not cause others in T's past to become as we are, Talented. We must use our new abilities only in emergency. Do ye agree?"

"Aye," she agreed, with no realization of how incongruous it was to hear a Russian girl speak with an Irish accent. "But if we buy a farm, we will not need to spend all of the money, I'm thinking, and did not the people of the town where T lived farm the land?"

"They did, but 'tis a land where it seldom rains. And few grow potatoes, I'm thinking. 'Tis all I really know about farming."

"But the winters are mild and the snow lasts but a short time," Kat pointed out. "And do the people not bring water from the mountains for their crops? I could have chickens and goats and sheep!"

"Aye, and cows, even horses," Patrick agreed. "And pigs! We could cure our own hams, so we could! I remember the how of it from when I was but a lad."

"But first, we need clothes," Kat pointed out. "And new names! I shall keep Kat, I think, but my father is dead and there's no reason to keep to his name. I could be Kat O'Brien, could I not? Or Kat Wilson, like the American president?"

"'Tis a thought! If we hold to our first names, why, we'll niver forget to respond when someone calls!"

"So let us go find clothes," said Kat. "There are many businesses still open, are there not?"

"It would seem so. A farmer would be abed by now, but city people are different. We'll walk for a bit and watch for a place we can change some of the gold coins for American money. A merchant would cheat us if we offered gold, I think."

"He would regret it," said Kat.

***

Many of the businesses had closed before they found a place that looked like it might have what they wanted. Patrick had spent most of his silver coins for the dinners and they hadn't found a gold buyer as yet, but maybe...

The proprietor was short, elderly, and judging by his name, Jewish. Moshe Abramson agreed to accept gold as payment, and invited them to look around while he examined the coin Patrick handed him.

Kat headed for the section with women's clothing while Patrick wandered the aisles. Mister Abramson apparently dealt in used goods as well as new. He found a section with guns and stopped for a moment. There were shotguns, mostly older double-barreled models best suited for black powder. But it was being replaced by the more-powerful smokeless powder that was less inclined to rust barrels, and an older shotgun might not be able to handle the higher pressures. Mixed in with the various brands of revolvers were several Colt M-1911s and a handful of Lugers. There were rifles too, including several Springfields. *Overpriced, and probably junk,* thought Patrick. But one of the old rifles, a Spencer carbine, appeared to have been well taken care of even if it was obsolete. It was cheap, but—

Regretfully, he shook his head and walked on. *We can always get guns, but until we buy our farm we'll not be needing them*, he decided.

He soon found what he was looking for, denims and a selection of warm coats. There were backpacks, too, just past the men's clothing. Most were used Army versions, but they'd be better than the awkward duffle bags. He added two backpacks to the growing pile on the counter just as Mister Abramson came out.

"Your coin is genuine," he said. "Sometimes they're not," he shrugged, "but I've seen this kind before. Souvenir of Japan, is it? And you have more like it?"

"Aye, souvenirs," agreed Patrick. "And how much would ye be a-givin' me for that one?"

"Well, it's a little smaller than an eagle, so it's not worth as much. Still, I think I could allow...how about five dollars?"

"How about ten dollars? Ye be making a profit on the clothes, 'tis not needful to rob me when ye change me money too!" He settled down to haggle with Mister Abramson while Kat wandered over to where Patrick had found his denim pants and jacket.

The final price for the coin was just short of ten dollars. Patrick changed several at that price, after paying for the things they'd bought. The old merchant would be making a healthy profit, but Patrick decided it didn't matter. Indeed, if his profit was high enough, he would be unlikely to tell anyone where he'd gotten the coins!

Patrick chatted with the old man while Kat took pants and a shirt to the rear of the store and changed. She would have to keep her Russian boots; none of the ones Mister Abramson had for sale would fit her.

"They're warm for California, the coats. I bought them from a sailor who decided he'd had enough of the sea, especially off Alaska," Moshe probed.

"Why, 'tis the very place we're going, my niece and I!" Patrick said. "'Tis said there's still gold to be found by an enterprising fellow, and I mean to try my luck."

"Your niece, you said?" asked Moshe. "But she's dressed like a soldier!"

"My sister's child, and my spare uniform was better than what she had. Died of the lung disease, my sister did. Her husband was killed in a coal mine explosion and there was no one to take my niece in. Family is important, ye know, and I know what the workhouses are like. I'd not be seeing her turned over to strangers."

"No, I can understand that. Well, she looks a proper young girl now, wouldn't you say?" Moshe beamed, as Kat joined them. "But what of your uniform, young lady?"

"I don't want it and 'twill no longer fit my uncle. "Tis glad I am to be rid of it! Will ye also change now, Uncle?" Patrick winked at her where the old man wouldn't see, then headed for the back to put on his own denim trousers and cotton shirt.

***

Ray popped into existence high above a flat, heavily-farmed plain. Confused for a moment, he realized that he was probably south of Chicago. Indiana had few cities in the area, if his teleport had been as accurate as he'd hoped, but in any case if he went due north he would eventually wind up in view of one of the Great Lakes.

Descending to just above the trees that skirted the fields, he consulted his compass and flew north. Fifteen minutes later, he spotted the lights of a town. Too small to be Chicago—

The town was an estimated mile ahead when he landed beside a gravel road.

The town appeared to be typical of small towns of the early 20th Century. There was a courthouse, closed now, and benches lining the street in front. He found a newspaper in a trash receptacle beside a bench, the Logansport Pharos-Tribune. It was dated August 12th, 1923. His teleport had brought him to just about where he'd intended, but a year or two earlier.

The front page consisted mostly of advertising; the few news articles were limited to one or two paragraphs with the remainder of the story inside on pages two and three. Ray returned the crumpled paper to the trash can and sat down to think. There was obviously some sort of 'port' here, but not on Lake Michigan. A river, perhaps? But it was Indiana, and that was close enough. Few people were about and no one paid attention to the nondescript stranger walking along the road.

Chicago would be north and probably slightly west of here. Best of all, there would be a restaurant open (the two he'd seen n Logansport were closed, the cardboard sign in the door proclaiming that fact) and a depot where he could board a westbound train. And maybe a place to exchange some of the gold ingots? If not, he could leave the train in one of the western states where mining was a major industry. An assay office might buy gold. If he stopped in a small town and made it obvious that he was only traveling through, he could exchange his gold and avoid questions he couldn't answer.

Finally clear of the town's outskirts, Ray levitated and flew north.

Chapter Twenty-five

"It is not much of a beard," said Kat.

"Give it time," grinned Patrick. "I only stopped shaving two days ago!"

"It is not even *black*, like a good Russian beard! It is brown and hard to see!"

"Ah, well. I'll just have to make the best of it, I suppose."

The two were walking south. Somewhere up ahead, according to the sign, lay the village of San Jose. Hopefully, they would find a deserted spot soon where they could levitate. They wouldn't go far, only to the depot where they would catch a train going east. But to do that, first they had to go south; Patrick had decided that catching the train in San Francisco would be too dangerous. He would have been reported missing by now, presumed lost at sea. Suppose someone recognized him? No, it was far safer to head south, then take the Southern Pacific east. All the way to New York, but they didn't plan to stay long. Patrick thought his father might have returned by now, so they would spend a few days in the city and ask around among the Irish. By then Patrick's beard would have grown out fully, they would have broken their trail, and they could head west and look for land.

They hiked, and endured the aches caused by the straps supporting the heavy packs that ate into their shoulders. When they stopped later that day in San Jose, they introduced themselves: Patrick Spencer and his niece, Katherine Wilson, called Kat.

The depot agent smiled as he handed over the tickets. What a nice young man! And his niece would be a real beauty one day, after she grew up! And added a few more pounds, of course. Why, she was as skinny as a boy!

***

Ray ruefully decided that taking the train had not been his best idea!

It was slow and bumpy compared to modern trains, not to

mention dirty. The car also leaked, not that that was a problem after they crossed into Missouri. The clouds vanished and the sun came out, but the passengers soon exchanged one bit of discomfort for another. Coal smoke inevitably found its way through unseen cracks, and the passengers could more often than not be smelled before he saw them! For that matter, Ray himself likely smelled as bad by now...if anyone noticed.

He wanted a shower, but a bath would have to do. He also wanted a change of clothes and a chance to stretch his legs and look around. The mountains were behind him now; this was a land of streams and pleasant valleys between hills. Ray left the train in Placerville, a small town that had survived the decline in gold production and was now the seat of El Dorado County.

Promising name, Ray decided. Not that they would need the money, but a section of land near a small town? This might be exactly what he was looking for!

The cook was Chinese, but the cuisine was standard American. Ray ordered a steak, which came with a baked potato and mixed vegetables. After eating, he walked up the single street, looking for a hotel. A number of houses stood empty, likely abandoned after the rush ended, but they were not what he was looking for. Strangers could not suddenly appear in the middle of a small town without attracting notice! The ideal property would be someplace out in the country.

There were apparently few good roads, or at least none that joined the town's main street. But that wasn't a problem, Ray thought; if anything, it was an advantage. He found a livery stable at the outskirts of town, and the liveryman did indeed have horses to rent. Ray picked out a sorrel gelding to ride and a bay gelding to carry supplies for a week. He paid in advance, then started a conversation with the liveryman as he expertly packed the bay.

"Bears up in them hills, this time of year. Been dry and they're hungry. You don't have a rifle?"

"Don't need one. I'll leave them alone if they leave me alone."

"They likely will, but watch out for my hosses! You're not a

220

prospector, are you?"

"Nope, just thought I'd take a look around. Seems pleasant enough," Ray said.

"It is. Good description, and east of here's a place called Pleasant Valley. Already a few farms there, and more up north. You a land speculator?"

"What makes you say that?"

"You're not a miner, and fishing around here ain't worth a fellow's time. You don't have a rifle so you're not a hunter either, not that we get many. Not here; better hunting up in the mountains. But if you're interested in land, a cousin of mine's got a ranch he wants to sell. Growing part of the country! Buy a place here and a fellow can't go wrong."

"You don't say!" Ray said enthusiastically. "What kind of a ranch does your cousin have?"

"Mostly valley land, with some bordering hills. He raises horses and cattle. Dependable water. Thinks he'd like to live in town, maybe move to Fresno. Neither one of us is getting younger. Say, you wouldn't be interested in a livery stable, would you? Hard work, especially shoeing the horses, but it brings in a good living. And people are always going to need hosses!"

"No, that's not what I've got in mind, but I may take a look at that ranch you mentioned. You sure he wants to sell?"

"He mentioned it a few months ago. Go east about ten miles to get to his place. Just follow the road; it's dirt, but pretty good except when it rains. You'll come to a tall ridge, timbered on top, and there's a track that skirts the ridge off to the south. The road follows the ridge for about five miles and you'll come to a log house that's just inside the tree line, north of the track. My cousin's name is Sam, just tell him Wayne sent you. If you like the looks of the country, I mean. Watch out for the dogs. Give Sam a holler from the gate. Likely he'll be out back, working in the corral."

"Sounds good, Wayne. I'll be glad to take a look at it. I figure two or three days."

"If you feel like looking around the ranch, just turn my hosses into the corral. Sam will outfit you and show you around. You'll like the place."

"He own it free and clear? No bank loan?"

"Well...be best if you talked to him about that."

Ray smiled to himself. Not only a nice stretch of country with a small town not too far away, but he could likely get it at a good price! The smile became a chuckle. Wasn't that what land speculators did?

***

As it happened, the post wasn't abandoned for more than a week. By then, the odor of decomposing bodies from the woods and the trench was almost overpowering.

Semenoff had complained via telegraph to President Wilson that the agreed-upon numbers of weapons had not been delivered. He boasted that only he could prevent the Bolsheviks from taking over the country, but to do that he needed modern weapons!

Wilson forwarded the message to the State Department, who sent it on to the War Department. A query was sent to General Graves, who responded. Lieutenant Thornton was ordered to delay leaving the camp.

Cables went back and forth for a day or two more, with State insisting that the arrangement they'd made with General Semenoff be honored and the War Department complaining heatedly about arming enemies in the field. But finally a message was sent to General Graves. Who in turn, sent instructions down the line to Colonel Morrow, who forwarded them to Major Avery. Who thought about it, realizing that the US Army would soon be out of this pesthole. What to do?

He issued his own orders, one to Lieutenant Thornton, the other to his Sergeant Major. He trusted the man, because they had served together a number of times, beginning when Major Avery was a green Second Lieutenant and Sergeant Major Mathis was a corporal.

So an order had been given to Lieutenant Thornton, and now it was time to carry it out. The men packed their belongings before dawn and lined up near the gate. Despite the lack of activity, they carried their weapons fully loaded and on safe. Mac notified the lieutenant the men were waiting.

"Got everything ready, Corporal Tyler?" asked Lieutenant Thornton.

"Yes, Sir. The explosives are in place and I'll light the fuses myself, right after everyone leaves."

"Give us time to get clear, but don't take too long catching up. I wouldn't be surprised if there were still a few snipers in the trees! There's something I have to do before we leave, but I'll only be a minute."

Lieutenant Thornton turned to the members of the detachment. Mac had formed them into two rows while the lieutenant talked to T, and now they were standing at attention, rifles held across their chests. Lieutenant Thornton nodded in satisfaction. The wound to his arm hadn't slowed down the old noncom. He raised his voice and addressed the men. "It's always a sad time when we abandon a post! But this one has served its purpose, and now it's time for us to go home. You are *veterans*! You confronted an enemy that heavily outnumbered you, and won! Be proud! You did what you were ordered to do, and served honorably in the best traditions of the United States Army. I am honored to have served with you. Some of you will be discharged when we reach home, others will remain in uniform. But some will remain here, good men all. They will not be forgotten. Detachment! Present....**arms**!"

Calloused hands snapped against stocks as rifles were brought to the salute. The pause lasted for several seconds, giving Lieutenant Thornton time to do an about face, salute the fresh graves in the small cemetery, then turn once again to face his troops. The maneuver was carried out awkwardly because of the clumsy cast on his leg and the crutch under his arm, but he managed.

"Order...**arms**! At **ease**! First Sergeant MacAuliffe, post the advance guard and the flank guards!"

Mac nodded to the waiting men he'd already detailed and walked with the lieutenant to help him if needed. But Lieutenant Thornton, face set, hobbled unaided to the two-wheeled cart. A pair of soldiers stood waiting, drawbars in hand. Three seriously-wounded men lay in the bed of the cart on folded blankets, taking up almost all the room. Thornton turned around and carefully backed into position at the front of the cart, then with Mac's help lifted his wounded leg and got his heel over the right-hand drawbar before sitting down. The leg had been throbbing; now it simply hurt.

Seated, he nodded to Mac. "I'm ready, First Sergeant. Take the column."

Mac gave the necessary orders and the cart moved off down the track. The remaining soldiers marched behind it. If a few looked back at the camp that had been their home for almost two years, it was not to be wondered at.

"Keep one hundred yards behind the column," T told PFC Skinner, his new assistant squad leader. "I'll catch up after I light the fuses. Don't worry if I'm a little slow, I want to make sure all the charges go off. I'll catch up before you reach the train stop."

T waited until they had gone around the curve, some two hundred yards away. The coiled fuses lay together and it was the work of a moment to light them. He made sure they were all burning, then slipped into the trees. Moments later he was airborne, but heading away from where the after guard had gone.

Behind him, plumes of dust and smoke shot up. The explosion's boom echoed down the trail as T disappeared above the trees.

***

The engineer impatiently sounded a long whistle. He had a schedule to keep.

Mac looked anxiously down the trail. "Damnit, Skinner, where is he?"

Skinner shrugged helplessly. "He stayed behind to set off the charges like the Lieutenant said. He told us he'd be along and not to wait, so we didn't." Worried, Mac headed for the railway car window where Lieutenant Thornton watched. "No sign of Tyler. I don't know what could have happened."

"We'll send a runner. Make that two men. Maybe he fell or something."

"Sir, we can't! The train *has* to go on. It's got to reach the side-track before the westbound passes."

"I don't understand this! Tyler knows—oh, the colonel is going to go ballistic when he hears!"

"Sir, we don't know that he had a problem. He could catch the next train. There'll be another tomorrow. You can tell the colonel he's delayed."

"Yes, but the colonel expects *Corporal Tyler* to report to him as soon as I dismiss the men! He wants to go over the ceremony!"

"You told Tyler about the DSC?"

"Why not? The colonel was going to tell him! Although Tyler didn't look happy. I wonder why? He's getting the first Distinguished Service Cross ever awarded to the regiment, and General Graves intends to personally pin it on him when we reach San Francisco. The colonel wants to meet him before we leave and go over the ceremony."

"It's a new award," commented Mac. "I can understand why the general wants to be involved."

"The colonel too, same reason. And Tyler's parents will be there! General Graves said he would have them meet us in California when we dock. It will be good publicity for the regiment and for the general too. God knows, we've had enough bad publicity! And now this!"

"Does Tyler know they're coming?"

"Of course! I asked where they lived and he asked why I wanted to know, so I had to tell him. He said he thought they'd moved since he joined up, but maybe the addresses were in his records. I think he just doesn't remember, part of the amnesia.

"He didn't look happy, but none of us really were! He was

close to PFC Smithers, you know; they shared a hut. But at least Smithers went fast. If Semenoff had waited just a few days..."

"He wanted the arms and ammunition, Lieutenant, but he didn't get them. Shame about them 'accidentally' blowing up, wasn't it? And just before the diplomats could do what they promised and hand them over!"

"Yes. The colonel may have some explaining to do, but..."

"There's no *proof*, Lieutenant. And there was a lightning storm not far away..."

"You're a good soldier, Mac! Well, I'll just have to tell the colonel Tyler's missing when we reach Vladivostok. Lord knows he's going to be mad!

***

T landed near a house on the outskirts of the city; he had spotted a baggy Russian shirt hanging from a line.

The temperature had warmed just enough for the clothes to dry, and the housewife who lived there was not the only one to have hung her freshly-washed laundry outside. Not that everyone bothered. Most Russians accepted the smell as part of living in Siberia.

T left a silver coin in place of the shirt; his uniform blouse he discarded in the woods. Someone would find it eventually, but by then he would be long gone. There was nothing he could do about the trousers or boots, and he would need to find a hat and a belt to cinch in the baggy shirt. It would never fit inside his fitted uniform pants, but that could wait. He walked into town and headed for the waterfront.

He had less than a mile to go when Ray commed him. <T? Are you headed back yet?>

<Yes, but not on the ship with the rest of the guys. I can't take the chance. Kat and Patrick left some time ago, so they should already be there.>

<What happened?>

<They decided to award me the DSC! It's kind of a publicity

award, so I couldn't say no, but then I found out they intended to have Tyler's parents there. I couldn't do that to them; the last they knew, their son was presumed dead, body not recovered. I'm just hoping the Army hasn't contacted his parents yet. Or if they did, that they'll just send an officer to present them with the medal. Who knows? He might have deserved it. These guys served a long way from home and too many died over here, doing their duty. They *all* deserve awards. As for the general, a dead hero will work at least as well as a live one.>

    <So what now? If you're not transferring back with the army, you're back to square one with no way to get out of Siberia.>

    <Not exactly. I know who I am, and I've got my Talents back. I know how to speak Russian, not well but enough to get along. The words are there, I just have to practice speaking it. The rhythm and accents are not easy. Right now, I'm heading down to the port to see if I can find a non-military ship going to the states. If not, I'll just take the first one headed out that will sell me passage. We're not the only ones whose ships come here; the Japanese have some 70,000 troops to support, so I may end up on one of their ships. Japan should be okay as a way-point, and no one will be looking for an American soldier named Tyler. Some of my gold came from there, so taking it back seems appropriate somehow. It might take a while, but I'll get home eventually.>

    <You'll probably arrive *before* I do, at the time you teleported east, but don't contact me! That would create a paradox. Wait until I get back and I'll comm *you*. Speaking of paradoxes, I haven't been able to comm Patrick or Kat. It's—I don't know, I sense something, but there's no answer.>

    <I wonder...could they have already tried to go into the future and ended up on an alternate dimension? Maybe they can't respond. Or it could be that they know not to overuse their abilities if there are people around. They might decide not to respond if they're in a city. But I wouldn't worry. They're together, they both have Talents, and they may even have abilities we don't know about. They'll be all right.>

<I suppose. They did get ashore, didn't they?>

<They did, and bought civilian clothes. I contacted them briefly two weeks ago. They were still in San Francisco at the time. New names all picked out too, Patrick Spencer and Kat Wilson. For the president.>

<Well...I suppose you're right. And if they had created a paradox here in the states, we would have known, wouldn't we?> sent Ray.

<*I* would,> responded T. <When my Talents first manifested, I looked up as much information as I could find. That's how I found out about the California investigations and Rhine's work at Duke.>

<Okay. What now?>

<There's no reason for you to stay in the past. I'm on my way and it may take a while, but I'll get there. See you in 2017.>

<I'll be waiting. Bobby was a busy fellow before he left. I took some of the gold and bought us another ranch. It's called Pleasant Valley Ranch, although I may change that, and the owner is the T and R Land and Cattle Company. I'll keep an eye on it, but if we ever again need to get away, we head into the past. It's the ultimate way to break our trail!>

Chapter Twenty-six

<I'm back!>

The replies were immediate, a <Welcome home!> from Shezzie and Ana Maria, a <Thumbs up> image from Bobby (how had he done that?), and Libby send a short message, a simple feeling that conveyed happiness.

<Where are you?> asked Ray.

<Albuquerque, and I'll be at the ranch in time for supper. I'll tell you all about it when I arrive.>

T found the necessity of watching for aviation traffic strange after so long in the past, but soon it became something he did automatically. He didn't dare teleport, not now, so it was levitate and fly until he got tired, land long enough to rest, then do it again. He passed Little Dry Creek that afternoon and half an hour later, landed in the ranch's back yard. Shezzie was waiting.

"You look fit! I was so worried!"

T relaxed the hug long enough to whisper in her ear, "I've missed you!"

"Then let's get caught up! I knew you were gone and I worried, even though it didn't take all that long subjective time."

She led him into the house.

***

T pushed his plate aside. "I can't eat another bite! Thanks, Ray."

Ray shrugged off the compliment and T's thanks. He handed T an after-dinner scotch and tapped the glass with his own.

"De nada, my friend. I'm just glad you're here. Time travel is just too dangerous; I suggest we keep it for emergencies only, say if the authorities begin to close in again. That analyst in Homeland Security...sometimes I worry about him! He's sharp and he's collecting more data all the time! But now, if he gets too close we just head for the ranch I bought."

"Tell me about it," said T.

"Just so you know, I didn't share this with Shorty or Max. They've pretty much given up on using their Talents anyway. Shorty's walking around now like a man half his age! From what I can tell, he *likes* walking, now that the limp is gone. As for Max, he got a good scare when the cops started asking questions that time. He's happy now to be running his restaurant and so long as he doesn't go flying around, he's safe. If his Talent extends to growing better vegetables, well, he's not even sure it's his doing. And if it is, most of his customers have been exposed to people with Talent. If they were going to change, they would have done so by now. Same with Captain Byrd. He understands the Talents but doesn't need to use them to do his job. His major ability is telepathy; he can listen without anyone noticing, so he's not going active at all. He telephones if he wants to talk.

"Libby's got a new interest, boys. She doesn't want to scare off the one she's spending the most time with...he's kind of a geek, she says, but even so. Plus she understands the dangers. The feds may have lost interest in us; they're busy trying to figure out how that fellow in prison can fly! So far, they're holding on to him, but not because he's stopped trying. The young woman, his girlfriend? Disappeared."

"I hope they don't get complacent. That guy might still find a way out! As for the girl, she got a real scare. I hope we never hear from her again."

"The prison people aren't particularly worried. He understands that even if he does escape, they'll never stop looking for him. He's just too dangerous. Captain Byrd visited him once and told him what would happen. He showed him the pictures of Solaris, what was left of him. I won't say his criminal days are over, but he'll be keeping a very low profile if he manages to get out! He definitely won't want to be put back in. He lives in a cage, there's no other word for it, and he's inside four reinforced concrete walls most of the time. The only exit is through a solid steel door that opens to an exercise yard. He's allowed out once a day, into an area that's enclosed top, bottom, and four sides with thick steel bars. The sun can get in, but the only way out is back to the room. And when he's outside, there are always two guards, one with a tranquilizer gun and the other with a stun-gun. He can exercise by doing calisthenics, but he's not getting out."

"Good enough, but we're still in someone's computer file so no slacking off and getting careless. About this ranch you bought?"

"We've visited there, everyone but you. We found out that teleporting east or west doesn't matter the first time. You can't go into the future, only the past. You might change to a different timeline—we've been afraid of that—but so far it hasn't happened. Not that we know of, anyway. I'll show you on the map after you've had a day or two to catch up. The original name was Pleasant Valley Ranch, but a year after I bought it I changed it to T and R Ranch. The owner of record is T and R Land and Cattle Company. There's a small village nearby; some of the residents work at the ranch and most are descendants of the family I hired in 1925. There are a few outsiders. One family runs a general store and there are support businesses too.

"The restaurant serves good coffee. It resembles Max's place. None of them are Talents and none of them know anything about us other than that we are part of the company that owns the place. We don't need the income, so the excess is shared amongst the employees. That keeps everyone happy, not to mention honest. A trust account pays their salaries, and whatever is left after taxes and expenses is divided up and paid out in Christmas bonuses. For operations, we've got a small herd of cows, some horses, a truck garden, and whatever the employees raise for themselves. There are dedicated plots of about five acres each and they share the ranch's irrigation water.

"We have a number of wells, but most of the water comes from Lake Tyler. I put in a dam and a diversion ditch that's big enough for our needs. I named the lake after your name while you were in the past. There are also springs up in the hills, and the creek that runs through the valley has never failed. We don't require much, and the excess goes into Jenkinson Lake. It's stocked with bass and panfish. Catfish too, now that I think about it. The employees sell the ranch's excess fruit and vegetables in Placerville. That income, and what we get from culling our herds, is enough to pay the taxes and keep the trust account healthy. They know they've got a good thing going and they also understand that one of the partners will show up from time to time to check on things; it keeps anyone from getting greedy. Only one of the original employees I hired is living now, but a grandson handles our finances. Graduated from UCLA with a masters in management, if I recall correctly."

"Sounds like a going concern. You're not worried about time paradoxes from visiting back and forth?"

"There's always a chance, but I've got a series of locations memorized. They're deserted areas up in the hills that are accessible through teleporting or levitating, but otherwise would be damned difficult to get to. If I teleport directly to the ranch, I'll end up in the early 1930s. If I teleport to one of the intermediate locations, I'm in the 1940s or 50s, and of course if I levitate to any of the locations, no time displacement happens. The 1960s are actually pretty nice if we decide to go back permanently.

"Depending on when I show up, I'm either a son or a grandson of the original owner. I've thought that we might want to just pack up and disappear from the 21st Century one of these days. The way things are going now..."

"Yeah. Well, I promised to catch you up on what I was doing," said T.

"What happened? I thought you had a plan."

"I did! But then Semenoff found out we were leaving. He was already in a financial bind, thanks to Patrick and me stealing that payroll, and the other thing he'd been counting on was getting the modern weapons the diplomats had promised. With money to hire people and modern weapons, he had a real chance to carve out his own little kingdom in southeastern Siberia. But a payroll didn't arrive and he found out the weapons weren't coming either. I'm guessing his soldiers, particularly the guerrillas and bandits, started deserting. The Cossacks may have given up on him too; they want leaders who succeed. Anyway, he was under pressure. He couldn't attack the battalion—that's where the weapons were—while we were in his rear, so he hit us first. I'm guessing he brought half of his remaining troops and probably most were the ones he thought he could do without. But we wiped out some, the rest ran, and by the time he got his main force to the battalion headquarters compound the weapons had been blown up. It was a pretty sharp action for a while, but it may have been worthwhile. I wonder if what we did might not have been enough to put him out of business? For a warlord, it's all based on reputation; one major failure and he's history. Semenoff had at least one when he failed to overrun our camp, not to mention that the Czech Legion outfought his troops at every turn. Anyway, the Army decided to give me a medal. I tried to talk them out of it, but the general wanted a hero."

"Used your Talents, did you?"

"No, not that time. It was strange, really; I think it had to do with what some of his people had done. You commed Kat, right?"

"I did, but only that one time I mentioned and only a few words then."

"I wish I knew what happened. They just stopped responding!" T fretted. "Anyway, some of Semenoff's men wiped out her family and took her captive. They mistreated her, I guess I don't need to explain further. I killed that bunch, but the rest were no better, and when I saw them coming over the wall I just snapped. I was out of ammo, so I went after them with the bayonet. Rifle butt, too, I'm pretty sure I killed at least one that way. Crushed his skull like a melon! So the First Sergeant wrote me up for the Medal of Honor. I didn't think much about it, and I probably don't deserve it. I overheard a conversation between Mac and the lieutenant, and the lieutenant said I would probably get the Silver Star. I was okay with that, I already have one from when I was in Afghanistan, but it turned out he was wrong. The general decided to make a big deal of it by awarding the DSC, which he had the authority to do. The award is...was?...still pretty new, and almost as big a deal as the Medal. The general was pissed at the War Department and State Department both at the time, which may have been why he decided to act.

"They thought I was Tyler. More than likely he'd been killed during an ambush, but his body wasn't recovered and when I showed up...I still don't know how I got to Siberia...they decided I might be their missing guy. So I couldn't go through with the medal ceremony. Someone would have realized I wasn't Tyler, and the general wanted Tyler's folks there which would have *really* caused a mess when they said I wasn't their son. Maybe Tyler's parents got the medal; I hope so. Not much, after losing a son, but something. Anyway, I blew up the camp and headed for Vladivostok. I still had a few American coins and some of the foreign coins we took from the Japanese paymaster. I paid a Greek captain for passage on the first ship leaving port. Having gold helped; he was heading for Yokohama with a cargo of beet molasses and wheat, and was glad to get the Japanese money.

"From there, I caught a ship going to Sumatra. That took the rest of my American money. The captain was Dutch and apparently they had regular trade with Japan, bringing in barrels of oil and bales of rubber and returning with Japanese manufactured goods. My money was almost gone by then, so I got a job on a tramp ship with a British captain. It was interesting, being a sailor, and it kept me in good shape. It's not a bad life, all things considered; there were a couple of bad storms, but we rode them out at sea.

"The first mate when I signed on was a bully, but he died early. Heart failure. We buried him at sea and I doubt anyone was grieving, not even the captain." T ignored Ray's speculative glance and continued. "I was rated able seaman by that time. The ship sailed mostly under canvas and only used the engine for entering or leaving harbor. I generally worked the mainsail when we were setting sail or reefing. Rough work, especially when it was cold, but the topmen had it worse. Still, they were proud of what they did. Took most of a year, but eventually he reached North America. We picked up a cargo in Mexico, mostly tequila, and smuggled it ashore south of Los Angeles. That's where I left the ship, in late summer of 1926.

"I had picked up a few dollars in wages by then, so I bought a ticket on a mail plane, a Ford Trimotor; trust me, planes have come a long way since then! He took me to Chicago, and from there I teleported to Albuquerque. That got me to 2016. The rest of the way I did what you said, short teleports until I reached 2017, and levitated home after that. So that's it. The trip was interesting, but I don't intend to do it again! If the government starts sniffing around, I'll head for your California ranch. With luck, I won't have to go back in time, but just in case, you'll need to show me the locations you mentioned. "

"Will do," agreed Ray. "Got a few other things to show you too. Bobby's gone, but he's monitoring what we do; I picked up that comm when he responded to you. I think he'll come back, one of these days, and probably with a wife or a serious girlfriend. He cleaned out that pocket you discovered, found a couple of others too, farther back, and he cleaned out at least one of them. He wanted you to know about another one farther back that he never got around to mapping. He also left a note; I'll show it to you when you're ready."

"Give me a day or two. I'll drive into town and see Shorty and Max. If you feel like coming along, we could have coffee and some of Max's pie."

***

Three days later T went with Ray to visit the mine.

"That's pretty amazing! I think Bobby's right, there's more gold farther back in the hills. Maybe one day I'll do a real survey, but meanwhile it's not going anywhere."

"We should take as much gold as we can carry when we visit the California ranch. Go back to 1925, bury it somewhere it's not likely to be discovered as a just-in-case cache," suggested Ray.

"Why not?" agreed T. "But leave enough here for Bobby, in case he needs more. He's entitled to a third, if I remember correctly. You said something about a note?"

Ray found it and T read it through. "What's this about a souvenir?"

"I don't know. I looked around briefly, but there's nothing in here but the gold ingots, and he wouldn't have called them souvenirs. I checked the machinery adit too, and the only thing there was the generator, the crushers, and the concentrator. I wouldn't call them souvenirs. The only other thing he did to the mine was replace some of the old supports. He had to do that in order to get to the new pockets he'd discovered, but he didn't just dump the old timbers, he put several near the rockslide that blocks the way into the cache location. It makes the collapse look natural. Now that I think about it, I did spot something once. No idea what, but I forgot about it before I got around to looking. Gold fever," Ray chuckled.

"Hand hewn timbers? Some could have been put in by early American miners, maybe even the Spanish. That might be what he had in mind. We never did figure out who first mined this place! They did lots of digging, though, so it stands to reason that old timer found something. Maybe Bobby found one of their picks. Let's take a look."

"Whatever that was I spotted, it looked more green than you'd expect from rusted iron. A copper joint reinforcement or something?" Ray played the beam from his flashlight over the timbers near the rockfall. Some were half-buried, only a part of the wood showing. Bobby had done well; a visitor would believe the cave-in was natural! No question, anyone poking around would probably decide the tunnel was too dangerous to explore.

Moments later, he spotted a faint metallic flash from one of the timbers in the back and pointed it out to T. Levitating, they eased deeper into the pile. "What the hell is that? Brass, you think?" asked Ray.

"Oh, yeah. Give me a second..."

The pile stirred as T worked, but no new rocks fell. Moments later, he held the object in his hands. "Lets go outside. I want a better look."

They exited the tunnel, blinking in the bright sunlight. T chuckled and then laughed out loud.

"What was the name of this place before we bought it?"

"The ranch, you mean? I don't think it had a name. They just referred to it by the previous owner. Apparently he went broke and just walked away."

"Oh, I doubt that. No, indeed. It was the old Spencer Ranch if I recall."

"I think you're right," agreed Ray. "But so what?"

"And what name did Patrick take?"

"Spencer. You don't..."

"Oh, indeed I do! I've seen this before, several times in fact. Take a close look. Patrick left me a message."

T held out the object, a triangular bladed dagger with a brass knuckleguard. The end of the blade, the part that had been embedded in the wood, was shiny; the portion near the handguard was heavily rusted, and the brass itself was green with corrosion. But T had no trouble pointing out the name scratched into the knuckleguard. "He left me something he knew I'd recognize, but no one else would." The scratches spelled out a name: O'Brien.

Below that were other scratches, a vertical line with a crossbar near the center and a second vertical intersected by two angled lines at right angles to each other. A plus sign, and a K.

"We know what happened to them after California. They came here. I don't think that 'K' stands for Kilroy!"

The End

As a reward for making it this far, I'm appending a short story I wrote after Siberian was published. Enjoy!

Angel

The heat had finally broken. California had survived yet another blistering summer and weeks of Santa Ana winds. The man walked purposely through the cemetery gate, then stopped in surprise. He knew where he was going, where he'd been going for months, but something new had been added since his last visit.

A statue of a young girl, life sized, perhaps a teenager, and carved from what appeared to be white marble now stood off to the right. It was some thirty yards away from the entrance and away from most traffic, but there was no way he would have failed to see it had it been there before. Intrigued, he walked over.

Wasn't there a policy about putting up monuments this large? It was beautiful, a work of art, so perhaps they had made an exception? The figure was facing into the cemetery, so Sam walked around where he could look directly at the face.

As he did, a slight movement caught his attention. A man, unseen until now, stood by the statue. He had been bent over, looking closely at a spot near the base. The movement Sam spotted had been when he stood up and touched the one blemish that marred the statue's purity. The man's fingers touched, almost stroked, the dark, almost black, streak on the face's left cheekbone.

The two stood silently for a moment, contemplating the statue.

"That's interesting. It's beautiful, but..." said Sam.

The other glanced at him for a moment, then turned back to examining the statue. "Thanks."

"You had it put here? The girl—she was a relative?"

"No. I never met her, but I carved the statue. I wish I could have done more, but I was too late. I *heard* her, but as hard as I tried she couldn't hear me!" The man's voice was low, his sorrow apparent.

"I'm Sam Jones. I didn't catch your name, mister..."

"I didn't say, but you can call me T."

"That's all?" asked Sam. "Just T?"

"Does it matter? Would it make a difference if my name was

Talbot? Or Temple, or Tipton, or Toles, or Tunney?" Sam half-smiled, recognizing that T had used his initial and the vowels to suggest names. For whatever reason, he wanted anonymity.

But a sculptor who didn't want to reveal his name? Was he already famous, but unwilling to take credit for this work? The face wasn't quite finished, but the rest was world-class! Sam had visited museums in Greece, in Rome, and the Louvre in Paris. This statue, despite the flaw, wouldn't appear out of place among the collections he'd seen.

"I suppose not. Easier to remember," acknowledged Sam. "You said you carved it? But there's no inscription! Confusing; I guess I understand why you don't want to reveal your name, but how are people supposed to know who it's for?"

"I didn't want a name, and I also deliberately left the face under-finished. The rest I smoothed out. It's for Sally, the girl buried here, but in a way it's for all of them. All the ones like her, the ones who were hurting and had nowhere to turn."

"I—can understand what you mean, I think. Symbolism, right? But why put it here? Is it some sort of religious thing? I've seen some in churches that are sort of similar. The women were always older, though."

"Not religious, just my own human response. And the figure is young, because Sally never got to grow up. I did that other monument too." The man pointed to a lumpy black mass a few yards away.

"I don't understand, Mister T. It looks like just a rock! A big one, but I can't tell that you carved it at all."

"I didn't. All I did was pick it up and bring it here, but it took me a while to find just the one I wanted."

"I'm sorry, I don't intend to sound critical but—well, it's kind of ugly! It's just rough and black and it doesn't shine at all. The one you carved is marble, isn't it?"

"It is. The ugly one is basalt, a black volcanic rock from deep inside the Earth. Kind of a metaphor too, but different. This one was born in hell, and it's common as dirt. The marble block I carved? I selected that piece too. It wasn't easy to find one with the blemish where I wanted, but for what I intended it was perfect."

"Admirable, Mister T—" but the other was no longer paying attention.

Sam cleared his throat. "What made you decide to do this?'

"A song. I heard it, and I couldn't get it out of my head. Pretty song, hasn't been written yet, and the woman who sang it probably hasn't been born, but I remembered Sally when I heard it and came back to do this. I think that's the only way I'll be able to get that song out of my head. So many kids..."

The other edged fractionally away. Was this strange man crazy? Perhaps dangerous? Not homeless, too well dressed, and no smell of alcohol so not drunk either...

T saw the movement and chuckled. "Oh, I'm sane, more or less. Sorry, I shouldn't have let that slip, but sometimes I just need to tell someone. It's how I cope with my pain. It helps if I share it, and you don't rush out to tell people things you hear. I like that."

"True enough, I *don't* tell secrets. If I made a habit of blabbing people wouldn't trust me, so I don't. But how could you have known that? I've never met you before!"

"I know."

Curiouser and curiouser. T seemed to not make sense, and yet...? "I know most of the folks who have family buried here." Sam swept his arm around, indicating the cemetery. "There's also a building at the far end that houses cremated remains. People like to know they'll be with family after the end, or some do; I never thought much about it, but I reckon if it's possible I'd like to be near my little girl. You live around here, T? "

"My home is off to the east a ways. I only come back here now and then for a visit. This is my first visit to the cemetery, and now that I've done what I intended I won't be coming back. Not like you; you've been coming here since your daughter died. I'm sorry for your loss, and I can see how you might want to be nearby."

"Thanks for the sympathy," said Sam. "Nothing to be done.

Medicine still can only do so much. For some..." he shrugged.

"Yeah."

"So...I don't like to pry, but how do you know so much about me and my daughter? And Sally? I remember when it happened, but I don't think it made news. Just another child, gone. So many!"

"It's better if I don't explain, Sam. Just let it go. I learned about you the same way I knew about this girl and her father. That's where *he's* buried, over there under the basalt."

"I didn't know statues or monuments like that were permitted." Sam looked at the lumpy black mass.

"They aren't, but the directors made an exception for me after I explained. The main reason they don't allow large monuments is because upkeep is more expensive. It takes the caretakers longer to mow around them, including these two, so I donated money to offset the additional cost. The directors know there'll be more, because I set up a trust fund."

"But—look, if I'm out of line, I apologize. But didn't the inquest say Sally committed suicide?"

"It might have, but she actually died of a broken heart. She just stole the sleeping pills from her mother to speed up the process. That's what the medical examiner found, because there was nothing more he *could* find. *He* couldn't find the real answer, but I knew why she killed herself because I heard her thoughts. I tried, but I couldn't get here in time, and I couldn't make her *listen* to me!" T's face scrunched up and he brushed at his cheek.

A tear? This crazy man was weeping for a girl he'd never met? "T, I'm sorry but I just don't understand," said Sam. "Look, can I call someone for you?"

"No, I'm all right. It's just depression, and it will pass."

"And you really did that sculpture?"

"Yes. There's a blemish on the back that most won't ever notice, but a chip popped off when the chisel shifted and that's what I was looking at when you walked up. I did that too, the mistake. I decided that it was better not to try to fix it, because it symbolizes my larger failure. But the rest of it's pretty good, I think."

"A chip? That's what that mark is, an *accident*?"

"Yeah. It's partially hidden by the fold of the gown. It wasn't easy to get that right, and I think I tried too hard. Michelangelo had the touch, but I don't. I'm nowhere near his level."

"I didn't mean to imply a lack of skill when I mentioned that rock. Sure, I noticed right away that the face is not quite finished but now that you've explained it, I agree with your reasoning. It's beautiful and a fitting tribute to the young lady. So much sadness! You captured that, I think. Had you finished and smoothed everything out, I think you'd have polished out the emotion. No, this way is better. You said she died of a broken heart? That's why you sculpted the head bowed and the face partially hidden by the cowl?"

"That's it. A short, sad life, and she kept her sorrow hidden. But her sister, the one she was concerned about, is doing better now. Sally didn't die in vain, because her little sister's safe now. If I hadn't heard Sally crying, I would never have known. That's why she killed herself; she knew what was happening, what was about to happen. And couldn't *do* anything, and couldn't face failure! Sometimes I wish I could end my own life! I'm a failure too, but I can't do what Sally did." T turned and for the first time, faced Sam. "I'm sorry to dump on you like this, but sometimes it just gets too much for me and I need to share. Don't worry, I won't harm you and you'll never see me again. It's better that way."

"No, it's okay if you feel like sharing," said Sam doubtfully. "I think I understand why you carved her statue. But that black rock...it has something to do with her suicide?"

"Yes. Her father is under there. He was the reason, you see. Childhood is already tough enough nowadays without what Sally had to face. Lots of kids can't take the pressures. Hell of a thing," T mused, "we've built a society our kids don't want to live in! Sally stole sleeping pills from her mother because she heard that a classmate had suicided that way. That's when I heard her, just before she slipped away. It's probably why I *could* hear her; just at the point of death, people's thoughts become clearer. As for the pills, Sally's mother knew what her husband was doing, but *her* way of coping was to drug herself into sleep so she didn't have to hear Sally crying."

"The father...he was...?" The man's face showed his astonishment.

"Yeah. He also beat Sally when she cried, and sometimes he left bruises. That's why I wanted to put the black mark on her cheek. Because she was bruised like that when she died. I don't think it was in the inquest, but it was mentioned in the medical examiner's report. I couldn't get here in time to help Sally, but her father's dead now. Heart failure." There was something of savage satisfaction in T's voice. "It was necessary, because he'd already started on the younger sister. Didn't get far, though; I was in time to prevent that, so maybe I'm not a total failure."

"This is so strange…and you mentioned a song? Not written, and the singer hasn't been born? How could you know that? And what song?"

"I've already said far more than I should, but you might as well know the rest. Not that anyone would believe you if you did make an exception this time and say something. It's called Concrete Angel, about a girl who had no place to turn. Or will be, the song I mean. She walled things off inside, and Sally did too, but then her father started on her sister. It was too much, she couldn't handle it, so she took her own life. Nobody knew about the father, they only know Sally suicided. Even in death he managed to take something from her, her reputation! There was nothing I could do about that, because it's better if people don't wonder why his heart suddenly stopped."

A brief look of satisfaction passed across T's face, but then his expression relaxed and for a brief moment Sam wondered if he'd imagined it. "Look, I hate to say this but you need help," said Sam. "You're just not making *sense*, T! Don't you have family I can call? Give me a few moments to visit Mary's grave, and I'll take you wherever you need to go. It's no bother and I'll be glad to help."

"Thanks for the offer, Sam, but I don't need a ride. I don't need help either; matter of fact, I'm feeling better now. Sometimes I just need to vent, and you made a good listener. You go ahead with your visit and thanks for listening. I'll be fine."

Sam shook his head, mildly dismayed. Despite T's words, h e resolved to report this strange conversation to the police as soon as he got to a phone. Maybe they could get care for the deranged man? President Reagan intended to close most mental facilities, but it hadn't happened yet, and maybe they would have someone who could help T. It was that, or believe that he was some sort of time traveler who had somehow known things about the girl Sally no one *could* know. And according to what he'd implied, the cause of Sally's father's death. *Mad of course, but probably not dangerous. And the statue he claimed to have carved? No, impossible! The statue revealed near-genius talent, maybe more than that! But weren't artists often troubled? Van Gogh had cut off his own ear, hadn't he? So he'd had to have been a little insane too.*

But not concrete, and not an angel. No wings. But...maybe. It could be! Wings were an allegory, weren't they? He turned, intending to ask T again if he would accept a ride.

Only to see him rise silently until he was floating above the trees. He had no wings either.

An angel, or something else?

Sam soon lost sight of the man called T, hidden as he passed beyond the trees at the far end of the cemetery.

End

Books by the author:

The Wizards Trilogy:

Combat Wizard
Wizard at Work
Talent
Veil of Time
Siberian Wizard
Magic

The Darwin's World Series:

Darwin's World
The Trek
Home
The Return
Defending Eden

The New Frontiers Series:

The Ship
NFI: New Frontiers, Inc
NEO: Near Earth Objects
BEMs: Bug Eyed Monsters
MARS: the Martian Autonomous Republic of Sol
Pirates
Terra

The American Southwest Series

Jacob Jennings
Edward Jennings
Edward Jennings: War and Recovery
Edward Jennings: Cattleman
The Territory

Fantasy

Jack L Knapp

The Wizard's Apprentice

About the Author:

Jack Knapp grew up in Louisiana and joined the Army after graduating from high school. He served three tours in Germany and traveled throughout western Europe before retiring. His current circle of friends and acquaintances, many of them fellow members of Mensa, live on every continent except Antarctica. Jack graduated from the University of Texas at El Paso before beginning his second career, teaching science.

Always an avid reader, he took naturally to writing. He's experimented with ESP (The Wizards Series) and woodcraft/survivalism. The deep woods of Louisiana were his playground, the setting for his Darwin's World Series. He's a knight of the Society for Creative Anachronism, so combat scenes involving swords, spears, and bows and arrows are reality based. Jack's recent novels examine the challenges humanity will face when we begin to spread out into space. Beginning with a startup company building the first practical spacecraft (The Ship), to growing a business in space while overcoming Earth-based obstacles (NFI: New Frontiers, Inc), to humanity's first contact with a non-human species (NEO: Near Earth Objects and BEMs: Bug Eyed Monsters) the novels are largely based on current events. A fifth novel in the New Frontiers Series, MARS: the Martian Autonomous Republic of Sol, was published in May 2017, and Pirates soon followed, as did Terra. A final novel in the series, Hybrids, will wrap up the story.

Jack's boundless imagination is evident in all his books. How imaginative? You'll have to read his novels to find out!

Jack L Knapp